MW01226117

SURPRISE PROPOSAL

IONA ROSE

AUTHOR'S NOTE

Hey there!

Thank you for choosing my book. I sure hope that you love it. I'd hate to part ways once you're done though. So how about we stay in touch?

My newsletter is a great way to discover more about me and my books. Where you'll find frequent exclusive giveaways, sneak previews of new releases and be first to see new cover reveals.

And as a HUGE thank you for joining, you'll receive a FREE book on me!

With love,

Iona

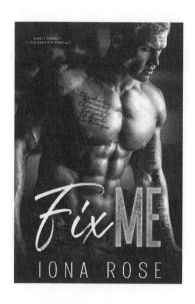

Get Your FREE Book Here:
https://dl.bookfunnel.com/v9yit8b3f7

Surprise Proposal

Copyright © 2023 Iona Rose

The right of Iona Rose to be identified as the Author of the Work has been asserted by her in accordance with the copyright, designs and patent act 1988.

All rights reserved. No part of this publication may be reproduced, stored in a retrieval system, or transmitted, in any form or by any means without the prior written permission of the publisher, nor be otherwise circulated in any form of binding or cover other than that which it is published and without a similar condition being imposed on the subsequent purchaser.

All characters in this publication are fictitious, any resemblance to real persons, living or dead, is purely coincidental.

Publisher: Some Books

ISBN: 978-1-913990-57-2

1

Savannah

I smiled secretly at the stares from a few of my colleagues as I carried the deliveries outside to my van. It was stinging cold but that was not an excuse not to dress well. Wearing my favorite skin tight jeans and high heeled boots, I felt like a million dollars.

Which was a good thing because my bank account was close to zero. Ethan, my six-year-old son, and I were surviving on the little money I'd saved back in Rogers and now, this job at the grocery store.

"Be careful out there, Savannah," Heather said, with a wave.

I grinned. "I will." While a lot of people only saw the disadvantages of my job, for me, it was perfect. I could pick my hours, which meant that when Ethan started his new school next week, I would be able to pick him up and drop him off.

I only had two deliveries but both were up in the mountains. I packed up the two deliveries in my minivan or rather my Aunt May's, and went to the driver's side. Sliding into the driver's seat, I said a silent thank you to my Aunt May. She was my mother's younger sister and my favorite relative.

I felt a familiar stinging in my eyes and pushed the feeling back down. I had promised myself not to cry again. I'd cried enough. Aunt May would not like it. After typing the first address into maps on my phone, I turned the ignition key and the van roared to life.

Ten minutes later, I was out of town and headed up the twisting road up the mountain. Thank God it was wide and even though the weather had been terrible, today it was mild.

My phone rang from the dashboard. A glance at the screen and my heart skipped a beat. It was my sister Ivy.

Ethan.

My chest tightened as I pulled over to the side of the road. I grabbed the phone and touched the screen to answer.

"Hey Ivy." My voice was deceivingly casual, hiding the fear coursing through me. I resisted the urge to blurt out if Ethan was okay.

"Hi," Ivy said cheerfully.

I squeezed my eyes shut with a surge of relief. She would not be this cheerful if there was anything wrong.

"I'm home today and I thought I would check up on you," she said.

"We spoke last night," I reminded her, though she didn't need any reminding. "I'm good, busy at work. How are the kids?"

"Good, they're upstairs in the games room." Ivy's house

was huge but she and her husband ran their own law firm in Rogers, Montana.

"Great," I continued. "I'll call you guys in the evening, okay?"

"Are you sure you're okay?" she asked, "I can send you something to tide you over."

"I'm fine, thanks." I hated to ask for help from my family and she was already doing enough keeping Ethan while I settled into our new lives here in Paradise.

We hung up and I continued my drive. Google maps told me to take the next left. I thanked God for technology. I was fine with a voice on my phone telling me which direction to go, but if you gave me a physical map, I was lost.

I took another left turn and followed the driveway that cut through a well taken care of lawn. Coming to a stop in front of a neat single-family home, I cut the engine and went to the back to grab the crate. I carried it to the house and gently deposited it at the front door.

Before I could ring the bell, heavy footsteps sounded and a second later, the door swung open.

"Hello. You must be the new delivery lady," an elderly woman said, a smile on her face.

"I am," I said, smiling back. "Do you want me to carry these in for you?" The instructions were to leave the delivery at the front door but there was no way I was leaving the heavy crate for her to carry.

"Yes please, that would be lovely," she said, holding the door open for me.

I lifted the crate and stepped into the house. I waited for her to lead the way into the kitchen.

"My name's Dorothy," she said, "and my husband's name is Rory." Her gait was slow as she led the way through an open plan space to the kitchen beyond.

"I'm Savannah," I told her.

"You must be new in town," she said, coming to a stop in front of the kitchen counter. She patted the space she wanted me to place the crate.

"I am but not so new. My Aunt May lived in Paradise and I came to visit her over the years. I've moved into her cottage."

"I knew May. She was a lovely woman," Dorothy said. "It's a small world. I always say, be kind to everyone you meet, you never know who they might be."

"Very true." I could see that she wanted to talk and I felt bad as I inched away from the kitchen. I really needed to get a move on since my next delivery was quite a distance away. "It was nice to meet you Dorothy. I'll see you next time."

My heels made a clicking noise as she followed me to the front door. "It was lovely to meet you too. Are you headed to Cameron's? Like us, he gets his deliveries done twice a week."

"Yes, I think that's him. How far is it to his house?" I opened the front door.

"Twenty minutes if the weather is good," she said. "Pass our regards. He's got a heart of gold, that Cameron."

"I will," I called out cheerfully as I made my way to my van.

I loved how people in small towns looked out for one another. It was one of the reasons why I'd decided to move into the cottage Aunt May left for me, rather than sell it or rent it out.

Dorothy's estimation was correct and in twenty minutes, I had reached my destination.

"Wow," I said aloud when I stopped the van in front of the two story, gorgeous, rustic house. My gaze swept over the landscaping which looked as if it had come straight from a postcard.

The views. If I lived in that home, I would have my groceries delivered too, as well as anything else that I needed. I would never leave it unless I absolutely had to. I gingerly got out of the van and went around to get the delivery.

I took my time walking to the front door, enjoying the views and the absolute peace that surrounded me. The house itself had windows which covered entire walls. The owner had brought the natural surroundings into the interior of the house. If by some miracle I ever became rich, that was the kind of house I'd live in.

I rang the bell twice but there was no answer. I deposited the crate on the ground. The temptation to look around was too great to resist and I walked around the house, following a gravel path. The garden surrounded the house, all the way to the back.

Beyond the neat grass were woods and just as I was about to turn back, I heard a soft but distinctive sound of someone chopping wood. I followed it, cursing under my breath when the heel of my shoe sank into the grass with every step I took.

The noise took me through to the woods until I came to an opening which looked like an open-air woodwork station. That's when I saw him. He had to be Cameron. Tall, broad-shouldered and deeply tanned.

My eyes followed the ripple of his arms as he raised the axe and brought it down with a loud thud. He was shirtless and clearly a man who spent his time outdoors, and not basking in the sun. Working. I imagined tracing each of those cut lines with my tongue.

An ache rolled through me and settled between my legs.

God. I'd not felt that way about a man, let alone a stranger, in a long time. He must have sensed my presence or heard my quick breathing, because he turned around abruptly.

He stood staring at me, axe in his hand, and a frown etched across his masculine face, as if at any moment he would swing that axe at me. If Dorothy had not mentioned he had a good heart, I would have turned around and ran to my van as fast as my heels would let me. My legs carried me closer. I realized I was waiting for him to say something.

His tightly muscled, broad chest gave off vibes of great strength and protection. It made me instantly think of resting my head against it, even if just for a moment, but when I moved my gaze up to his face and his icy blue eyes, I almost gasped. There was no warmth or kindness there. Just a barren space of terrible emptiness.

"What do you want?" he asked coldly, the frown on his face intensifying.

For a few seconds, I couldn't speak. A sudden chill hit my core. I couldn't believe his rudeness. No hello or any form of politeness. He couldn't be the good-hearted Cameron that Dorothy had referred to. There was nothing remotely good-hearted about the ruggedly handsome man glaring malevolently at me.

"I brought your order from the grocery store," I blurted out.

"Leave it at the front door," he instructed abruptly, and turned his back to me.

I watched dumb-founded as he raised his axe in the air and continued chopping as if I wasn't there at all.

For a few seconds I was so stunned by the unnecessarily rude way he had dealt with and dismissed me, I just stood there staring at his back. Even though I wanted to say something, I couldn't. He wouldn't hear my voice above the noise of the axe meeting wood, anyway.

Grinding my teeth, I turned away and made my way back to the front of the house. My breathing returned to normal when I entered the van. What was the matter with him? And why did he live here all alone? I answered the last question myself. With that kind of attitude, who would want to live with him?

What a first impression!

I moved my hand to the ignition key, but I was shaking too much to turn it. A fresh wave of anger went through me. If I was honest, I would have admitted it wasn't just the way he treated me that had affected me so much. It was the way I had responded to him that bothered me, but I wasn't being honest right then.

I turned all my focus to fuming at him.

He wasn't going to speak to me like that. How dare he? That was not the right way to treat people. Maybe no one had ever told him that. Well, that was about to change right now. I got out of the van again, propelled by righteous anger and indignation.

I marched back to the woods wishing I'd worn sneakers as my progress was slower than I liked. The sound of chopping wood had gone and it was silent, except for the sounds of insects and nature.

He had obviously heard my clumsy footsteps because he stood staring at me. The axe was now leaning against the trunk of a tree.

"Maybe no one has ever told you this, but you are a rude human being," I said.

His gaze seared me, moving down my body before returning to my face. A hint of amusement pulled at the corners of his mouth, incensing me further. "You're right.

Nobody has ever told me I'm rude, but then again, I've never had someone walk onto my property and stand there, gawking at me, saying nothing either."

He had a deep, authoritative voice that distracted me from my anger for a second. "I was not gawking." Maybe I had been. The man was super hot, after all, but I wasn't about to admit that. As a matter of fact, my cheeks flushed when I remembered the insane way my body had reacted to him.

"Don't you have any more deliveries to make?" he mocked, "Or are you paid to stare at random men you come across in the woods?"

I pointed a finger at him. "You—" But I was at a loss for words. I hated his guts, but he was right. I *had* been staring at him, and still was. In my defense, he honestly was the most physically tempting male I'd ever come across in my whole life.

I tore my gaze from the intriguing V line that ran down until it disappeared down the low waistband of his jeans. I shook my head. In my state there was no getting the better of him. Embarrassed and still deeply furious with him and myself, I whirled around, and without another word, marched to my van.

This time for good.

2

Cameron

I craved a cup of coffee at the end of the shift and not just any coffee. I wanted the kind that Joe's coffee house in town made. I hated going into town and rarely did, but good coffee beckoned. I had just done a shift, hiking with visitors. It was not too bad. None of them had wandered off and gotten lost.

As I parked my Jeep in front of the coffee house my gaze moved to the grocery store next door. I'd thought of that woman more than I liked. She'd even invaded my dreams. Savannah. I'd found out her name from Dorothy when I passed by to check if there was anything they needed.

Just remembering how she had stood up to me to let me know how rude I was, made me smile. I pushed her out of my mind and crossed the road to Joe's. I grabbed the door at the same time as someone from the inside yanked it open.

The next thing I knew, hot liquid was splashed all over my jacket. Thankfully, my field jacket was thick and other than looking unsightly, it didn't get through to my skin.

"Oh my God, I'm so sorry," a familiar voice gasped.

I shifted my gaze from the dripping mess of my clothes to Savannah's absolutely horrified face. Her hand was slapped over the mouth that I had been face-fucking in my dream. She was trouble with a capital T and I didn't want no trouble in my life at the moment. I wanted no strings. Of any kind.

"It's fine." I shook off the excess and side-stepped her to enter the coffee house.

I strolled to the counter while everything in me demanded I have a conversation with the woman who had been invading my thoughts for longer than I cared. But for what purpose? I reminded myself the only kind of female I was interested in was one I could have sex with and immediately forget about.

To accomplish this successfully, she had to be from another town. Someone who I would never see again. As sexy and delectable as she was, Savannah simply did not fit into that criteria. Dorothy had already mentioned that Savannah was the late May's daughter, and she had moved into town permanently. Savannah wasn't right for me, not even for a quick roll in the hay.

"Hi Liz," I greeted the dark-haired woman behind the counter. She was Joe's wife and they ran the coffee house together. Before them, Joe's father, Joe Senior, had run the coffee house.

Liz smiled at me. "Well, well, well. It's nice to see you again, stranger. You disappear in those mountains for too long. What can I get you? The usual?"

"Yes please."

"Let me buy that for you, please?" Savannah urged, sidling up next to me.

Remembering she had spilled half her coffee, I said to Liz, "And her coffee to go as well."

"Oh please, don't make me feel worse. I should be buying the coffee," Savannah cried frantically.

"Don't worry about it," I muttered curtly, not even looking in her direction.

"I'm so sorry. I was... distracted."

"It's fine."

Blessed silence. Not for long, though.

"Are you headed to work?" she persisted.

I hated small talk, but for some reason, I found myself turning towards her and responding to her question. "I'm coming off work."

"We haven't properly introduced ourselves," she mumbled, a smile trembling on to her luscious lips and her hand sticking out towards me. "I'm Savannah Hayes, just moved into town."

I considered ignoring the hand, but that uncertain smile got to me. I took the peace offering she held out, but as soon as our fingers brushed, sparks shot up my arm. Fuck, what the hell was that! That had never happened to me before. No woman had ever affected me so viscerally. I could see she had felt it too. She snatched her hand back as if she had been bitten by a snake.

"Cameron Elliott," I said, blood and heat rushing to my cock.

"It's nice to meet you," she said, her eyes flitting from my face to my chest. Her cheeks were flushed and she seemed and she looked as if she wanted the ground to open up and swallow her whole.

I didn't need anyone to tell me the intense attraction was mutual. Savannah Hayes wanted me just as much as I wanted her. Not that, that improved the situation one bit. I was glad when Liz brought our drinks. I grabbed mine, gave her a twenty-dollar bill and turned to leave.

"Have a nice day," I called over my shoulder.

She couldn't accuse me of being rude after that, could she. In my truck, I was embarrassed to find that my cock had swelled even more. The more I dwelled on her, the more I grew.

I drove home with thoughts of a naked Savannah in my mind.

No matter what I did, I couldn't stop thinking about her. I could picture her even though I'd looked at her for less than thirty seconds. Her red hair had been covered in a beanie and she had worn those tight jeans accentuating the curve of her ass and thighs.

I pictured myself pulling her jeans down over those curvy, thick hips and grew harder. Savannah had a body that made you want to toss her on a bed and ravish her. I found myself wondering if she would do my delivery again.

And that was where I drew the line.

It was stupid to fantasize about her. I needed to completely stop thinking about her. There was no future there. She was a good girl and all I ever want ever again is bad girls. Fuck em and leave em, kind of girls.

I got home and went outside to chop firewood in an effort to get her out of my mind. Bad decision. I kept visualizing her in those jeans that molded her body just right.

I FINISHED CHOPPING wood for the day and headed back to the house. I usually worked four days a week from Monday to Thursday and I looked forward to the three days of downtime. Heading straight up to my bedroom for a shower. It was a big house. I could still remember the first time my family saw the house.

They couldn't believe it was for one person, especially my mother. She kept walking into every room musing at the size of it. At the end of it, she had commented she couldn't live in a house this big. She lived alone with Cassie, my youngest sister, and she already thought that my old childhood home was too big for them.

As I stepped into the shower an image of Savannah popped into my head. It was so long since a woman did that. And just like that Amanda rushed into my being.

My chest constricted as the familiar pain spread from a core point to the rest of my chest. It was true what they said, the pain of grief faded over time but it never went away. It has been five years now since I lost her and it still hurt deeply. With a sigh, I stood under the hot rivulets of water and allowed my mind to empty. Experience had taught me to push the sadness away before it invaded my mind and took root.

Slowly, slowly, I turned my mind to other things, until I was once again a functioning human being. No one would be able to tell the difference.

I got out of the shower and was picking out clean clothes to wear from my walk-in closet, when the doorbell rang. I frowned, wondering who it could be. Grocery delivery was the day after tomorrow. Probably someone else who had lost their way.

I wrapped the towel around my middle and went downstairs. I opened the door and Savannah stood there, looking like a Christmas gift that had been delivered early. She held a cake box in her hands. Her eyes moved down to my bare chest, then below to my lower region and to my shock, my cock visibly jerked.

That had never fucking happened before. Her eyes widened as she raised them up to my face.

"Hello," I said as calmly as I could, as though my erection was not causing a tent in front of my towel.

"Hi." Her eyes dropped to my cock again.

I suppressed a grin. Her discomfort and obvious reaction was fun to watch. She roused herself and held out the cake. "I brought this for you as a measure of my apology. I'm sorry for pouring coffee all over you and ruining your obviously expensive jacket."

The only thing I remembered about that incident was how hot she looked. I shrugged. "Thanks for the cake but it's completely unnecessary. I have more jackets than I need."

"I made it myself," she put in hopefully, a small glint of pride coming into her eyes.

I raised my eyebrows.

"It will make me feel better if you take it," she said, almost pleading.

I nodded and put my hand out, ready take it without touching her skin, but instead of letting go, she held onto the box.

"Do you want me to take it to the kitchen for you?" she asked, staring pointedly at my naked chest.

I'd forgotten I was nearly naked. "Sure thanks. I'll go get dressed, then we can have some together."

As she made her way to the kitchen, I sprinted up the stairs. I whistled as I dressed. It surprised me how happy I was to have some company. But not just any company. Her company as I actually preferred spending hours upon hours alone.

I dressed in record time, grabbing some jogging pants

and a t-shirt. Back downstairs, I found that Savannah had found the coffee maker and was making us some.

"I hope you don't mind, but I didn't want cake without something to wash it down with."

"Not at all. Would you like me to hang that up for you?" I nodded towards her jacket.

She smiled and unzipped her jacket. "Okay. Since it looks like I've more or less invited myself in."

My eyes were glued on her chest when she took off the jacket. She was wearing skin tight jeans like the other day and a low-cut spaghetti strap top that was showing a whole lot of cleavage. She had full, perfect breasts and her skin was like cream, smooth and silky. She looked good enough to eat and I could feel the familiar stirring in my cock for her.

I distracted myself by fetching mugs and side plates for the cake.

"Where can I get a knife?" Savannah asked.

I directed her to the right drawer, while staring at her shapely ass. I'd never seen a woman so perfectly made for my hands and mouth.

The moment that thought formed, guilt quickly followed it. How could I think that about another woman? Amanda had been perfect for me. I turned away from the sight of her. But Amanda was gone. Lost forever and Savannah was here. I mourned my dead wife for so long and maybe I just wanted a little comfort for me, for a while.

"How long have you lived here?" Savannah asked, breaking into my thoughts. She'd settled down at the island with our coffee and two slices of cake.

"Five years," I said slowly. Had it really been that long? Where had the years gone? Even as I asked the question I knew very well where the years had gone. I'd been buried in grief unable to even contemplate that one day, I would feel alive again.

Without realizing it, the darkness had slowly lifted. In last few months I had a lot of not great, but good days. Days when I felt content to be alive. Days where I could tolerate being around other people.

"Dorothy told me that you are a park ranger?" Savannah commented, as I took my seat next to her.

"I am," I replied as I became aware of her floral scent. It reminded me of sunshine and summer. So she had asked about me too.

"It sounds like an interesting job." She fidgeted in her chair and then reached for the fork. Her arm brushed against her mug, sending it sliding across the island. She muttered a string of curses.

I quickly got up and hurried to the counter to grab a kitchen cloth.

"I'm sorry," she said, trying to stem the flow of coffee down the island.

"It's fine. It doesn't matter. There's more coffee."

She grabbed the towel from me and moped it all up, moving back and forth until the surface was dry.

Savannah sat on the chair with her back to the island sinking her teeth into her bottom lower lip. An irresistible urge to see her happy and laughing came over me. I moved to her and placed a hand on her knee. A fairly innocent gesture, but it stopped being innocent when she looked at me with her large softly brown eyes. I could feel myself drowning in the velvety depths.

"I'm so clumsy," she whispered.

"No, you're not." Without conscious thought, I moved between her legs until her face was a couple of inches away from mine. "It was an accident and can happen to anyone."

Her gaze dropped to my mouth and I knew she was thinking about kissing me. That's all I needed. I crushed my mouth to hers and she draped her arm around my neck and pulled me to her.

I slid my hand to the back of her head and a tiny moan escaped her lips. She parted her lips and I slid my tongue into her mouth. She had a coffee taste in her mouth and beyond that, a strawberry one, as though she had sucked on one before entering the house. I bit and sucked her lips until they were swollen.

Every time she moaned into my mouth, the fire in my blood increased, almost consuming me. I felt as horny as a fucking teenager. I moved my hand from her knee to her chest, cupping her full breast, her stiff nipple grazing the palm of my hand.

She let out a loud moan, but suddenly grew still.

I understood immediately, backed away and caught the look of horror in her eyes. It was as if icy cold water had been poured over her... and me. Without saying a word, she swung her legs to the side and slid off the stool unsteadily.

"I'm sorry I have to go," she gasped.

I didn't say anything. Not that it would have mattered anyway, she was already halfway out of the kitchen. She grabbed her jacket and without looking back, disappeared through the door.

I raked my fingers through my hair.

Fuck! What had I been thinking? I didn't even contemplate going after her. What was I going to say? Sorry for kissing you? Sorry I couldn't control myself around you?

I was an idiot. I had allowed her to light a dangerous fire inside me.

I listened to the quick taps of her shoes until the front door opened and shut with a soft click. I looked at the slices of cake on the plate. Chocolate. So she made it herself. I collected some icing on my finger and put it on my tongue.

Delicious.

Still, it was not sweeter than her mouth.

But that was taboo. Or was it?

3

Savannah

"I just listened to the news. There'll be a storm today," Heather said. "Be careful out there."

"I will," I told her. My biggest problem was not the weather. I'd been dreading this day since yesterday when I left Cameron's. I shook my head free of that memory and carried the crates to the minivan, one at a time.

I settled in the driver's seat and inhaled deeply before turning the ignition key. My insides were shaking and as I started to drive, memories of that kiss invaded my thoughts and I couldn't shake them off.

What had been wrong with me? How would I have kissed a stranger? It didn't matter how attractive he was. Sane women did not go around kissing men they did not know. What kind of woman must he think I was?

I had done a lot of stupid things in my life, including getting married to Finn. The only thing that made me not regret the marriage was Ethan. I loved my little boy with all of my heart and he was the only reason I got up every morning.

Heather had not been wrong. The weather was not great. A light snow was falling and the wind was picking up but it wasn't too bad. I drove slowly and carefully, grateful that my Aunt May's van was sturdy enough to navigate the slippery roads.

I had a few deliveries to make along the way to Dorothy's and by the time I got there, snow had started falling in earnest. I hurried out of the minivan and went to the back to grab her delivery.

She must have been watching out for me at the window because by the time I got to the front door, it was already open.

"Hi Dorothy," I said. "Can I come in?"

"Yes of course my dear," she said. "It's terrible out there. I wasn't sure you were going to come."

"It's not too bad," I told her. "I'll be done in a few hours." I carried the crate to the kitchen and found an older man, I assumed was her husband stirring the contents of a pot.

"This is Rory, my husband," Dorothy said.

Rory smiled and nodded at me, then he continued what he'd been doing.

"Stay with us until the storm is over," Dorothy said.

I was touched by the concern in her voice. "I'll be just fine. Besides, Cameron's place is not too far off from here. Plus, my minivan is made for this weather," I said with a smile to reassure her.

It really was cold I thought as I entered the warmth of the minivan. I couldn't wait to finish my deliveries and head back to the cottage. I had two more days to get it in order before Ethan came home from my sister's place.

The closer I got to Cameron's place the more that stupid kiss haunted me. Except that it was not stupid. It was the hottest kiss I had ever shared with anybody. Cameron kissed as if he was dying of thirst and I was his oasis.

I couldn't forget how my body had come alive at the touch of his lips or the way his hand had cradled my head to hold it in place. My panties had been completely soaked by the time I fled the house and that night I had barely slept and when I did, I had dreams, erotic dreams that left me feeling unfulfilled in the morning.

I swallowed hard as Cameron's house came into view. I turned off the engine and inhaled deeply before reluctantly leaving the safety of the van. I was going to apologize to him and then hopefully, with my dignity intact, leave.

Just as Dorothy had done, Cameron had the door open when I got there. I saw him and my breath hitched.

"Hello," I said and tried not to look at him, but it was impossible not to. Our fingers brushed as he took the crate from me. Immediately our gazes locked. I could have bet my last dollar that Cameron was thinking about that kiss too.

"This is not good weather to be out in Savannah," he said.

"I know but I'll be done soon," I told him. "You are my last delivery." I followed him into the house staring at the muscles on his shoulders as he carried the crate through to the kitchen. He dumped it on the counter and then moved to the coffee maker.

I hoped he didn't think I was going to stay for coffee. It was embarrassing enough that I had to see him again without making it worse by spending more time in his company.

"Make yourself comfortable," he said. "This storm is going to be here awhile."

I shook my head. "I can't stay. I have to go but before I do I want to talk to you about something." I folded my hands into fists and forced myself to continue.

Cameron moved closer to where I stood. I wished I could take a step back but I couldn't without looking like a coward. I raised my gaze to meet his eyes. "I wanted to apologize."

A puzzled look came over his features. God he was handsome. Concentrate.

"Apologize for what?" he asked.

My heart pounded so hard I was sure he could hear it. I tapped my thigh with my left hand. "I shouldn't have lead you on the last time I was here."

Cameron's features relaxed and a hint of a smile pulled at the corners of his mouth. He cocked his head to one side and contemplated me. "I kissed you, Savannah. And I must say that I enjoyed it. I was actually hoping we could do it again."

My jaw fell open. Before I could say or do anything Cameron took a step forward and wrapped his strong muscular arms around me.

I should have stopped him but instead I looked up into his eyes. Big mistake. I felt as if I was falling in the icy blueness of his eyes.

"We should get rid of the coat. It's hot in here."

He gave me a few seconds to respond, but when I didn't, he removed his hands from my waist and began to unbutton my jacket. I needed to say something. But I couldn't bring my mouth to move. On the last button, he looked at me as if giving me one last chance to say no.

Again, I did not respond because my body was dying to feel his hands on me. I was helpless to say anything. I wanted this so badly. I hadn't been touched or held by a man in almost two years.

Unfortunately my ex-husband had been a terrible lover so I didn't think I was missing out too much. At least, until I laid eyes on Cameron.

Cameron peeled off my jacket and helped me out of it. Then he draped it over a chair and ran his callused hands over my bare arms while his eyes hungrily raked over my body.

I'd worn a halter dress that I had no business wearing with my cup size. But I loved halter dresses. I found them cute and to be honest I think there was a part of me that had been hoping Cameron would get to see it. That he would find me irresistible. Foolish, I know.

"You look beautiful," he said, his voice thick with desire.

I felt beautiful.

Cameron pulled me close, crushing my breasts against his chest. My nipples came alive, aching and longing for his touch. He brought his mouth to me and brushed his lips against my mouth.

I inhaled his manly scent and with a moan I closed my eyes and draped my arms around his neck.

I parted my lips inviting him into my mouth. He groaned and depend the kiss then without warning he dropped his hands to my hips and lifted me, placing me gently on the kitchen counter.

"God, you're so sweet," he muttered in between desperate kisses to my lips that left me wanting more.

Cameron ran his hands over my thighs, pushing my dress farther up and all the while our lips were locked on each other. My chest rose and fell with every breath I took.

His hands moved all the way up past my belly to my breasts. He cupped them and rubbed my nipples with his thumbs over the material of my dress. A moan escaped my mouth and at that point I didn't care about anything except getting rid of the deep ache between my legs.

"I need to taste you, Savannah," Cameron snarled suddenly, as if he no longer bear the wait.

His words went straight to my pussy. I was so aroused my whole body felt as if it had been lit on fire. Cameron stared at me, waiting for an answer.

The rational side of me tried to kick in. I should stop him, but I pushed that voice away. No, not this time. I wanted this man so badly. Just this once, I told myself. It had been so long. I deserved one moment of passion. Of forgetting all my responsibilities and having a bit of fun.

"Yes, yes, I want you to taste me," I whispered feverishly.

Cameron groaned and shoved the rest of my dress up. "Spread your thighs and show me your pussy," he ordered.

4

Cameron

From the first moment I laid my eyes on that red halter dress I knew I had to see what was underneath. Savannah wore tiny panties that matched her dress and her hair. As sexy as her panties were, I wanted them off.

I needed to look at her pussy and see how wet she was.

I hooked my thumbs on the hem of her panties and slowly dragged them down. I loved the expression on her face.

"Raise your hips, sweetheart."

She anchored her hands on the counter and raised herself up. I pulled her panties down the rest of the way and tossed them to the end of the counter.

Savannah sat back down again and parted her knees wide giving me a perfect view of her pussy. She was exactly how I had imagined she would be: pretty, and pink, and dripping wet. Her eyes blazed with passion and desire. She wanted this as much as I did and she wasn't hiding it or acting coy.

"You're so fucking gorgeous". I lowered my head between her legs and used my tongue to tease her folds. Her moans filled the room and with every lick to her clit Savannah groaned louder.

I licked her greedily with my tongue and teased her clit with my mouth and my lips. Arousal juices seeped out of her and I licked all of it. I slipped a finger inside her pussy while keeping my tongue on her clit. Savannah raised her hips to meet my finger as I slid it in and out.

Her walls squeezed my fingers and when I added a second one, I moved slowly so her pussy could adjust to having two fingers. I was going to regret this later but at the moment it felt so fucking good to hear her moans and to inhale her scent.

Savannah wraps her legs around my neck, imprisoning me and holding me captive.

"Cameron, please," she cried as I pumped my fingers and flicked my tongue over her clit faster.

The tone of her moans grew softer and turned to whimpers. I knew she was close.

"Please... please... I need to come," she moaned out.

"Come for me."

Savannah let out a loud moan and the walls of her pussy contracted, trapping my fingers. Her whole body trembled, including her legs, which were wrapped around my neck.

I pulled out my fingers which were coated with her wetness, and locking gazes with her, I licked them dry. My cock ached to be freed from the confines of my pants and join in on the action. But I didn't want to fuck her in the kitchen.

I wanted Savannah on my bed, spread-eagled, so that I could feast my eyes on every inch of her, kiss and lick every part of her skin. I gently lifted her off the counter and carried her upstairs to my bedroom.

I laid her out the bed and stood for a moment looking down at her hungrily taking in her beauty. She was mine. For the moment at least. She stared right back at me without a shred of embarrassment or regret. I loved that about her.

"I'm going to fuck you so hard, you'll never forget this evening," I said.

"It's already imprinted in my mind," she purred, driving me crazy with that sultry voice.

I got between her legs and pulled up her dress. She sat up, giving me the space to pull it over her neck.

"I hate to get rid of this dress. You look beautiful and sexy, and I couldn't resist you the moment I laid eyes on you," I told her.

"Thank you," she said.

In the next moment, the dress was off and my eyes roved over her gorgeous full cleavage on display. I lowered my head and planted kisses over her skin moving lower each time. I licked the top of her breasts and then gently bit on her nipples over her bra.

She thrust out her chest and moaned softly. Reaching back, I snapped her bra open and slid it off her shoulders. I tossed it to the floor.

Fucking hell. She was gorgeous with her chest bared for me. Savannah resembled a Greek goddess of water. The dress, even though gorgeous, did not do justice to what was underneath it.

She lay back on the bed and I draped my body over hers. My cock strained in my pants, jerking about, demanding to feel her. But first, I needed to lick her nipples, which were calling for me to put my mouth on them.

I caught one between my teeth and bit gently, then shifted to the other, marveling at how big they were.

Raising my head, I said, "You have beautiful breasts."

She smiled in a way that told me she was aware of this. Maybe a previous boyfriend. A jolt of jealousy shot through me, leaving me feeling uncomfortable. I had no right to feel possessive towards Savannah. She was not mine and I wasn't interested in claiming her as mine.

I dropped my head back down and worked on her nipples and breasts, loving them and drawing back to look at the effect of what I was doing. They had become hard peaks. I lowered my attention to her belly, trailing kisses all the way down until I was between her legs again.

I gave her clit a teasing swipe and then stood up. Savannah kept her eyes on me as I undid three buttons and then pulled my shirt over my head. My pants were next to go.

Savannah's eyes widened at the sight of my tented boxer briefs.

"You're big," she said.

I'd heard that comment before from Amanda and other former lovers. It didn't make me proud. It was just a fact. I was well endowed. I pulled down my boxer briefs and my cock bobbed up and down as if it couldn't wait to be nestled inside Savannah's wet heat.

I pulled open the bedside drawer and grabbed a packet of condoms. I took one out and opened it with my teeth, then rolled it over my cock.

"I want you so badly," Savannah said.

"I want you too." I couldn't wait to get my cock into that

sweet pussy. I moved to the bed and arranged myself between her legs. I gripped my cock and teased her with it, rubbing it over her center.

I wanted it to last and to be good because it was not going to happen again. This had to be a one off. Savannah lived in town and we'd be seeing each other a lot. I didn't want a relationship and I hoped that she didn't either. If she did, things were going to be very awkward between us.

I hoped that she would see it for what it was. Two adults pleasuring each other. Nothing more. I pushed my cock in slowly, hissing as her heat drew me in. Savannah threw her head back and moaned loudly.

My moan followed when my cock was buried to the hilt.

"So big," Savannah said. "And so good. Fill me with it. Fuck me with your big cock."

I loved that she was outspoken in bed. I loved my women loud and vocal. There was nothing as great as knowing I was pleasing her.

"You feel so fucking tight," I told her. I pulled my cock in and out slowly. Savannah wrapped her legs around my waist and squeezed my ass. I plunged in all the way again, until I was married to the hilt.

I couldn't remember feeling so good in a long time. The pleasure was almost unbearable. I thrust in and out while staring at Savannah's face as she takes in every inch of my cock.

Soft moans escape her mouth, inflaming me further and bringing my orgasm closer. No way. I wasn't going to come any time soon. This night had to be seared into our memories. I didn't question why that was important. It just was.

She slid her legs up and down my ass, tightening them and then loosening them, depending on whether I was thrusting up or down. At the edge of my mind, I worried about tomorrow. It was stupid to worry. Not when my cock was buried in her delicious pussy.

After tonight, Savannah and I would end it but for now, we were both going to enjoy ourselves. I increase my movements fucking her harder and deeper. She cried my name over and over again.

"Oh God, Cameron. I'm so close," she said.

I wasn't ready for her to come. Not just yet.

I pulled out my cock. "Turn around babe. Get on all fours."

She changed positions without a murmur of protest. I trailed my hand up and down her spine and then grabbed her ass cheeks and spread her open. Holding my cock in my hand, I used it to spread her wetness to her clit.

Savannah arched her back and wiggled her ass, enticing me to bury my cock inside her again.

"You want this Savannah?" I asked her, slapping her pussy gently with my cock.

"Oh God, yes. If I didn't, I wouldn't be in this position right now," she said over her shoulder.

I laughed. That was a first. I'd never laughed during sex with a woman. Sex had always been a serious business of rendering and receiving pleasure. I gripped her hip with one hand and lined up my cock against her slit.

She was wet enough for me to thrust into her hard. She let out a scream and urged me to keep going. I drove my hips forward at a rapid pace that she loved. Sounds of our moans filled the room. I lost myself in her as we moved together so perfectly.

I rode her hard, taking us both to our releases.

"It's too much," Savannah said.

"Fuck, yes." I desperately needed my release but she had to come first.

Reaching around I pinched her clit. She screamed my name and then her arms collapsed on the bed. Holding her hips up I kept pounding until I burst inside her, my cock gushing into the condom.

5

Savannah

I woke up with a start and sat up, startled, at the unfamiliar surroundings.

"It's ok," a familiar voice said.

Cameron. The fog in my brain lifted and the events of the previous couple of hours came flooding back. I inhaled deeply as pictures filled my mind. Cameron and I first in the kitchen and then moving to his bedroom.

"Did I fall asleep?" I asked him.

He flicked a switch and the room was illuminated with light. I lay down flat on my back and Cameron propped himself on his arm and stared down at me smiling.

"You did. You must have been very tired."

I went to sit up but Cameron pushed me back, gently.

"I have to go," I said.

He put a finger to his mouth. That's when I heard it. The sound of the wind howling angrily. There was no way I could drive back to town with that kind of weather.

"It's not just the wind. It's snowing heavily," Cameron

said. "We haven't had a storm like this in years. It's not safe for you to be out there."

He moved his hand to my chest and stroked my nipples, reminding me of the hot sex we'd had a few hours earlier.

"You're so beautiful and coming inside you was amazing," Cameron said casually as if he was talking about the weather.

My face heated up. I was rarely embarrassed by anything but for some reason with Cameron I felt a little shy. His hand played with my nipple, pinching it until it beaded, before moving to the other one. My body began to stir.

Unbelievable, considering how long we had been at it. He lowered his hand and ran it over my skin, stroking my belly in feather-light movements. My breath hitched when he dropped his hand between my legs.

"Your pussy is so sweet and tight," Cameron murmured.

"I'm surprised by how chatty you are in the sack. You don't say much out of it."

He chuckled. "That's because I don't need to say much out of it but here, I need to tell you how you make me feel and I need to know how you're feeling."

I swallowed hard and looked into his eyes. What was I thinking? I was wondering where this was going to go. I wanted to tell Cameron I wasn't interested in relationships. I had just come out of a horrible marriage and I didn't want anything to hold me down again.

His fingers, however, were doing things that were distracting me from my thoughts. I lost it completely when he started drawing circles around my pussy with the tip of his cock. I remembered the size of his dick and how it felt pushing against my walls. I'd never felt that kind of intense, mind blowing pleasure.

I wanted to feel it again. I wanted his cock to stretch me

so hard it was almost painful. I was already stuck in his house and I wasn't going to go anywhere so I might as well make the best use of it.

As for the conversation we needed to have, I'd wait for the storm to clear up then I'd talk to him. Nothing was going to come out of this and I was not interested in a relationship. That was the last coherent thought I had.

I pushed myself up and thrusted a finger at his chest. I said, "It's my turn now to be in control."

He raised his hands in mock surrender. "You're not going to get any arguments from me."

I straddled him and dragged my pussy over his belly, leaving a wet trail. I moaned as I moved up his chest until my pussy was directly above his mouth. He stuck out his tongue and pressed it against my slit. He gripped my thighs and I moaned as he moved his tongue expertly over my folds.

I let him pleasure me for a bit then slid down and kissed him. His mouth tasted of me. It was erotic and a huge turn on. His hands caressed my back moving down to my ass to squeeze it. I moved away from his mouth and poised my pussy above his cock. Wrapping a hand around its width, I sank down, letting out a loud moan as his cock stretched and forced its way through my folds.

Cameron was definitely the biggest man I had ever had. "At this rate you're going to spoil me for any other man." I sank into him, feeling a mixture of pleasure and pain as his big cock pushed back at my walls.

Cameron's hands gripped my hips and easily lifted me until only the head of his cock remained buried inside my pussy. He locked gazes with me as if to ask if I was ready.

"Yes," I cried in response to the question he hadn't asked.

He slammed me down on his cock and before my moan

ended, he pushed me up and slammed me back down. I felt as weightless as a ragdoll as I bounced on his cock.

So much for being in control but I wasn't complaining. I loved that Cameron liked to be in charge. He had let me believe I was the driver but all along, he was the one who was in control.

His eyes hungrily locked on my breasts as they bounced up and down on my chest. I loved knowing that he found me attractive. It had been a long time since I'd had a man look at me as though I was his favorite meal.

This was going be my last night of freedom and I wanted to smile when I remembered it. I wanted to have Cameron in every way I could. I draped my body on him so that my nipples were grazing his chest. With his cock buried deep inside me, Cameron took a nipple into his mouth.

I gyrated my hips, needing to feel the friction between us. Cameron gave the same attention to my other nipple then raised his head and kissed me hard on the mouth. He sat up with me in tow, his cock sheathed in my pussy, and gently lowered both of us until I was flat on my back.

"I'm going to fuck your tits first," he said, pulling out his cock.

I grabbed my breasts and squeezed them together. His cock, still coated in my wetness, slid smoothly between my breasts.

"You look so hot," he said, his gaze on my hands as they played with my nipples.

After a few strokes, Cameron slid off my breasts, and lowered his body to kiss me. I wrapped my hands around him, holding him close to me. Balancing himself with one hand, he used the other to guide his cock inside me.

"I'm going to make you sore so when you're doing your deliveries, you'll remember this the whole time," he said.

I laughed softly. "I don't need to be sore to remember." I stroked his back and shoulders. Cameron knew his way around a woman's body. Sex with him was an experience I was never going to forget.

He slid inside me while kissing me. Hit by sensations from all angles, I moaned into his mouth and rocked my hips to get his cock as deep as it could go. Cameron pulled back and stared into my eyes. His ice blue eyes cut through me, as if he could see into my soul.

He went still when his cock was completely buried in me. "How does that feel, babe?"

I still couldn't get over how vocal Cameron was in bed. "It feels so good." I said, my breath staggered. "Please."

He eased his cock out and then slammed it back in. I gave a sharp cry of pleasure and dug my nails into his shoulders.

"I love it when you're rough like that," I told him when he paused to look down at me with an expression of concern.

His features relaxed and he slammed into me again and again. I clung to his shoulders for dear life. I was overwhelmed with need as if it was the first time he and I were having sex.

"More," I whispered to him and he gave it to me.

"You're so beautiful," he said, without breaking a beat.

"I need to come," I said, sweat dripping down the sides of my face.

"Come all over my cock." Cameron commanded and my body started to unravel as though it had been waiting for permission from him.

Waves of orgasm rolled off me, and as I screamed his name, he growled and a gush of thick cream filled me as he came with me.

"HOW IS THIS ONE?" Cameron said, holding out a t-shirt.

It looked like I was going to spend the night and I was borrowing something to wear. I didn't feel like wearing my clothes and just needed something to relax in.

"It's perfect, thanks," I said, swinging my legs from the bed until they hit the floor. I took the t-shirt from Cameron and made my way to the bathroom. I could feel his eyes on my bare ass and I gave a little more swing to my hips, grinning as I imagined the expression on his face.

"I'll be in the kitchen," he said before I shut the bathroom door.

I looked around the massive, gorgeous space. The claw tub was tempting but I opted for the shower instead. It was one of those huge shower heads that felt as though you were under a warm waterfall. Glorious.

My body felt like a guitar that had been fine-tuned after years of neglect. Or maybe even for the first time. I had no regrets. I hadn't been laid in ages and I'd forgotten how pleasurable good sex could be. Not that sex with Cameron could be classified as good sex. It was out of this world.

I hummed as I wiped myself dry and then pulled on the t-shirt that Cameron had loaned me. It made me feel naughty knowing I was wearing nothing underneath. Teasing Cameron was quickly becoming my favorite thing to do. I loved how he obviously found me attractive and didn't bother to hide it.

The house was warm, almost toasty and the t-shirt went down to my knees. I didn't need anything else over it and nobody was going to come with a storm and this time of night. I straightened the bed and then made my way downstairs, making a mental note of calls I needed to make.

The most important one was to my sister to check in on Ethan. My purse was on the table at the foyer and I got my phone and checked my messages. Heather had texted like a million times asking if I was okay. I texted her back and told her that I was marooned at Cameron's house.

She sent three question marks which made me laugh. Afterwards, I called my sister.

"I'm glad you called. We saw in the news that there was a terrible storm in Paradise," Ivy said.

"All true but I'm okay. I'm at a friend's place," I said.

There must have been something in my tone of voice because Ivy picked up on it immediately.

"A friend?" she asked. "You mean a man." She sighed. "Savannah, you just got to Paradise. Can't you focus on getting your life back on track first?"

Defensive feelings came over me. I'd made a mistake once in my life but since my marriage and subsequent divorce to Finn, my family treated me as though I was a walking disaster.

Ivy's words hurt. "I'm an adult Ivy and I know what I'm doing."

"Adults don't sleep with someone they've known for two hours," she said.

That stung. So now I was a slut? I bit on my bottom lip to stop myself from saying something that I would regret later.

"The way you dress doesn't help either," Ivy said. "It's like you're asking for it."

"I like how I dress," I hissed. "I like looking and feeling good." If I couldn't feel good about myself, then who would make me feel good?

"I thought that leaving Finn had changed you. Made you grow up," Ivy said.

Tension filled silence came over the phone. Sometimes I

hated my sister and her superior ways. But the fact was she helped me a lot with Ethan when I needed someone I trusted to stay with him.

"How is Ethan?" I asked coldly.

"Fine. He misses you," Ivy said in a matching cold voice.

"I'll be there on Sunday. Thanks for having him."

"It's fine. He's my nephew and we love him so much. He's a special kid." My sister's voice had softened.

That was one thing we could agree on. We ended the call and it saddened me that we couldn't get along. I meant what I said to Ivy. I was an adult and could sleep with whomever I wanted.

Cameron had already started on dinner and wonderful smells were coming from the kitchen. I should have been upset with myself especially after the conversation with Ivy, but I tried to live my life fully and with no regrets.

So I had sex with Cameron. It was amazing and I enjoyed every second of it but after that, we'd go our separate ways. My life would continue and hopefully we could remain friends.

"Hi," he said, turning around when he heard my soft footsteps on the dark wood floors. His features had softened and a slight smile lifted the corners of his mouth. Sex was good for everyone, even the grumpy Cameron.

"Hi. What can I do to help?" I said.

His eyes dropped to my legs and lingered, before returning to my face. It had been that way between Finn and I. After we got married, he had gotten insecure about the way I dressed. When I wore skimpy clothes in the house just to have a little fun, he called me a slut. So I stopped but I missed it.

"I've got the chicken in the oven," he said. "You can make the salad while I sort out the potatoes."

"Sure." We were comfortable with each other, which was another surprise. We were practically strangers, but being marooned with Cameron, with snow falling hard outside and the wind howling, created intimacy between us.

It felt like being with an old friend. I went to the sink and rinsed my hands and then washed the vegetables that Cameron had placed on the counter for the salad.

"You don't look like the type that knows how to cook," I said to him as I diced the carrots.

He chuckled. "You can't be a park ranger and not know how to cook."

I loved his laugh. And his broad, muscled shoulders. And his butt.

6

Cameron

I was aware of every movement that Savannah made. Why did I think it was a good idea to give her my t-shirt to wear? She had gorgeous legs and I kept stealing glances at them and remembering what was above them.

When she moved her full breasts jiggled as well, reminding me how it had felt to slide my cock in the deep valley between them. It was also nice to see her so comfortable in my house after we had sex. With the way she had run off the other day when we kissed, I expected her to be shy and withdrawn.

"How is it being a park ranger?" she asked.

I shrugged. "I like being outdoors all day but mostly I like the solitude." In my former life, I had been a social human being but when I lost Amanda, and... nope. I wasn't going to think about that.

"I'm the opposite. I love being around people. I would go

crazy if I had to spend all day alone. I'd probably start talking to the walls." She giggled.

I grinned. It was easy to picture that. From the little I knew of her, Savannah loved chatting and interacting with people. Dorothy and Rory had loved her. She was the type of person who everyone loved, and to be honest, I was no exception.

The only problem was I wasn't interested in relationships. I had vowed I was done with love. It hurt too badly when you lost someone and there was no way I could survive that kind of pain again.

"Did you always know you wanted to be a park ranger?" she asked.

I waited for my chest to constrict painfully, but it didn't. "I became a ranger five years ago." The words leapt out of my mouth, without giving me time to rethink them.

Whenever a woman I was seeing became inquisitive and asked personal questions, I brushed her off.

Savannah stopped what she was doing. "Really? What did you do before that?"

I shrugged. "I worked in the city. I was a high-flying trader, making in an hour more money than most people earn in their lifetime." Success and money had been the most important thing to me at the time. My goal was to give Amanda and our unborn child the best life I could.

"Oh wow. I could never have guessed it," Savannah said, staring at me as if trying to understand me.

There was not much to understand. My goal in life since losing Amanda was to survive. When she died in that car crash, I had died as well. I'd become a shell of a man.

"Why did you change careers?" she asked.

I had said enough and she didn't really need to know about Amanda. My family were the only ones who knew and I preferred to keep it like that. I shrugged in response to her question. "Just needed a change."

My answer seemed to satisfy her. She tossed the salad and then carried it to the fridge. The potatoes were already in the oven and now all we needed to do was to wait for dinner to be ready.

I got a bottle of wine from the fridge and two wine glasses from the cabinet, and set them on the table.

"You know, that gives me hope," Savannah said, tapping the table with her fingers. "If you can change your career and change direction completely, then so can I."

"What do you mean?" I poured the chilled wine in both glasses, figuring if she didn't like wine, I could drink both of them. I usually limited myself to two glasses anyway.

She took the wine and sipped on it. "Thanks, this is lovely. What is it?"

It was one of my more expensive brands. I was a bit of a wine collector and over the years, I'd developed a taste for rare expensive wines. I handed the bottle to Savannah and she whistled.

"This one's special," she said.

I smiled. Few people cared about wine and it was nice to see she could tell the difference between the different brands.

"You were saying?" I prodded her, wanting to hear her career plans.

"I've always wanted to work in a beauty salon. Maybe even my own someday." Her cheeks reddened. "I know, it's a crazy goal for someone who delivers groceries..."

"Don't say that and never put yourself down," I said sternly. "You're smart and driven and you can be anything you want to be."

She smiled and my heart lifted. "Thank you. Those words mean a lot."

"It's true." I never said things that I didn't mean.

She laughed softly. "I know you are curious but are too much of a gentleman to ask why I never followed my dreams."

It had crossed my mind but I had trained myself to mind my own business. I hated being asked personal questions and I imagined other people did as well. Add to the fact I had never been interested enough in another person to ask personal questions. The only life I'd been interested in for the last five years was mine, and mine alone.

I didn't confirm her statement but I kept my gaze on her very pretty face.

"I got married too early," she said and when she saw the look of horror on my face, she quickly added, "But divorced now."

I let out an audible sigh of relief and she laughed.

"I'd gone to college for only six months when I got pregnant and we had a shotgun wedding," she said, a tone of sadness in her voice. "So that was my dream crushed but having Ethan made it all worthwhile." A soft smile came over her features.

She had a child. By the sounds of it, her child was just about or a little older than my daughter would have been. "You have a son?"

"Yes. His name is Ethan and he's six years old," she said.

The pain came then. I'd almost accepted losing Amanda but when I thought of our unborn child who died even before she got a chance at life, I wanted to punch something.

"Hey, are you okay?" Savannah said, placing her hand on my arm.

"I'm good. Dinner must be ready." I got up abruptly and busied myself with getting the chicken and potatoes from the oven. Silence filled the room and I knew Savannah was wondering what had happened.

I couldn't explain to anyone the pain I carried on a daily basis. The pain of knowing I would never see my daughter. I placed the plates and the food on the table and invited Savannah to serve herself.

We couldn't eat in silence. "What made you move to Paradise?"

"I wanted space from my ex and his new girlfriend. I guess I needed a fresh start for me and Ethan and Paradise held good memories for me. I'd come to stay with my Aunt May every summer when I was a kid and I loved this small town."

"It's not so small now," I said.

She laughed. "It is compared to my home town. City really."

I viewed her with new eyes. Savannah could laugh and move on with her life after a divorce, which in some ways resembled grief. She had lost too but you couldn't tell from being with her or talking to her.

A thought crossed my mind. "Your ex, he didn't hurt you, did he?" I held my breath as I waited for her answer. In my eyes, there was nothing more despicable than a man who hurt a woman. There was never any excuse for it. Never. Women needed our protection and love.

I hadn't been able to protect Amanda and our baby. A sharp sword pierced through my chest, slicing my heart in half.

"Not physically but over the years, he bashed my self-esteem until I forgot who I was. By the time we divorced, I was a mess." She spoke in a matter of fact way, with no trace of emotion. The only time her emotions came to the surface was when she spoke about her son.

"Where is your son now?" I desperately hoped she wasn't one of those horrible mothers who left their children to fend for themselves. If she was that mother, I didn't give a fuck if there was a storm. She was going to leave.

She smiled. "With my sister. I'm picking him up on Sunday so he can start school on Monday."

We ate quietly for a few minutes. I pictured Savannah as a mother and she fit the role perfectly. Not that there was physically anything motherly about her. She dressed sexier than normal people did and she reveled in her sexuality. Clearly, she was a woman who was proud of her body.

But it wasn't just her perfect body and how she carried herself. It was the joy she emitted and her caring nature. Dorothy had told me how Savannah carried her groceries into the house and always asked if there was anything else she could do. You couldn't be all that and not be a good mother.

"What about you," Savannah said. "Do you have family around?"

"Yes. My mother, sister and brothers all live around."

"How lovely for you," Savannah said enthusiastically.

Shame came over me. What would she say if I told her the last time I'd seen my family was over two months ago? And before that it had been four months. That my phone was full of messages inviting me for Sunday lunch at my mother's house which I never responded to.

"Are they married?" she asked.

I shook my head. "No. My sister lives with my mom but my other siblings live alone." Career wise, we had all done well for ourselves. Cassie lived with my mother out of choice as she owned the largest beauty salon in Paradise.

An idea came to me then. I would ask her for advice about Savannah's situation. College was not an option for her right now but I knew a lot of Cassie's employees had learnt on the job. The only problem was that I had isolated myself so much from my family, I wasn't sure if Cassie would have it in her heart to do me any favors.

"You look so thoughtful," Savannah said and then cocked her head to one side. "You're a difficult man to read Cameron."

A lot of people said that. If only Savannah knew. I had spoken more to her in a day than I had spoken to all other people combined in a month. There was something about her that had slowly broken my barriers. Maybe because she was a very open human being herself. She had disarmed me with her raw honesty, starting with the day she scolded me about my rudeness in the woods.

We finished our food and side by side, we washed the dishes.

"Let's drink this in the living room," I suggested, carrying the wine and fresh glasses.

"This is so cozy," Savannah said when she entered the living room.

I had lit a fire in the living room chimney and an orange glow lit up the room. It seemed right that Savannah and I were sharing this moment. I set the wine bottle and glasses on the table and sat down.

Savannah unselfconsciously sat next to me. I poured the wine and handed her one glass. I took a sip of my wine and then unable to resist the lure of her thighs, I placed my hand on her calf. A tremble went through her leg.

I raised my hands up to her thigh and softly stroked it, moving my hand up to the hem of her t-shirt. She breathed through parted lips and desire flared in her eyes. She took a sip of her wine and set the glass back down. I planned on seducing her until she asked me for it. The night was going to be long and fun.

7

Savannah

Cameron took his hand away and I wanted to beg him to return it to its former position on my thigh.

"Tell me about your son?" he said.

Asking me about Ethan was the best way to distract me. "He's a sweet little boy and so kind. He loves the outdoors and he's a little man's man, which I love."

"Was he close to his father?" Cameron asked.

I shook my head. "Finn was too demanding of Ethan and I was glad when he got into another relationship and shifted his attention from Ethan."

"My father died when we were teenagers," Cameron said and didn't say any more.

"Did that affect you?" I worried that not having a father in his life would affect Ethan. I tried my best to do the stuff he liked with him but let's be honest, I wasn't a man.

"It did but not in the way you might think. He had given

us a good foundation but I really missed him. Still do. My father was a great father," Cameron said.

"I wish I could say the same for Finn. He's a bully, of women and little boys. I can't tell you how happy I was that I had the option of moving to Paradise, thanks to Aunt May."

"I'm glad for you too," Cameron said.

I was curious about him but I didn't want to ask too many questions. I could already tell that Cameron was a very private person and I didn't want to make him uncomfortable.

Silence fell between us. Cameron drained his wine but did not pour more for himself. Instead, he inched closer to me and shifted his body to face me. I forgot to breathe as I waited for his next move.

He raised his hand and brushed my nipples with his fingers in a feather light movement. My nipples peaked and became visible through the t-shirt. Lazily, Cameron did it again. My chest rose up and down as my breathing changed.

I lifted my glass and drained my glass as well, then set it on the table. With a finger, Cameron drew a circle around one nipple and then moved to the other. Fire lapped at my insides and my whole body came alive.

He leaned forward and took a nipple into his mouth and gently bit it. I let out a moan and when he bit the other nipple, I cried out. My nipples were super sensitive normally but with Cameron, they were like spikes of nerves.

I bit on my lower lip to contain my moans. I needed his mouth on my bare skin but he wasn't making a move to remove my t-shirt. After a while, it dawned on me what Cameron was doing. He was teasing me. Waiting to see how long it would take before I begged him to tear off my t-shirt and fuck me senseless.

Two could play that game. Excitement coursed through

me. "More wine?" I asked him and instead of waiting for an answer, I stood up. I experienced a feeling of loss when his hands fell off me.

"Wine?" Cameron said, momentarily confused.

"We need fresh glasses," I announced and picked up the used glasses from the table. It was completely unnecessary of course to get fresh glasses but I needed an excuse to sashay across the room.

As I slowly walked, swaying my hips, I could imagine the hungry look that Cameron was giving my back end. In the kitchen, I took my time rinsing the glasses, then I found clean ones and returned to the couch.

I stifled a smile at the sight of Cameron pacing the living room, a huge tent in front of his jogging pants. I bent to pour the wine, counting down seconds as to how long he could keep away. I counted up to five seconds before his hands were on my waist and his cock was pushing against my ass.

A soft moan left my mouth as Cameron dry humped me. Wine forgotten I stood up and kept my hands by my side, giving him freedom to do what he wanted with my body. He growled close to my ear and slipped his hands under my t-shirt.

"Do you have an idea how fucking sexy you are?" Cameron said.

"Hmm," I murmured.

His hands skimmed over my belly, making me tremble and cry out his name softly. He turned me around, cupped my bare ass and kissed me. Liquid heat trickled down my thighs. Without warning, Cameron lifted me and without breaking the kiss, he started bouncing me on his cock.

"Oh God, Cameron," I said when we came up for air. "Please." I needed more.

"Tell me what you want, Savannah," he said, his eyes blazing with passion.

"I want you to fuck me with your big cock," I said unashamedly.

He growled and carried me around the couch. "I love a woman who knows what she wants." He lowered me to the floor gently and turned me to face the couch.

I knew what he wanted. I gripped the back of the couch and spread my legs. Behind me, Cameron lifted my t-shirt and bunched it around my waist. My breath hitched as I imagined the sight I made with my ass spread out for him.

"Fuck you look hot like that," he said, his voice husky. He gave my ass cheeks a gentle slap that made my flesh reverberate all the way to my clit.

My pussy clenched, needing him inside me. Swishing sounds filled the room as Cameron took off his pants. The next thing I knew, he was sawing his cock across my slit, touching my clit but barely. I adjusted myself, bending further for more friction.

"Soon, I'll fill this pussy with my big cock," Cameron said.

"Yes," I said. "Do it now."

He chuckled. "Not so fast. I'll make you come first without fucking you. How does that sound?"

"Mmm, yes." I didn't care what he did or didn't do. The desperate urge to climax was growing stronger by the minute.

When the orgasm came, it thundered through me, and if I hadn't been holding on tight to the couch, I'd have slid to the floor. Before I could recover, Cameron slipped his cock inside me and took on a fast, punishing rhythm that immediately started a fire inside me.

I screamed as his thrusts took me closer and closer to

the edge. I bucked against him, needing his cock deeper and deeper. When I came, it was like fireworks going off inside me. I screamed and dug my nails into the leather couch, hoping that I wouldn't leave scratch marks, but unable to do anything about it.

Cameron came with a roar, and hot cream flooded my pussy. Cameron buried his face on my neck, his breath like a hot fan on my skin. We stayed that way for a few minutes, waiting for our breaths to go back to normal.

He stood up, gently pulled out his cock and guided me to the couch. He sat down and I followed, sitting on his lap. He wrapped his big hands around me protectively and I wrapped my arms around his neck and lay on my head on his shoulder.

It was an intimate pose for people who barely knew each other but there was something about Cameron that made me trust him. He was grumpy and rude, but he had a tender side, which I'd seen that evening.

"You're perfect Savannah," he murmured, stroking my back.

"So are you," I said back. I wasn't a fool and I knew that all the sweet words we were saying meant nothing. They were words brought by the intimate moments we had shared. In the harsh light of the morning, we would go back to being the strangers we had been to one another.

We stayed that way for a good ten minutes, then Cameron suggested we wrap up for the night and head upstairs. Outside, the storm was still raging and it felt good to get into bed. Cameron surprised me when he pulled me close to rest my head on his chest.

He wrapped his hands around me. I definitely would not have pegged him as the type that likes to cuddle. His body was like a warm blanket around me. With his free hand, he smoothed my hair back in slow, soft movements.

I wondered what Cameron was thinking. I knew so little about him.

"Can I ask you something?" I said, breaking the silence.

He cleared his throat. "Sure."

"Why are you single? Surely it's not for a lack of women. Paradise is not that much of a small town."

He took so long to answer I thought he had fallen asleep. When he did talk, his voice sounded so sad.

"It's a choice," he said. "My wife died in a car accident five years ago. When she passed on, she took my heart with her. I don't have it in me to love another woman."

I covered my mouth. "I'm so sorry." I tried and failed to imagine the kind of pain he had gone through. "That must have been terrible."

He grunted.

I mused over his words that he didn't have it in him to love another woman. That suited me perfectly. I wasn't interested in a relationship either. Why then did I feel a crushing disappointment?

8

Savannah

Saturday deliveries took longer than usual because of the weekend traffic. It was the one and last Saturday that I was working because of Ethan. My manager at the grocery store was awesome and a mom herself. She was happy to give me the shifts which worked well with my schedule.

I got back to the store in the afternoon to grab my schedule for the following week. Heather had just finished her shift and was getting ready to leave.

"Want to grab a coffee?" She asked as she wrapped a scarf around her neck.

"Sure, give me a minute." I headed to the notice board, outside the manager's office and removing my phone, I took a picture of the schedule.

Heather was waiting for me at the staff entrance in the back. We left together and headed to Joe's Coffee house next door. I was lucky to have made a friend so quickly in Paradise. Heather had taken me under her wing on the first day, giving me tips on doing deliveries, as it had been her first job.

Warmth and delicious scents of coffee and pastries hit us as soon as we entered the coffee house. It was packed but we found an empty table when a couple got up to leave. The server, a friendly girl, Cathy, wiped it down and we sat down.

"You have a glow to you," Heather said after we gave our orders and Cathy left.

I grinned. It was difficult to deny it because I felt wonderful. "I feel like a car that has just gotten serviced." I laughed as soon as those words were out of my mouth.

Heather laughed too. "That good huh? How did you get so lucky and you've only been in town for a couple of weeks? I live here and no one has asked me out in months."

"We both know you give off keep away vibes," I said casually. Heather was not interested in going out with anyone after coming out of a four-year relationship. The last two years had been long distance and it had taken a toll on her. "Besides, Cameron never asked me out. I just happened to be stranded in his house during a storm."

"Lucky you. But there's something special about you Savannah if you got Cameron to talk to you let alone sleep with you," she said.

Cathy brought our coffees and we waited for her to leave before continuing with our conversation.

"I'm still shocked to be honest," I told her. "I told you about the first time we met and how rude he was. But yesterday, he was like a different person. He was very worried about me being out in the storm and wouldn't hear about me driving in that weather."

"Rightly so," Heather said, sipping on her coffee.

I kept my hands around the mug to warm them up. The

weather had become mild with a hint of sunshine but it was still very cold. I lifted the mug to my lips and took a sip. Heaven.

"So are you two in a relationship now?" Heather asked.

I shook my head. "No. It's nothing like that. Neither of us wants to be in a relationship. I have enough on my plate and Cameron..." I didn't know how much Heather knew about Cameron's life and I didn't want to disclose his private matters.

"It was so sad what happened to his wife," Heather said.

I let out a sigh of relief. "Something like that scars you for life."

"I remember when he first moved back to Paradise. Everyone was talking about it but we never saw him. We still don't except when he makes the rare stop at Joe's for coffee and that takes less than two minutes. Then he disappears again."

I already knew he never went to the grocery store. His order was more or less the same every week and if there was a change, he called. Heather told me a little about his family but it was stuff I already knew from Cameron himself.

"Tell me the juicy stuff," Heather said with a mischievous smile. "Is he good in bed? He has to be with a body like that."

I laughed. "He's a fifteen out of ten. That's all I'll say."

Heather's eyes widened. "I've never met one of those except in romance books."

My face heated up as my mind returned to that morning. I'd woken up to something wet and delicious lapping at my pussy folds. It had been heaven, waking up in the midst of ecstasy. He had fucked me with his tongue until I came.

"I know that look," Heathen said, bringing me back to

the present. "Get your mind out of the gutter. So now that's it for the two of you? No seeing each other?"

"Pretty much." The morning had been glorious and we'd even taken a walk in the woods after breakfast and a shower. But when we returned to the house and it was time for me to leave, it had gotten weird.

I blamed myself. I'd told him something to the effect that he needn't worry about me clinging to him or whatever. I cringed when I remembered the conversation. He'd simply nodded and said nothing. I felt like an idiot.

Heather stared at me in admiration. "I don't know if I could do something like that. I mean I can have a one-night stand and I have, but not with someone I'm likely to see again. You deliver his groceries for goodness sake."

I shrugged. "I can always leave them outside his door." I wasn't that confident in my ability to move on after that weekend.

For one, I'd seen a gentle, sweet side of Cameron that made me like him a whole lot more. If things had been different, he was a man I'd have loved to get to know better. But they weren't and I had to move on with my life.

CAMERON and I had exchanged numbers in case of emergency as he put it but I never expected him to call or text me. That's why it irked me so much that I kept glancing at my phone on the two-hour long drive to Ivy's place.

By the time I pulled into the driveway, I was pissed off with myself for my weakness. Why was I waiting for him to text or call? There was nothing to say to each other and I had made sure of that by telling him before I left. I could have kicked myself for my big mouth but I'd wanted to say it to save him the discomfort of saying it himself.

I killed the engine of the minivan and got out. I never ceased to admire my sister's home. It was one of those houses that were featured in interior design magazines and I loved visiting to gawk and admire. That afternoon however, I wasn't in the mood for it.

I wanted to leave as fast as I decently could. Our last conversation had left a sour taste in my mouth. I wasn't a person who held grudges but combined with the fact that I hadn't heard from Cameron at all, I wasn't in a friendly or forgiving mood.

I made my way to the front door and before I could ring the bell, it flew open and Ethan hurled himself at me.

"Mom," he cried.

I laughed and hugged him tightly. "Hey buddy. I missed you." My bad mood evaporated. We entered the house hand in hand and Ethan led the way to the kitchen, talking a hundred words a minute.

"Uncle Sam took us fishing mom," he said. "And I caught a fish."

My throat constricted painfully. Those were the things that Finn should have been doing with his son. Ethan loved being outside, either riding his bike or just being out in nature.

"Hi," I said to Ivy, her husband Sam, and their son, Liam. I went to him and ruffled his head.

"Hi," they chorused back.

"I heard you guys went fishing," I said to my nephew. "Did you catch a fish?"

"I did but it escaped," he said in a pouty voice.

I laughed. "Next time you'll catch another one. Get your stuff," I said to Ethan and the boys left together.

"Coffee?" Ivy asked and I said yes.

I made myself comfortable at the island and chatted with Sam. Ivy brought the coffee and gave it to me.

"Thanks."

"Savannah, I need to tell you something," Ivy said, throwing a nervous glance at her husband.

What now? She wouldn't dare ask me about the mysterious man I'd spent the night with in front of Sam would she? I was friends with Sam but that's not to say I would be comfortable discussing my sex life in front of my brother-in-law.

I looked at Ivy and waited for her to speak. She wore a nervous look and I immediately became worried.

"We bumped into Finn in town yesterday," she said.

There was nothing odd about that as they lived in the same town. That was one of the reasons why I'd left. I hated bumping into Finn and his new girlfriend every time I went to town. Worse than that, I hated the promises he made to Ethan and the disappointment by not showing up.

I figured if I left town, my little boy would not have any expectations of his dad and he would not get his little heart broken over and over again.

"Ethan told him that you guys had moved to Paradise. He seemed more interested than usual in your lives."

It was odd and honestly, a little worrying. I didn't trust Finn's renewed interest in Ethan. He'd never been interested in his son. "Thank God that we're in Paradise. I don't trust him either but I'm not going to worry about it," I said with more bravado than I felt.

"That's what I said," Sam said. "There's a law and remember he didn't contest custody. He wasn't interested and I'm sure that hasn't changed."

Sam's words reassured me. Ethan and I left after I finished my coffee, and Ivy walked us to the van.

"Does your new m know about E?" Ivy asked, gesturing at Ethan who was skipping ahead.

I sighed. I should have known that Ivy wasn't going to let it go. She was like a dog with a bone. "He's not my new man. He's just someone I met and we were attracted to each other." I seared her with a look. "Adults do that, you know."

"I just hope you know what you're doing," she said.

"I do." I didn't. Well, my brain did but my heart was clueless. I missed Cameron. Stupid, I know. How did you miss someone you had met for a total of four times?

Ethan and I got into the minivan and waved goodbye to Ivy. It was a relief to leave and I couldn't wait to get back to our little cottage. Ethan seemed to like Paradise when we first arrived and for that I was glad.

He spoke non-stop for an hour and then fell asleep, his head leaning against the window. My heart burst with love for him. Finn floated into my mind again. Why had he been asking about us? I hated that he now knew where we lived.

Paradise was not small but it wasn't so big that you couldn't find someone. We were divorced and he had moved on with his life. I had hoped when the divorce became final, he would marry Nancy, the woman he left me for. That would make me feel safe.

We drove through town and to my shame, I slowed down as I drove past Joe's coffee house, hoping that I would catch a glimpse of Cameron. Such things only happened when you were not waiting for them.

9

Cameron

I t was about two in the afternoon when I drove my truck out of the garage and headed towards town. My destination was my sister's salon, something I hadn't done in years. My conversation with Savannah bugged me and I wanted to do something about it.

Savannah needed a push in the right direction. The weather was mild and it hadn't snowed again since the day when Savannah spent the night. I took a turn off the main road in an automatic action. I never drove past Dorothy and Rory's home without checking in on them.

Their only son lived in another state and I'd taken it upon myself when I first moved back home, to keep an eye on them. I parked my truck and headed to the front door. I gave three rap knocks and several seconds later, the door swung open.

"I thought it was you," Dorothy said, a wide smile on her face. "Come on in for coffee."

I was about to refuse then thought better of it. Ten

minutes would not make a difference to my time and besides, my sister Cassie was not expecting me.

We exchanged pleasantries as I followed her to the living room where Rory was reading a newspaper. He folded it and placed it on the table.

"Hello sir," I said to him.

He grinned. "Hello yourself," Rory said. "It's nice to see another face apart from Dorothy's."

"Are you complaining," Dorothy asked as she headed to the kitchen.

"Never."

She turned to look at her husband and they exchanged a look of pure devotion and love. A pang went through me. That was the kind of future I had imagined with Amanda. We would have raised children and then grown old together.

I hadn't just lost Amanda, I had lost a future as well. Savannah jumped into my mind uninvited. She was different from Amanda but they both shared an excitement for life. That was what had drawn me to Savannah... and that hot body of hers.

"How's life in the park?" Rory asked. "Any new adventures?"

He loved hearing about my work and I always had a story or two to entertain him. It was no different today. I told him about a tourist who had gotten lost but had been found after two days. This was not the best weather to get lost in especially when it was snowing or raining.

Dorothy brought the coffee and we sat around and chatted. I left shortly after, promising to drop in on them soon. I enjoyed the picturesque road through the mountains and stupidly wished that Savannah was with me.

I was thinking about her too much. We were done and

thinking about her was pointless. After I was done talking about her to my sister, that was it.

Cassie's salon was at the end of Main Street and I got a parking spot at the front of it. I found myself straining my eyes to see if I could catch a glimpse of Savannah. It had become a habit but one I needed to wean myself off soon. There was no space for a woman in my life.

I pushed the glass doors open and entered the cool interior. I was impressed with what my sister had done with the space. I had only come once and at the time I'd been thick in the mist of grieving for my wife and hadn't really paid attention to the décor.

The reception area had oak veneer paneling and arched blue shapes that were the theme in the whole salon. I let out a sigh of relief that my mother was not behind the reception desk.

"Hello," the woman behind the reception said. "Welcome to Cutting Edge beauty salon. How can I help you?"

"My name is Cameron Elliott, I'm here to see Cassie," I said.

Her eyes widened. "Cassie has another brother?"

I almost smiled at the expression on her face. "Yes."

She shook her head. "I'm sorry. I've only met Asher and Dr. Elliott." She picked up her phone. "Please have a seat. I'll let her know that you're here."

I sat down and as people walked in and out of the salon, it dawned on me how much I had isolated myself in the last five years. I couldn't even remember when I had last spoken to either Asher, who was a firefighter or Thomas.

"She's in her office," the receptionist said. "It's the last room on your right down the hallway."

"Thanks." It was a good thing that she gave me directions. I don't remember an office or even a room upstairs.

I bounded up the stairs and strolled down the wide hallway until I got to the last office. I knocked and Cassie's voice called for me to enter.

"I didn't believe it when Daisy told me you were downstairs. I was sure it was a mistake." Cassie stood up and walked around her desk to hug me.

"No mistake," I said and held her close. "It's good to see you, sis."

"It's wonderful to see you Cameron." She kept her hands on my shoulders and stood back to inspect me. "You look well. Very well."

I know what she meant. Something had happened since meeting Savannah. I felt happier and more optimistic about the future. It was as if she had sprinkled me with some magic that had lifted the veil of grief that always surrounded me. I felt more alive than I had in years.

"Mom will be sorry she missed you," Cassie said. "Can I make you some coffee?"

"No, I'm good, thanks." I sat down on the visitor's chair. "You've done well for yourself. This place looks amazing."

"Thanks," she said. "It hasn't reached the level of Cutting Edge in Helena." There was a wistful note in Cassie's voice.

She had gone to college in Helena and settled there, getting a job in a beauty salon. A few years later, Cassie had her own beauty salon. And then our father had gotten sick and she had sold the salon and returned to Paradise to help my mother take care of him.

When he had passed on, she had not returned to Helena and had instead opened a beauty salon in Paradise. Cassie was thoroughly ambitious and I knew that Paradise would not be enough for her. At one point in the future, she would probably return to Helena.

"Helena is a city, Cassie. You can't compare the two," I told her.

She smiled. "You're right."

I cleared my throat. "I need some advice."

She sat up straighter in her chair. "I'm intrigued. You of all people wanting advice from me?"

She would understand why I needed her expertise when I told her. "It's about a friend of mine. Her name is Savannah. She's new in Paradise and she's currently working at the grocery store."

"Go on," Cassie said when I paused.

"She did six months of beauty college then life happened but she's always been interested in the industry. What would you advise?"

Cassie tried to hide a smile. "First of all, I must say that I'm intrigued. I didn't think you met actual people let alone spoke with them."

"Cassie."

"Okay," she said and grew solemn. "I would advise her to apprentice in a beauty salon and it so happens that we have a space and we would be happy to have her."

"Really?" I said, smiling broadly. My next question would have been if she had space for Savannah.

She nodded. "Anything for you bro."

My chest constricted painfully and guilt bubbled up my throat. I had more or less cut off all of my family from my life and Cassie was being so good to me. "Thanks."

"You said that she's working at the grocery store. She can come whenever she's free and if she likes it, we'll give her a paid apprenticeship position."

"She'll be so happy to hear that."

A mischievous look came over her features. "I have something I want you to do for me in return."

"Sure, anything," I said.

"We're having a family lunch at Mom's next Sunday. Please come. It's been so long and everyone will be so happy to see you."

I inhaled deeply. I loved my family and to be honest, I'd missed them. My brothers and I had been close, texting and calling each other. But when Amanda died, I cut myself off and I knew that must have hurt them. Maybe it was time to rejoin the world of the living.

"I'll be there," I said and pushed the chair back to stand up.

She came around and we hugged again. When Cassie drew back, she had tears in her eyes. "Mom will be so happy."

The guilt bubbled up again. I hated that I'd pushed my mother away as well but at the time, surviving alone, day by day had been all that I could manage. I smiled at Cassie, kissed her forehead and waved goodbye, promising to see her in a few days.

In my truck, I held the steering wheel, conflicted over what to do. I had a delivery due the following day, which meant that I would see Savannah. However, the thought of waiting over twenty-four hours felt unbearable at that point. But only because I had some good news for her. Nothing else.

I hadn't been to her side of town for years and I drove slowly, reacquainting myself with the area. I slowed down when I got to Savannah's cottage. It's just as I remembered it. Colorful and pretty, except now, it was a little run down and it could have done with a lick of paint.

Savannah's minivan was not in the driveway and disappointment flooded me. I brought my truck to a stop in the street parking to consider my next move. I really wanted to see her face when I gave her the good news.

Just then, her minivan approached and relief surged through me. I pulled the key from the ignition and waited for Savannah to get out of the van. She went around to the passenger side, opened the door and a dark haired boy got out. All the air left my lungs as an image of a girl popped into my mind.

My daughter would have been a year younger than Savannah's son. Sadness came over me and I wasn't sure if I wanted to leave the truck, after all.

Don't be a pussy. All you have to do is to tell Savannah that she has a position at The Cutting Edge Salon, if she wants it.

My heart hammered with nervousness as I got out of the truck. By then, Savannah and her son were at the front door. They heard my footsteps and turned. Savannah smiled and I exhaled a breath I hadn't known I'd been holding.

"Cameron, what a nice surprise," she said.

I noticed the boy was in a school uniform. She must have come from picking him up from school. "Hi." I got to the front door and smiled at the boy. He looked up at me with a curious expression.

"This is my son Ethan," Savannah said in the cheerful manner she had of talking. She ruffled her son's head. "This is my friend from the woods. The one I told you about."

Ethan's face lit up. "Is it true that you have a house in the woods?" he asked.

I laughed at the wonder in his voice. "Yes, I do. You can come and visit anytime." My response reminded me of the person I had been before Amanda died. I'd been friendly and outgoing and I'd loved kids. I guess that person was still in there, somewhere.

"Can we Mom?" Ethan said, turning to his mother.

"We'll see," Savannah said and unlocked the door. Ethan ran in. "Come in for coffee."

The plan was to tell her what had brought me around, as soon as I got the chance. Instead, I accepted her offer and followed her into the house. In the kitchen, she filled a pot of coffee and leaves it brewing, then pours a glass of milk for Ethan.

She excused herself to take it to him along with a cookie. I looked around the kitchen. It was cozy and homely, but like the exterior of the cottage, it needed updating.

10

Savannah

I t was odd but exhilarating to have Cameron in my house. I'd been missing him terribly and just seeing him walking towards us had felt like a dream. I wanted to pinch myself to be sure it was real. He was seated at Aunt May's old kitchen drinking his coffee.

"I came by to give you some news," Cameron said, after we'd been quiet for a few minutes. Not that it was uncomfortable. It felt restful. Cameron was restful, when he wasn't making me feel so aroused that I wanted to tear off all my clothes.

I waited for him to continue.

"I went by my sister's salon. It's called The Cutting Edge and it's no—"

"I know it," I said, interrupting him. "That's your sister's beauty salon?"

He nodded. "Yes. Anyway I told her about you and that you have done six months of college."

I didn't know how to feel about Cameron telling his sister about me. I'd told him my past in confidence.

"She wants you to apprentice with them in a paid position. It can be part time, when you're not working at the grocery store," Cameron said. "She asked me to give you her number and when you are ready, you can give her a call."

I was touched that he had gone to the trouble of talking to his sister. Knowing Cameron, it couldn't have been easy. I smiled. "Thank you for doing that for me." I was a little uncomfortable knowing that someone else knew my story.

"You're welcome," Cameron said. "I'll text you her number."

"Okay," I said. "That's really kind of you and her."

He nodded, tipped his cup to drink the last of his coffee and set the mug on the table. "I'll get going now."

I wasn't ready for Cameron to go. It felt good having him in my cottage. "I'm just about to start preparing dinner. Please stay."

"Are you sure it's okay with Ethan?" Cameron asked.

"Absolutely. I'll just change out of these clothes." I peeked on Ethan who was playing happily in the living room with his toy cars. In my bedroom, I stripped out of my day clothes and changed into a pair of fresh yoga pants and a crop top. I ignored the tingling between my legs and hurried back.

I grinded to a halt in the living room at the sight of Cameron on the floor with Ethan. They were each driving a car around the coffee table in what looked to be a race.

Ethan was the first to see me. "Mom, look. Me and Cameron are racing and I'm winning."

"Of course you are," Cameron said. "You're a better driver than I am."

The grin on Ethan could have split his face. Warmth spread across my chest and tears filled my eyes. Ethan was my life and having Cameron give him the male attention he so desperately needed meant the world to me. Cameron winked at me and continued playing.

As I prepared dinner, I mused over Cameron's sister's offer to work in a salon. I should have jumped at it but it felt like too much happening in a short amount of time. We had just moved to Paradise and Ethan had just started school. I needed to catch my breath before jumping into something else.

There was also the discomfort of a stranger knowing my story. It's not that I was embarrassed about my past but I didn't want everyone knowing I dropped out of college and got married too soon, and to a jerk at that. All that stuff was nothing to be proud about.

Soon, the kitchen was filled with the delicious scents of chicken. Dinner was chicken fried rice and in forty-five minutes, it was ready. Ethan and I usually ate at the old kitchen table and after setting it, I went to the living room.

I heard Cameron's voice before I saw him and when I did, my heart melted. He and Ethan were seated on the floor with their backs resting on the couch, and Ethan was reading Tarzan, his favorite story book. The rapt attention on Cameron's face told me he was really listening to the story and not pretending to.

Ethan loved reading and when he had an audience, he enjoyed it even more. He liked to imagine that like Tarzan, he lived in the woods.

I waited for a pause in the story. "Dinner is ready gentlemen," I said.

"Can I just finish this chapter Mom?" Ethan asked.

I looked at Cameron.

"I'd love to hear the end of the chapter. Tarzan is lost in the woods and I won't enjoy dinner if I don't find out if he'll find his way back home," Cameron said.

Ethan looked at him as if he had discovered the secret of aging.

I laughed. "Okay then. Five minutes. You still need a bath before bed, young man."

I was still smiling when I returned to the kitchen to serve dinner onto the plates. Ethan and Cameron came soon afterwards and as we ate, Ethan more or less told Cameron how the rest of the story unfolded.

I would not have pegged Cameron as someone who liked children. He was too reserved for that, or so I'd thought. In the company of a child, he became chatty and more comfortable than I'd ever seen him, except of course, between the sheets.

After dinner, Ethan insisted on helping with the dishes, as did Cameron, so I let both of them clean up. When they were done, I made another cup of coffee for Cameron and left him drinking while I supervised Ethan's bath.

"I really like Cameron Mom," Ethan said as I tucked him into bed. "Is he your boyfriend?"

His question took me aback and I didn't know how to answer it. "What would you say if he was?"

He grinned sleepily. "I'd tell you to marry him. I like him. I like him very much."

I like him too, I said internally. I kissed Ethan, turned off his lights and shut his door. Cameron had turned on the small TV that had been Aunt May's and he was watching the news. When he saw me, he turned his attention to me.

"Is he asleep?" he said.

"Yep. He's usually tired by the end of the day and as soon as his head hits the pillow, he's gone."

I'd been dying to kiss Cameron ever since I saw him walking towards me. But we'd parted with the tacit understanding that what had happened that night was a one off. Instead of straddling him like I ached too, I sat at the very end of the couch.

"Thanks for dinner, it was lovely," Cameron said.

"You're welcome," I said. "It's nice for us to have some company. Thanks for playing with Ethan." I'd stayed with Finn for Ethan's sake. My little boy had needed a father, even a shitty one like Finn. Then he had left us and I'd realized sometimes it was better not to have a father than to have a shitty one, who criticized you all the time.

"You don't have to thank me. I enjoyed it. You have an awesome boy."

Cameron's voice held a wistful note. Maybe he and his late wife had plans for having a baby. My heart went out to him. I couldn't imagine going through the kind of loss he had gone through. No wonder he had pushed everybody away.

"Ethan's the only reason I don't regret my marriage to Finn," I said.

Cameron moved to the edge of his seat and I knew he was preparing to leave. In the next moment, he stood up. "I have to go. Think about my sister's offer."

"I will," I said and stood up.

Sudden tension sprouted between us as I walked him to the truck. Suddenly, it felt as though we were strangers, not people who had shared intimate moments together. We stood next to his truck awkwardly.

"I'll see you tomorrow when you bring my groceries," he said.

"Yeah. See you then." I watched him as he unlocked his

truck and after one more lingering glance at me, he entered his truck.

Before Cameron could turn the engine, my phone rang loudly from my waistband. I pulled it out and glanced at the screen. The number was unfamiliar.

"Hello," I said.

"Hello Savannah."

A shiver went down my spine. My blood turned to ice. Finn. Just the sound of his voice was enough to frighten me. Cameron must have seen my reaction because he got out of the truck and placed his hands on my shoulders.

"Finn. Why are you calling me at this time?" I said, fighting to keep my voice from trembling.

"I'm in town," he said.

"Which town?"

"Paradise."

My whole body shook. "What do you want?" I asked him, willing myself not to be cowered. Cameron's hand went around me and pulled me close. His strength seeped into me.

"I want to see my boy," Finn said. "Nancy and I want to raise him ourselves. We're getting married and since Nancy doesn't want to get pregnant, we figured we'd raise Ethan. Besides, we don't think you're the right person to raise him. You work part time at a grocery store, Savannah. You live in a dilapidated cottage and you're single. Nancy and I can give him a good home with two parents who have a stable job."

It felt as though I was living in a nightmare. This could not be happening. "Finn, you knew all that about me before you signed away your custody rights. You can't just change your mind." My voice had become hysterical.

"I can. He's my son and that will never change. When can I see him?"

"He's in school during the day," I said.

"Nancy and I can come back on Sunday. Wait." I could hear muffled voices as he spoke to someone. Then he came back to the phone. "Nancy said Sunday won't work. We'll come back on Saturday and we'll spend the afternoon with Ethan. Then after Nancy and I get married, we'll go to the courts for full custody."

He disconnected the call before I could respond. I wanted to cry. That was the very thing I had dreaded. Finn was not interested in Ethan. It was just a plan he and Nancy had hatched and I didn't know what they wanted. Sobs broke out from me and my body shook violently as I cried.

"Let's get back into the house," Cameron said and led me back in. We sat on the couch and he held me until my sobs subsided.

"What's going on Savannah? It's your ex, isn't it?" he asked.

"Yes." Hysteria rose up my throat again. I fought the urge to race into Ethan's room to make sure that he was okay. "He wants to take Ethan." I told him everything that Finn had said.

"We'll get the best lawyers," Cameron said. "He's trying to get you to give up without a fight. The courts will be on your side Savannah."

"He's right though, isn't he?" I said. "When he and Nancy get married, they'll look like the better parents as far as the courts are concerned, won't they?"

Even Cameron couldn't deny that. "Then we'll beat them to it. We'll get married."

At first, I thought I'd heard him wrong. "What did you say?" I asked Cameron, staring into his eyes for signs that he had been joking.

"If getting married will guarantee you win custody of

Ethan if Finn goes to court, then I'll marry you. You're an awesome mom and Ethan is a great kid. I couldn't bear it if anyone did anything to hurt either of you. I'll do whatever I can to ensure that you remain together."

His words brought a fresh wave of sobs. No one had ever offered to do something that was entirely for me.

11

Cameron

"This is crazy," Savannah mumbled for the fifth time since I picked her up from her cottage. I felt her gaze on me. She didn't voice it, but I knew what she was thinking. What was in it for me?

Nothing. Savannah had the bad luck of getting married to a jerk. She couldn't see how someone would do something good for her without expecting anything in return. I hated bullies more so when they targeted women and children. If I could do something about it, I would. Even getting married.

I would feel safer with Savannah and Ethan under my care. Plus, I had nothing to lose. After Amanda, I vowed that I'd never marry again, but with Savannah, it wasn't going to be a real marriage. The one way I knew I could protect her and Ethan was to marry her.

I'd invested wisely over the years and could be considered rich by a lot of standards. I'd hire the best lawyers for

Savannah and keep them physically safe. The security in my home was top notch and I'd feel a whole lot better when they were with me.

The weather was pretty good for a winter day. Savannah should have been doing deliveries, instead, we were headed to an elopement chapel in Helena to get married. I'd organized everything via email and over the phone and the only thing remaining was to show up.

"We don't really know each other," Savannah said, speaking up after almost ten minutes of silence.

"We have an hour and a half to remedy that," I teased, then realized it was a major concern for Savannah. "What do you want to know?"

Her deep inhale filled the truck. "I don't know. Let me think. Why did you decide to be a park ranger?"

That one was easy. "I've always loved the outdoors and when Amanda died, I felt tired of the city and I needed something different. A change. Being a park ranger was perfect for me."

She nodded. "Your turn."

"What have you always wanted to do but never got a chance to?" I asked her.

"Traveling. I've always wanted to travel the world and I hope that one day, I get the opportunity to. Have you traveled a lot?" she asked.

Pain sliced through me. I waited for it to abate before answering Savannah's question. Amanda and I had traveled a lot before she got pregnant. We had visited a lot of European countries, Asia and Africa. We had both loved traveling and had a lot of fun planning for our trips.

"Yes."

To my relief, she didn't pursue the conversation further

to ask where I'd been. "If you could travel, where would you go?" I asked her.

She let out a soft laugh. "It's got to be Paris. The city of romance."

I'd been to Paris and it really was a romantic city. Amanda and I had done all the touristy things, but the moment that stood out for me was having dinner while cruising on The Seine.

I never thought I'd ever want to travel with another woman but I wished that Savannah and I were on our way to Paris. I'd get to show her the city and enjoy looking at the expressions on her face.

"My turn," Savannah said, sounding relaxed. The tension had left her voice and she seemed as though she was enjoying the game of getting to know each other. "What was it like growing up in Paradise?"

"Idyllic," I answered without giving it a second thought. My siblings and I had had the perfect childhood. "Paradise was not as large as it is now and at the time, everyone knew everyone else."

"Compared to Rogers, Paradise is a small town," Savannah said with a laugh.

"I'm sure. In those days, if you got up to some mischief with your friends, by the time you got home in the evening, your parents knew about it," I said, smiling at the memories.

It was a shame that I'd lost touch with my old friends who still lived in Paradise. A good number of them had left but several remained, but I had not kept contact with them.

I lost myself in my memories. Savannah must have done the same because we were both lost in our thoughts.

"How long are we going to stay married for?" Savannah asked quietly.

I shook my head. "I haven't thought about it." I hadn't

thought beyond marrying Savannah and keeping her and Ethan safe.

"I have Ethan to think about and I can't have him thinking that his mother is a serial wife," Savannah said.

"I'll be in no rush for a divorce," I said.

"What if you meet someone you want to marry?" she said.

"Not going to happen," I said. "Unless you do."

She shook her head. "Marriage is not on my radar. My focus is on getting my life back on track and raising Ethan."

"Then it's settled," I said. The thought of being married to Savannah indefinitely did not bother me. I was just glad that I could help.

"What about the..." her words trailed off. She cleared her throat. "The physical side of things?"

I glanced at her in amusement. Her cheeks were flushed, which amused me further as Savannah was not the type of woman who got embarrassed easily. "We're two adults Savannah and we can't deny the attraction between us. If we want to pleasure each other, fine. If we don't, that's fine too."

"Okay," she said in a small voice that made me want to stop the truck and wrap her in my arms.

"You look very pretty by the way." Savannah had worn a strapless soft pink dress and held up her hair in a gorgeous bun, with tendrils falling to the side of her face.

"Thanks," she said. "Are you sure we'll be back in time to pick up Ethan from school?"

"Absolutely," I said firmly. "With a couple of hours to spare."

We drove silently for a few minutes, then Savannah spoke up. "I'm really grateful for this. I don't have the words to express my gratitude. I already feel safe, as if Finn can't take Ethan away from me." Her voice shook with emotion making me even more determined to take care of them.

"It's my pleasure." I barely got the words out. My throat was strangely constricted.

We got to Helena in good time and we found the chapel easily enough. I parked my truck and killed the engine. "Ready?"

She smiled at me and acting without thinking, I leaned across and kissed her lightly on the mouth.

"I'm ready now," Savannah said and we both laughed.

We got out of the truck and I straightened my suit jacket. The last time I wore a suit was when I worked in the city. I was glad I'd dressed formally especially after seeing how well dressed Savannah was.

I took her hand and as we strolled in, I noticed she was trembling. I squeezed her hand. At the entrance of the chapel, Savannah stopped walking and turned to me. "Are you sure you want to do this Cameron? You don't have to. I'm sure there's another way."

"I'm fine," I told her.

She nodded and smiled. "Okay, let's do this."

"WE DID IT!" Savannah said when we emerged from the chapel an hour later. She glanced down at her ring and then looked up at me.

My heart skipped a beat at the look of wonder on her face. "We did." The whole thing had gone smoothly and very fast. The package we had gotten had provided witnesses and extras like flowers and music. It felt like a real wedding, except for the lack of family and friends.

"Congratulations!" A woman walking by said to us.

"Thank you," Savannah and I chorused back.

Hand in hand, we made our way to the truck. The marriage certificate sat safely in the pocket of my jacket. I was glad we had gone through with it. All the while, I'd worried Savannah would get cold feet. Without us being married, I didn't know how else I could take care of her and Ethan.

I opened the passenger door for Savannah and gave a little bow. "Mrs. Elliott."

She giggled and entered the truck. I went around to the driver's side feeling as if I'd suddenly become ten feet tall. Which was insane seeing that our marriage was of convenience. It wasn't real.

I slid into the driver's seat and glanced at Savannah. "What's wrong?" Worry was drawn across her face.

She looked at me with big light brown eyes. "What are you going to tell your family? They're going to hate me."

"They won't hate you." No one could hate Savannah. She had the purest heart of anyone I knew and an innocence that made you want to protect her. That innocence was the reason why I had offered to marry her the night her ex called, threatening her.

"You're saying that but look at it from their point of view. First you ask your sister if I can work in her salon and then the next thing, you've married me. How do you explain that?"

I took Savannah's hand and held her gaze. "I'm an adult Savannah. I don't have to explain myself. Even to my family. The only person I now owe explanations to, is you, as my wife."

A shiver went through her and I held her hand tighter.

"Don't worry about what people will say. They don't

matter. You and Ethan and your safety are what matter now."

She nodded but I could see the fear in her eyes. Trust was hard won but with time, she would begin to trust me. I leaned forward and planted a light kiss on her lips, then inserted the key into the ignition hole.

"Let's go celebrate and I know just the place," I told her.

I'd seen the restaurant when I was researching eloping packages. It was an hour's drive away, right between Helena and Paradise. I pulled onto the main road and drove at a leisurely pace, in no rush, now that the main business of the day had been done.

A giggle broke out from Savannah.

"What?" I asked her, already smiling in anticipation.

"I just thought of how my family will react to the news that I'm married," she said. "I'm the black sheep of the family but this will cement that reputation forever. They'll get even more shocked when they meet you."

I didn't know whether that was a good thing or not. "Why? I hope I won't embarrass you."

"On the contrary," Savannah said. "You're not the kind of man they would expect me to be with."

I let it go. If my main competition was her ex, I reckoned I was a few points ahead with Savannah's family. "What about Ethan? Are you worried about his reaction?" I didn't know much about six year olds and how they reacted to such sudden, life altering news.

"I'm not worried about Ethan. He's a kid and he trusts my decisions. He'll just be happy that we'll get to move into a house in the woods. Plus, he likes you."

Relief surged through me. It was important that Ethan was comfortable about his mom's new marriage. I made a silent vow to myself. That boy had gone through a lot with his parents' bad marriage and a father who didn't care. I was going to change that and be there for him.

Our marriage of convenience had nothing to do with him. All he would know was that he had a stepfather and I was going to act like one in the way I knew best.

12

Savannah

"I still can't believe it," Heather said as we had a cup of coffee together at Joe's before starting our shift.

I showed her the ring on my finger. I'd intended to remove it yesterday after Cameron dropped me home but I couldn't. I liked it on my finger a lot better than I'd liked wearing Finn's ring. I felt a stupid pride to be Cameron's wife, even though it was only in name only.

"I know and even though it's only been a day, I don't regret it. I think I made the right decision." I wasn't frightened of Finn's visit on Saturday. I wasn't fighting him alone. I had a husband by my side, and not just any husband. I had Cameron.

Already, he'd put me into contact with his lawyers and I had an appointment with them the coming week. Just thinking about it made me want to cry. He had meant everything he had said when he proposed and there was nothing in it for him. Cameron just wanted to keep Ethan with me. He was the real deal.

"It's so romantic," Heather said, staring at me over the rim of her mug.

I laughed. "That is so opposite of what this is. There is nothing romantic about our marriage."

"Think about it. This man hears a conversation between you and your ex and when you're done, he offers to marry you to keep you safe." She let out a dramatic sigh. "I'd call that fucking romantic."

I laughed. "I suppose when you phrase it like that, it kind of is."

"When are you moving into his place and meeting his family?" she asked.

My stomach tightened with anxiety. I was dreading meeting his family, irrespective of what Cameron had said. "We're moving in on Friday after school. Cameron wants us to be already living with him when my ex comes on Saturday."

"Protective. That's my kind of man," Heather said. "Why hadn't we all noticed Cameron before you came around."

I laughed. "Probably because you had a boyfriend." She made a face. "As for meeting his family, they have a Sunday lunch, so Ethan and I will meet them then."

"They're good, solid people," Heather said. "I was friendly with Cassie in high school but we drifted apart when she went to Helena for college."

"They might be the best people but anyone would react suspiciously when your son or brother introduces a wife you knew nothing about." I grimaced. Saying it aloud made it sound even worse.

"Relax. They'll love you. We all do," Heather said.

That wasn't reassuring but there was absolutely nothing

I could do about it now. We finished our coffee and headed to the store to sign in. I grabbed my delivery sheet and perused it. Cameron had a delivery and his place was the last on my route.

Too bad he wasn't around. He had swapped his shift around with a colleague and he was working for the next two days. I had a few deliveries around town before I headed to Dorothy and Rory's house. I considered slipping my ring off but I figured there was no point since eventually, everyone would know.

I parked my van and went to the back to grab the delivery crate. I carried it to the front door and as always, it swung open and Dorothy stood there smiling.

"Hello and congratulations!" Dorothy said.

I paused in surprise and raised a questioning eyebrow. The older woman's gaze dropped to my left hand where my ring sat gleaming on my finger.

"Cameron was here yesterday and he told us about you two tying the knot," she said excitedly. "You two are perfect for each other. I teased him about it being a shotgun wedding but he wouldn't say a thing." Mischief shone in her eyes as she stared at my flat stomach.

I laughed, relieved that Cameron hadn't divulged the real reason for our marriage. I didn't want to be the object of sympathy for everyone in Paradise. Dorothy was so excited for us that she didn't let me put a word in and she kept up an excited chatter as I carried her groceries to the kitchen.

I emptied the groceries, storing them in her pantry and fridge, then carrying the empty crate I made for the front door. Dorothy was misty eyed as she said goodbye.

"He's a good boy. Take care of him."

"I will," I said, touched by how much she cared about Cameron.

I drove to Cameron's place next without much enthusiasm knowing he wasn't home. I parked and carried his groceries to the front door. He had texted to let me know where he would hide the key as well as the security code to disarm the alarm. I found it and opened the door, then keyed in the code on the security panel.

The door shut behind me and I padded past the stairs, down the hallway to the kitchen. I loved how peaceful and spacious his home was. Ethan was going to enjoy living here and let's be honest, so was I. I felt like a fraud as soon as the thought formed. I wasn't Cameron's real wife and had no right to be living in his gorgeous home.

I emptied the crate and as I put away everything, a note pinned on the door of the fridge caught my eye. I moved closer.

Hey wife, I wish I'd been home. Would have loved to see you. Cameron.

Simple words but they made me smile and I couldn't stop rereading the note. It was a shame that our marriage was fake. Cameron would have made an awesome real husband. Too bad I'll never find out. I shook my head free of fantasies and chided myself on the present.

Glancing at the time, I saw that I still had a lot of time before I had to pick Ethan up from school. I opened the fridge and stared at its contents, before deciding what to cook. It would be a nice surprise for Cameron when he came home after work and found dinner waiting for him.

I pulled out the ingredients from the fridge, settling on meatloaf and mashed potatoes. Half an hour later, the kitchen was filled with delicious smells and in no time, I was mashing the potatoes.

When I left Cameron's to go and pick up Ethan, I was grinning like a fool. I wished I was there to see his face when he saw the note telling him his dinner was in the oven.

"WHEN DO we move into the house in the woods?" Ethan asked.

I smiled. Despite what I'd told Cameron, I was a little worried when the moment to tell him I was married came. I ruffled his head, glad that all he wanted to know was when we would move in with Cameron.

"Friday," I said. I hoped I was doing the right thing. We hadn't been in our own cottage for long and now we were moving again.

"Cool," he said, totally unperturbed.

My chest squeezed as I stared at his trusting face. My darling Ethan. I hoped I wasn't messing him up for life but marriage to Cameron was my best bet of keeping him safe from his father.

The next few calls I planned to make when we got home were not going to be that easy. I was dreading it but it had to be done. I took Cameron's attitude and told myself I was an adult who made her own decisions.

What was I going to do with the cottage when we moved in with Cameron? I wasn't going to sell it for sure but I couldn't just leave it empty. I could rent it out but it wasn't in great condition and it wouldn't attract good renters. No point in giving myself a headache over that now.

I settled Ethan in our small living room with a snack and went to my bedroom to make the calls to my family. I started with Ivy who I was in constant contact with. For the first time, I hoped she was too busy to pick up the call.

No such luck. She answered on the second ring.

"Hi," she said cheerfully. "Was going to call you guys tonight. How's Ethan?"

One thing about my sister was that she loved Ethan like her own son. That was one of the reasons why I tolerated her criticism. "He's great, loving his new school. Kids are friendly and the teachers are kind."

I held the phone away and took in rapid quick breaths. It was harder than I thought it would be. "How are you guys?" I asked.

She gave me a rundown on her family. My nephew had hurt his knee on the playground but it was nothing serious and he'd be okay.

"So, what's new with you?" Ivy said.

"A lot actually," I said as a nervous laugh escaped my lips. I held up my ring as if she could see it and said a silent prayer, I plowed. "I got married the day before yesterday. You are talking to the now, Mrs. Cameron Elliott."

The phone went dead quiet, but I knew Ivy was still there because I could hear her rapid breathing.

"I know I did not hear that correctly," she hissed into the phone.

"You heard correctly. Cameron and I—you remember Camer—"

"Isn't he the guy you were sleeping with on the first day you arrived in Paradise?" Ivy said in a cutting tone.

Her words were like a sword, tearing and hurting as it plunged deep inside my chest. I remembered Cameron's words.

I'm an adult Savannah. I don't have to explain myself. Even to my family.

I repeated them to myself.

"That's him," I said, refusing to let Ivy know how much her careless words had hurt me.

"What is wrong with you Savannah?" Ivy exploded. "We leave you for one week and the next thing we know, you're married to a stranger. Mom and Dad are going to be so disappointed in you."

"What's new?" I quipped, unable to keep the bitterness away from my voice. I'd been disappointing my family for as long as I could remember. I'd stopped caring whether I disappointed them or not. The person who mattered now was my son, Ethan.

I'd planned on explaining to Ivy the circumstances that led me to agreeing to marry Cameron. I changed my mind. She already thought the worst of me. It didn't matter.

"Can you tell Mom, Dad and Rebecca?" I asked in a cowardly moment.

"Hell no!" Ivy's voice thundered down the phone. "Handle your own mess." The phone went quiet and it took a moment to realize she had hung up on me.

With a sigh, I called my other sister, Rebecca.

"Hey stranger," she said when she answered the call.

"Hi," I said. There was a seven-year gap between us and we'd never truly bonded like sisters. It didn't help that during the years I'd been married, she had been in college studying medicine.

We exchanged pleasantries and then I told her without a preamble. "Just called to let you know that I'm married now."

"Oh," Rebecca said. "I didn't know you were seeing someone."

"It's a long story but yes, I've sort of been seeing him," I said.

She was quiet for a moment and then she spoke. "I'm going to trust you know what you are doing and I look forward to meeting him."

Relief surged through me. I couldn't believe her reaction. It was the opposite of what I'd been expecting. Sudden tears filled my eyes and I couldn't speak for a few seconds. It meant so much to have a member of my family say positive things.

13

Cameron

I was a fool for getting excited over my wife who wasn't really my wife moving into my house with her son. My house was too big and I looked forward to sharing it with Savannah and Ethan. I loved how enthusiastic Ethan was to move into the house in the woods. Not that he had ever seen it. I hoped the reality would live up to his imagination.

I parked my truck behind Savannah's van in her driveway. I glanced at the time. Eleven. A little earlier than we agreed but I'd convinced myself it was a good thing, after all, I had a lot of work to do, helping with the move. Not quite true. Savannah had said most of the stuff was in suitcases. Still, I liked being early and I'd never once been in a situation where being early hurt you.

I knocked on the door several times. No response. She was probably in the backyard. I walked around the cottage to the back door which was open. Before I could knock, I heard a muffled voice coming from inside the house.

Gripped by worry, I hurried in and found Savannah on the couch, crying loudly.

"Savannah," I said, going to her. "What happened?" My first thought was Ethan. "Is Ethan okay?"

She nodded. "Yes, he's in school." She wiped her eyes and then tried to smile at me. "I'm sorry, it's just me being silly. I just got off the phone with my mom and she gave me another scolding. It got to me, that's all."

"Is it about our marriage?" I said.

"Yes."

I didn't want to say anything negative about her family but I didn't like that they were causing Savannah so much sadness. I took her hand. "Come and sit on me." The only thing I could think of to comfort her was to hold her.

She slid onto my lap, threw her hands around my neck and laid her head on my shoulders. I held her tightly as soft sobs filled the room. Every sound was a slice of pain funneled into my heart.

I rubbed circles on her back as her sobs slowly ebbed away. She sat up and looked at me, her eyes red stricken.

"I'm a mess. I'm sorry you found me this way."

"Don't apologize for being human," I told her.

She stared at me solemnly. "Did you cry when you lost your wife?"

I swallowed hard. "I don't know. I might have. All I remember is this thick fog that came over me which lasted for years."

She brought her head down and kissed me lightly on the mouth. She drew back and stared into my eyes and then kissed me again. This time, it wasn't a chaste kiss. She parted my lips and slipped her tongue into my mouth. I groaned as our tongues slid against each other and tangled together.

Savannah slid up my thighs until she was seated on my cock. It had been so long since I'd kissed her and held her like this. I was so hard, it felt as if my cock would explode. She grinded on me as our mouths and tongues ravaged each other.

I caressed her bare arms. Savannah drew back and with a wild look in her eyes, she took off the crop top she was wearing and tossed it to the floor. I hungrily soaked in the sight of her breasts before descending on them with my mouth.

Savannah gave a sharp cry when I gently bit her nipple and arched her back, giving me herself. I moved my attention from one to the other, feeling as if I would never have enough of her.

"I love what your mouth is doing, Cameron," she said.

I loved the way she tasted and how she wasn't afraid to say what she was feeling. Without moving my mouth from her nipples I dipped my hands under the skirt she was wearing and caressed her thighs. I slid my hands up to her ass and caressed her skin over her panties.

"Take these off," I growled.

"Only if you pull down your pants," Savannah murmured. "I want your big cock inside me."

All my blood dropped to my cock. Savannah got off my lap and holding my gaze she raised her skirt giving me an eyeful of her gorgeous thighs, and then pulled down her panties.

I unbuttoned my pants and pulled them down along with my boxers. Savannah straddled me again, holding her skirt up. I gripped her waist and guided her to my cock. I wrap one hand around the base as Savannah lowers herself.

Raw need blazes in Savannah's eyes as my cock stretches

and expands her. She rocks on me but it's not enough. I grip her hips and raise her, then slam her back down to the hilt.

She whimpers and begs me to do it again. I lean forward and kiss her deeply, allowing her to rest on my cock with no movement. Then I grip her hips and lift her until just the head is inside her slick heat. I bring her back down, picking up a quick, sharp pace.

Savannah dug her fingers into my shoulders as I hit the perfect spot. "Right there Cameron... yes... oh God please."

I thrust upwards, deeper, harder.

"Cameron," Savannah screams as she unravels.

"Fuck, you're beautiful," I said to her as I explode deep inside her. I held her tightly against me, listening to her quick breaths, as I waited for my own to get back to normal.

"Do you think that he'll like it?" I asked Savannah as she walked around what would be Ethan's room.

She didn't speak at first as she looked at all the toys I'd bought for Ethan. She stared at me in disbelief before continuing with her inspection. Okay, I admit, I'd gone a little wild at the toy shop but everything I'd seen had been perfect for a six-year-old boy.

Savannah picked up a T-Rex head flashlight and started to giggle which soon turned into a sob. I assumed that it was a happy cry. "He's not going to believe this. Oh Cameron. You didn't have to do all this, spend so much money."

"I wanted to, besides I'm not short of money. You and Ethan will always be taken care of financially." I needed her to know her money worries were now permanently over. The joys of investing wisely.

She sat the flashlight down and came to me. "You've

already done so much for me Cameron. I'll take care of my and Ethan's expenses."

Everything in me revolted against the idea. "I know we got married to protect you and Ethan but you're still my wife and Ethan my stepson. I take care of my people. Okay? Let me. Please. It's the only thing that gives my life meaning at this point."

She nodded. "Okay. Thank you. If we ever become too much, please tell me. I'd never want to abuse your generosity."

That was never going to happen but that's not what Savannah wanted to hear. "Okay."

I left Savannah to arrange Ethan's clothes and stuff in the closet and went to the hallway to carry her suitcases to our bedroom. It had been easier to carry Ethan's things into his bedroom. I carried the four suitcases to the walk in closet. Thank God for the storage space because Savannah had a lot of clothes.

I returned downstairs to get preparations for dinner started. Tonight was the first night we would have dinner together as a family. The image of a smiling Amanda popped into my head. She didn't look upset that I'd married another woman but how could she when it was like nothing she and I had.

Savannah came downstairs twenty minutes later, in time to go and pick Ethan up at school. We'd worked out the time she would need to leave as it was a longer drive than when they had lived in town.

She stood a few steps away from me and wrapped her hands around herself. She looked vulnerable and so pretty.

"Are you okay?" I said.

She nodded but it wasn't convincing. Her face reflected the worry that was niggling at her. That was one of the things I loved about Savannah. She was an open human being and had no secrets. If she was unhappy, you saw it in her face and when she was joyful, which was the majority of the time, it reflected in her face.

"What if it doesn't work out Cameron?" she said. "What if we end up hating each other?"

No one could ever hate Savannah unless there was something seriously wrong with them. "We'll always be friends, Savannah and this is not a real marriage, so how can it not work out?"

A slow smile pulled at her very enticing lips. "That's a good way of looking at it. It's not a real marriage so there's nothing to work out." She dropped her hands to her side. "I'm about to go and pick up Ethan. Bet he's been looking at the time all day."

I laughed, glad that he was excited about coming to live with me. "Can I come with you?"

"If you like," she said. "But I don't want you to feel obligated."

"Savannah. Stop. I want to."

"Okay, thanks. Let's use my minivan. Ethan doesn't know your truck yet."

We left the house and headed to her minivan. I let out a stream of curses as I folded my body into the passenger seat. "It's so fucking small."

Savannah laughed. "Why am I not surprised at your complaining? Your truck has spoiled you, making you think that all cars are made to accommodate your size."

"They should," I grumbled.

I tensed as soon as Savannah started to drive. I gripped the dashboard as she took the corners too fast for my liking.

"Are you okay?" she asked with laughter in her voice. "Don't tell me you're scared of being driven?"

The terror I felt made me more honest than I would have been in normal circumstances. "Amanda was driving when we got in the accident." I said and as soon those words left my mouth, Savannah slowed down.

"I'm so sorry. I wasn't thinking."

My heartbeat slowed down and the tension left my body as she drove at a slow, nice pace. I knew my reaction had been over the top but it wasn't the first time it had happened and there was not much I could do about it.

"It's okay. It only happens when a female is driving me," I said, remembering once when my sister drove me and I'd gone ballistics on her.

"Your mind probably associates accidents with female drivers," Savannah said.

"I'll get used to it over time," I said.

We got to Ethan's school and joined the pick-up queue. Ethan came to the van a few minutes later and when he saw me, a smile lit up his face.

"Hey buddy," I said as I got out of the van to help him get buckled up.

"Hi," he said and got in. He kissed his mom.

"How was your day sweetheart?" Savannah said.

It was relaxing listening to their exchange which I imagined happened the same way every day. Ethan told us about his day, relaying an argument that had ensued with his best friend. He wanted to know who had been right, between the two of them?

"It depends on how you look at it," Savannah said carefully.

I was going to enjoy having a family.

14

Savannah

Dinner was fun with Ethan regaling us with his never ending stories of school and then harassing Cameron to take him for a walk the following day.

"I'll wear my flashlight to see in the dark," Ethan said. He looked so intense it was funny and sweet.

"It's not going to be dark," I said with a laugh.

"It will be in the woods," Ethan insisted.

Why was I arguing with a six-year-old? After dinner, I cleaned up as Cameron had made dinner, then it was time for Ethan's bath and bedtime.

"I have my own bathroom Mom," Ethan said as I shoved him into the shower cubicle.

I was happy he was happy but as he showered, the magnitude of what I had done slammed into me again. By getting married to Cameron, I'd now exposed Ethan to another way of life. A way of life that was above my means and definitely unsustainable.

I hated when I questioned my decisions like I was doing now. What would Cameron say to that? The question popped into my mind from nowhere. The answer was easy. Don't worry over things you have no control over. Cameron had an extremely practical nature and I'd come to value his opinions.

My insides tightened with tension when I said goodnight to Ethan. Tonight was going to be the first night that Cameron and I were going to spend together as husband and wife. I headed downstairs to let Cameron know I was going to take a bath and head to bed early.

I was physically and emotionally exhausted. Cameron was stretched out on the couch watching the news channel on TV. I went to him and kissed his forehead.

"I'm going to take a shower and call it a day," I said to him.

"All right," he said. "I won't be too long either."

A bath is exactly what I needed. As I soaked my weary body in the perfectly hot water, the exhaustion melted away. Despite the impulsiveness of my decision in marrying Cameron, I believed I'd done the right thing for Ethan. I had no other way of guaranteeing his safety and Finn did not bluff.

He'd meant what he said. He planned on fighting me for custody and under the previous circumstances, he would have probably won. I couldn't work with probabilities. Not when it came to Ethan. Yes, I'd made the right decision.

After my bath, I dried myself and slipped into a sexy lacy nightdress. It wasn't a deliberate move. All my night dresses were sexy. Before slipping into Cameron's huge king sized bed, I went next door to check on Ethan. Opening the door slowly, I tiptoed in and peered at his sweet face.

He was sound asleep. I kissed his forehead lightly and

tiptoed out, shutting the door behind me. Cameron was still downstairs and I entered bed and turned off the lights.

Despite my exhaustion, sleep refused to come. My mind felt energized, as if the day was just beginning. I mused over the following day. The plan was to go for a walk and then get ready for Finn's visit. Cameron had insisted on him seeing Ethan here at home.

His reasons were to let Finn know what or who he was up against. I was all for anything that gave me an advantage. I was more grateful than ever for Cameron's help. I'd just started to fall asleep when the door opened slowly and then shut. I could picture Cameron as he went to the bathroom, then returned to the bedroom and entered bed.

He moved close until he was spooning me. Heat engulfed my whole body as he pressed against me. His hand caressed my body softly before moving up to my breasts. A sigh escaped my lips as he played with my nipples over my silk night dress.

I moaned as incredible sensations coursed through my body. My nipples became hot, aching peaks as he flicked them with his thumbs. A need to touch him came over me and I turned around to face him.

His chest was bare and I ran my hands over his muscles. He let out a groan and pulled me closer until my breasts were pushing against his chest. The room was illuminated by the moonlight and I could see the hunger in his eyes. He slid off the straps of my night dress and tugged at it, exposing my chest to his eyes.

He cupped my breasts and gently squeezed them, letting his thumbs rub my peaked nipples. His cock pushed against my thighs and I reached between us. To my surprise, he was naked and my breath hitched when my hand came up against his thick, erect cock.

"I want to taste you Cameron," I said to him. "I want to suck your big cock."

He let out a long rugged breath as I slid under the blankets, until my face was level with his pelvic region. I threw back the covers to get a better view. Cameron forked his hands through my hair as I got my first taste of him, cleaning the precum gathered at the tip of his bulbous head.

I stroked his length, marveling at the sheer size of his cock. I'd never thought of men's penises as beautiful, but Cameron's cock was beautiful. Thick and long, with veins streaking down, it was a work of art. We were always in a rush to have sex and I'd never had a chance to look at it up close.

I flicked my tongue over a new drop of precum and swallowed it. I loved the taste of him. Salty and manly. Then I opened my mouth and took him in my mouth a little at a time and with my free hand, I stroked his tight balls. I almost gagged as his cock hit the back of my throat.

Sounds of his deep groans filled the room as I sucked him, hollowing my cheeks every time I took all of him in. The hold of his hand on my head grew firmer as he held me in place. He had given me so much pleasure in the weeks we had known each other and I wanted to repay him. Not that I ever could.

Cameron had given me more than sexual pleasure. He had given me peace of mind and hope that everything would be okay.

His hips moved in time with my movements, rocking into my mouth. His groans grew deeper and louder. His balls tightened some more in my hand and movements became more urgent. I sucked harder and faster. My own pussy flooded with arousal and it felt as if I was also on the verge of orgasm.

Cameron gripped my head and half rose, before a choked groan left his mouth and he came, flooding my mouth with hot cum. I swallowed every last drop, then licked his cock until it was clean. He rolled onto his back and I laughed to see that his cock was still hard and standing at attention.

"You're insatiable," I said to him as I happily straddled him and bent down to kiss him. Cameron took that opportunity to pinch my nipples until they peaked again.

"You're amazing Savannah," he said.

I brushed my pussy over his cock and then holding it in position with one hand, I lowered myself on it. I closed my eyes as his cock stretched me, inch by inch. It felt so good and so intense. I sank down until I felt his balls resting on my ass.

"I want you to ride me hard," Cameron said as his hands moved to my ass. He let me ride him for a few minutes, his breath growing labored. He moved his hands to my hips and he raised me a few inches off him and then thrust upwards, hard.

I groaned loudly, hoping my noises would not wake Ethan up. Cameron held me in place, poised in the air and fucked me. He drove his cock in and out of me until my groans became one long moan. The orgasm built up in me as my body tightened.

I rode him faster and faster clenching my muscles around him. My body exploded, making me momentarily lose my vision but I didn't stop riding Cameron until I heard his groan as he came inside of me. I collapsed on top of him and he held me tightly.

～

I LOVED HIKING but I wasn't feeling too hot for it the following day as I trudged behind Ethan and Cameron. I didn't understand how Cameron was so energetic and cheerful considering the night we had.

We'd had sex all night as if we only had one night together. Every inch of my body ached and my pussy was so sore, I didn't think I'd be ready to have sex again for a long time. Lies of course. As we were wearing our jackets, my eyes had been on Cameron's tight ass and I recall thinking how nice it would feel to touch him. So much for never having sex again.

Our feet made crunching noises as we walked over the fallen leaves. I loved how peaceful it was in the woods. As if the three of us were the only people remaining in the world. An eerie thought but I wouldn't mind if Finn disappeared from my life.

I raised my hand and looked down at my ring. How different things would have been if I hadn't had it. For one, I would have been stressed beyond imagination, knowing that Finn's chances of winning custody of Ethan would have been high.

It wasn't for sure but I was almost guaranteed of keeping Ethan. And that was all because Cameron had offered to marry me. He had to be the kindest, most selfless man I had ever met.

The walk took almost two hours with Ethan stopping to inspect every insect and crawly he saw. He couldn't stop talking as we entered the house.

"Mom, did you see the giant spider that was hiding under the leaf?" he asked, a look of wonder on his face.

My heart squeezed happily. "I did. Too bad you and Cameron frightened it away."

"We didn't," he protested. "Cameron said it had to go back to its family."

I rolled my eyes at Cameron and stifled a giggle when he winked at me. God, he was sexy. And he was mine. For the time being. It had to be enough. I quashed thoughts of the future which kept popping up in my mind. I fantasized that Cameron had fallen in love with me and wanted to make our marriage permanent.

What was possessing me to entertain such thoughts when Cameron had been very clear from the start. He was not capable of loving another woman. When his wife died, she had taken all his love with her. I needed to be grateful for the sacrifice he had made for me and Ethan and not be greedy for what he could not give.

After a glass of water each, Ethan and I went upstairs to his room. I wanted to remind him that his father was coming in two hours. I wasn't sure if he remembered.

"Hey buddy, come and sit down for a moment," I said, patting his bed.

He came carrying a robot toy and sat down. He looked so handsome with his face flushed from the exercise.

"Do you remember what day today is?" I asked him.

His eyebrows drew together. "It's Saturday, Mom."

"Yes, and what's happening today?" I prodded.

He didn't answer but his whole demeanor changed and my heart squeezed painfully. I hated to see my boy so torn up over his father. One part of him craved to be loved and accepted by his dad but the other hated the constant criticism that Finn threw at him.

"Daddy is coming to see you but Ethan, we'll all be here so you have nothing to worry about," I said.

"Daddy said that he'll take me to live with him," Ethan said softly.

I stiffened. "When?"

"When we were in town with Aunt Ivy," he said. "I don't want to live with him. I want to live with you, Mommy." Ethan usually called me mom but when he was stressed her reverted to mommy and it tore at my insides.

"Look at me," I commanded and waited until his eyes, which were the same shade as mine, lifted. "Nobody is taking you away from me, okay?"

"Promise?" he said.

"I promise." That was one promise that Cameron had given me the power to make.

A smile lit up my son's face and I had to fight the tears that were threatening to fall from my eyes.

15

Cameron

F inn was nothing like I expected him to be. For one, he did not look like a bully, with his short compact body and almost mild manner. The only thing that gave him away was his beady, restless eyes that kept darting around the living room.

As I'd suspected, coming to my home had destabilized him and so had seeing the diamond ring on Savannah's finger. She had gleefully introduced me as her husband and you could have picked Finn's jaw off the floor. We had locked eyes and he had understood the significance of that. Savannah and Ethan were now under my care.

His fiancée Nancy looked pissed. She glared at Savannah and her ring. Knowing that my point had been made, I excused myself, and left them in the living room. I went upstairs to my study where I had a view of the front lawn. I didn't entirely trust the bastard.

As I logged in to look at my investments portfolio, I kept an eye on Finn who was outside having what seemed like a heated discussion with Nancy. As long as it wasn't Savannah. Then he went back in and seconds later, he and his fiancée left and marched to their car.

This is just the beginning Finn, I said inwardly. Next week, Savannah had an appointment with my lawyers, who were the best in our side of the country. Half an hour later, a soft knock came on the door. It was Savannah.

"Come in," I said, when she peered in.

Savannah was heavy footed when she entered my office, as if the weight of the world was too heavy for her to carry. I shot to my feet and went around my desk to stand near her.

"Are you okay?" I asked her.

"I'm fine, just so sad for Ethan. He usually has such high hopes and then bloody Finn crushes him. He'd been looking forward to taking his dad to the woods and showing him around. Finn told him that he couldn't. He's too busy."

I didn't know what to say. I folded my fists automatically and if that sorry ass of an ex was there, I couldn't have promised to keep them to my side. "I'm sorry." There was nothing else to say. Finn was an asshole who had no business being a dad.

I closed the distance between us and folded my arms around Savannah. She clung to me as painful sobs shook her body.

"I have an idea," I said to her when her sobs subsided. "I know this place that Ethan will love."

She wiped her eyes. "Where?"

"It's a surprise."

I took them to the entertainment center in town and Ethan loved it. We played a lot of the games with him and by the time we left for home, everyone's spirits had been lifted.

"Does your mom live in a house in the woods as well?" Ethan asked me on the drive towards town.

I laughed, grateful that unlike adults, children bounced back from their problems fast. I glanced at Savannah. She was smiling too but she still had an air of sadness about her. I understood her emotions. Dealing with people like her ex was an emotional suck.

I'd gotten the whole story from her later in the evening after we got home from the entertainment center. Finn had been livid to discover that she was married and had hissed a few choice words to her when no one was listening.

He had told Savannah that he was going to fight for Ethan and even after reassuring her that we had the resources to fight him, she was still worried. Understandably so. It was a threat to her child.

"No, she doesn't," I said to Ethan. "But she has a pretty neat house with fun places to explore."

"Cool," Ethan said, pressing his nose against the window.

"You good?" I said softly to Savannah.

She turned up the volume of the radio. "They're going to hate me."

"No, they won't," I said to her and reached for her hand to squeeze it.

She was silent after that. Ethan chattered all the way to my mother's house, distracting us with his funny observations and questions. The boy was like a sponge. He wanted to know everything and when you answered his question, he took a moment as though to absorb it.

I pulled up in my old childhood home and noticed my brothers' cars already there. It dawned on me again how far apart we had grown in the last five years. We had been so close once, and now seeing their cars, it brought a longing for simpler days.

"Relax," I told Savannah. "It will be fine."

She smiled bravely and I leaned across to kiss her lightly on her mouth.

"Yuck," Ethan said and we both laughed.

As we walked to the front door, memories slammed into me as if they had been unleashed from a locked space. Me and Amanda, the first time I'd brought her home to introduce her to my parents. My dad had been alive then and I remembered how proud I'd been to show her off to everyone.

They'd loved her from the beginning and she and Cassie had become like sisters. It seemed so long ago. Another lifetime. I'd become a different person and I wondered what Amanda would make of me. The answer to that shamed me.

She would have scolded me at how I'd chosen to live my life or barely live my life. Like Savannah, Amanda had been full of life and she would have wanted me to find happiness after she died. Easier said than done.

The door swung open and my mom appeared, smiling at me with tears in her eyes. She looked older but that was to be expected. The last time I'd seen her was almost six months earlier when she had come to my house. Over time, her visits had decreased and we went for long periods without seeing each other.

"Cameron," she said and then noticed Ethan and Savannah by my side. Her eyes widened with delight when they fell on Ethan. "Hello," she said to him. "Please, come in, everyone's already here."

I kissed her cheek. "Mom, this is Savannah and her son Ethan," I said, keeping it simple.

"It's a pleasure to meet you Savannah," she said warmly

and just then, her golden retriever, Jack, came up behind her, wagging his tail.

"Wow!" Ethan cried. "Is that your dog?"

Mom laughed. "Yes. His name is Jack and he loves visitors. Show him your hand."

Ethan looked at his mother and when she nodded, he stretched his hand. Jack went to him and sniffed his hand, then licked it. Ethan giggled and then he was all over the dog, patting and hugging him.

"Looks like Jack has made a new friend," I said as we followed Mom into the house.

My brothers sat talking animatedly in the living room and when we walked in, they fell silent. You could have cut the tension that suddenly grew in the room. They both stood up. Asher, our youngest brother, stepped forward.

"Hey," he said with a nod but did not offer a handshake.

"Hey," I said back.

His gaze moved to Savannah and he smiled at her. "I'm Asher, Cameron's brother."

Savannah smiled and offered him her hand. "It's nice to meet you both finally. Cameron has told me a lot about you."

Asher's eyebrow rose up. He was right to be skeptical. If I never returned his calls or texted back, what were the chances that I spoke about my brothers? But I did.

"And I'm Carter," our oldest brother said, pushing his spectacles up.

"Doctor Elliott," Savannah said, awe in her voice. She had been so impressed to hear that my oldest brother was a medical doctor. "It's a pleasure to meet you."

"Where's Cassie?" I asked.

"Here I am," my sister's cheerful voice sounded behind me.

I whirled around and hugged her, then I introduced her to Savannah. I looked around for Ethan.

"He's playing all over the house with Jack," my sister offered. "You have an awesome boy."

Savannah smiled. "Thanks. I'm Savannah," she said.

I waited for the introductions to be over and seeing my moment, I dropped my bombshell. "Savannah is my wife."

Silence followed my abrupt announcement. There could have been a better way to say it, but the information would be the same, however I dished it.

"Wife?" my mom asked from where she sat on the couch.

"Yes."

I took Savannah's hand. She was trembling slightly. I wished we were alone so I could reassure her. She was safe with me and besides no one in my family would say anything hurtful or offensive. They were good people.

"What the fuck Cameron?" Asher exploded.

"Language please," Mom said sharply.

Ethan chose that moment to come running into the living room with Jack closely behind him.

"Mom, can we get a dog?" he said, looking up at Savannah with huge eyes that would have melted anyone's heart.

"We'll talk about it, okay?" Savannah said.

Ethan's arrival broke the tension. My mom shepherded us all to the living room and I made sure that I sat next to Savannah. Ethan's presence stopped anyone from asking about my marriage but I could feel my family's gazes on me, as if I'd now completely lost my mind.

"I'm going for a walk around the compound. Anyone want to come?" Carter said, throwing a pointed gaze at me.

"I'll come," I said.

"Me too," Asher said.

The three of us left the house via the back kitchen door. I was happy to note that my mother had kept the house in good shape. Winter was slowly giving way to spring and though none of us was wearing a jacket, we were not cold.

"Remember this?" Carter said as we walked by the old oak tree with a tire made swing on it.

I laughed remembering how we used to fight over who would go first. Carter, as the first born, always won that fight.

"When did you get married?" Asher said in a harsh voice.

Our youngest brother was a firefighter and the feistiest of all of us. His choice of career fit him perfectly as he always had too much energy. I'd already known that question would come up and Savannah and I had agreed to stick to the truth.

"Less than a week ago," I said.

"I suppose the right question would be, when did you two meet?" Asher continued.

"None of your business," I snapped. I was prepared to answer a few questions, if politely worded, but I owed no one an explanation, including my brothers.

"We are just worried about you," Carter, ever the peacemaker, said.

I sighed. "I know but I'm fine and Savannah is a fine woman." We were not going to tell anyone that our marriage was fake. That would have been humiliating for Savannah and we had Ethan to think about.

"I'm worried about Mother," Asher said. "You hurt her very badly when you cut yourself off Cameron. And now you're back, walking in here as if you have every right—"

I turned around and in two steps I was standing chest to

chest with Asher, anger coursing through me. "Are you sure you want to finish that sentence?"

"You bet I do," Asher said, his eyes flashing with anger. "Someone needs to tell you. Yes, we get it. Your wife died but guess what, we all loved Amanda. She was family. But you punished everyone for it, but mostly Mother."

Carter pushed both of us away from each other, then turned to me. "Asher's right Cameron. You can't hurt Mother again."

"I won't," I growled, guilt almost drowning me.

16

Savannah

I could feel Cameron's mom and sister's eyes on me as soon as the men left. I resisted the urge to glance at the door, willing Cameron to walk in and save me. There was no chance of that happening. I was sure that his brothers were grilling him outside.

"Cameron told me you would call me with regards to apprenticing at the salon," Cassie said warmly. "You never called."

I fidgeted in my chair. "I got a little busy." I smiled but I was afraid my smile reflected the discomfort I was feeling.

I tried to put myself in their shoes. How would it feel if one of my sisters showed up with a man we had never met and introduced him as her husband? A shocker for sure and trying to figure out what was going on.

"I understand. Sometimes, life overwhelms us," she said kindly. "Please feel free to come when you're ready. We could do with the extra help."

I wondered again what Cameron had told her about me

but I quickly pushed it away, deciding not to stress myself further. I swung my gaze to Cameron's mom. Her eyes were coolly assessing me.

"This is a surprise to all of us, as I'm sure you can imagine," she said. "But I have to say that I haven't seen Cameron look this happy ever since we lost Amanda."

I held my breath.

"For me, that's enough," she said softly. "I'm grateful that he has you and Ethan in his life, Savannah."

Guilt grabbed me by the throat and squeezed. These people did not deserve what we had done. I hadn't given a lot of thought to Cameron's family. My worries had revolved around Ethan and nothing else. It dawned on me how many people our fake marriage was going to affect.

"I'm with mom," Cassie said happily. "I'm happy to have a sister-in-law and I can't wait to get to know you better."

"Me too," I choked out.

"So, how did you and Cameron meet?" Cassie asked.

Panic rose up my throat. I hadn't hashed out the details with Cameron as neither of us had envisaged a situation where I would be left alone with his family. I'd stick to the truth. Inhaling deeply, I told them about how rude Cameron was to me when we first met.

"That sounds like Cameron," his mother said.

When I told them about marching back to the woods to scold him for his rudeness, they laughed and cheered.

"I bet that must have surprised the hell out of him," Cassie said, wiping stray tears from the corners of her eyes.

By the time Cameron and his brothers returned, we had become quick friends and I'd become comfortable in their company. Cameron looked at me with a question in his eyes and I smiled at him. He looked relieved.

The brothers did not speak to me much during dinner

but us ladies kept the conversation going. We talked about Aunt May which brought tears to my eyes to hear how well she had been loved by everybody.

After dinner, I helped Cassie wash up.

"Please come to the salon," she said. "We really could do with an extra pair of hands."

Anxiety came over me. How much had Cameron told her about me?

"Cameron said you really loved our industry and honestly a lot of my employees have learnt on the job. I have a feeling you'll be really good at it. And I promise that we'll be very patient," she said.

A moment of insight came to my mind. There was no way Cameron would have told her too much about me. He wasn't that kind of person. Cameron said as little as he could get away with.

"Say yes?" she said. "It can't be that much fun delivering groceries in this weather. In the salon, we have hot coffee and snacks delivered from Joe's every day."

I laughed. "You're very persistent."

She winked. "I've been told that before. I tend to go with my gut and right now, they're telling me we would be lucky to have you."

I compared the atmosphere she had described with my delivery job. Plus, the chance to actually learn a skill. "Okay, I'll do it. Give me a week or so to finish the month and give notice at the grocery store."

She grinned. "Yes. I'm so happy."

I beamed back. Cassie made me feel as if she really wanted me to work with her and that gave me hope and excitement for the future. I imagined being able to say that my profession was a hair stylist. "Me too."

"YOUR FAMILY IS WONDERFUL," I told Cameron on the way to the cottage. We hadn't given much thought to what we were going to do with it. I'd simply packed my and Ethan's stuff and moved into Cameron's house in the woods. A lot had happened in a short time, and I'd not had time to plan.

"They loved you," he said.

"Except for your brothers," I pointed out without bitterness or anger. Cameron's brothers had every right to be weary and suspicious about me and our new marriage.

"It's not you," Cameron said.

We spoke softly because Ethan was dozing in the back seat of the truck. "What do you mean?"

"I'm sure you've figured out by now that I isolated myself when I lost Amanda. It hurt my family but mostly of course, my mother. My brothers are concerned, rightly so, that I might hurt her again," Cameron said in an emotionless voice.

Except that I heard the tightness in his voice that told me it hurt him that he had hurt his family. "You didn't do it deliberately. It's the only way you knew how to survive."

He brought the truck to a stop in the driveway and looked at me. "I never expected anyone to understand but that's exactly it."

We shared a look of perfect understanding.

"Where are we Mom?" Ethan asked in a sleepy voice.

"The cottage sweetheart," I said, snapping my seatbelt open.

"Aren't we going home?" Ethan asked.

He said it so innocuously but the words slammed into me like someone had physically punched my chest. My son had already started thinking of Cameron's house as his home. What if Cameron got tired of us? After all, he was gaining nothing from our marriage. If anything, it was a hindrance for his social life.

Ethan stayed in the truck while Cameron and I made our way to the entrance. Cameron took the keys from me and opened the door. Walking in after him, the cottage seemed to have shrunk.

"It looks so small," I murmured.

"It is small," Cameron said matter of factly.

Except that I'd never thought of it as small. It had been enough for me and Ethan but living in Cameron's house made every other house look tiny by comparison. It was not just Ethan who had gotten used to a new way of life. I had too.

It looked more run down as well. We walked through the living room, bedrooms and bathroom before returning to the kitchen.

"I want to do a few repair jobs, if it's okay with you," Cameron said.

I turned to him in surprise. "What about work?"

He touched peeling paint on the wall and it fell off. "I'll do it on my days off." He looked at my face and continued. "I'll enjoy it."

He was already doing so much for us but if he was going to enjoy it as he said, then why not? I'd come to learn that Cameron was not the type of person that said something when he did not mean it.

"Okay," I said. "But you are not to use your own money. If you need anything, please let me know."

He nodded solemnly. "I will."

We left moments later and headed straight home. Ethan had school the following day and I wanted him to get enough rest.

Later, Cameron came with me to tuck Ethan in. We turned off the lights and returned downstairs together. To my surprise, Cameron took my hand as we walked down the stairs. In the living room, he pulled me onto his lap and slipping his hand around my neck, he pulled me in for a kiss.

I closed my eyes and allowed his mouth and tongue to do their magic. My tension of the day ebbed away as I melted into him. He kissed away all my doubts and fears. I cupped my hand on his day old scruff, loving the male roughness of it against my hand.

Heat enveloped my body and I found myself grinding against his hard cock which felt like a huge plank of wood. God, it felt good. I ran my hands all over his body, my movements becoming more frenzied by the minute.

Cameron moved his mouth to my chest and nibbled on my breasts over my blouse, as he urgently undid the buttons. I was sure that he had ripped off a few of them. I shrugged off my blouse and raked my hands through his hair.

"You have perfect breasts Savannah," Cameron murmured, pushing down the cups of my bra.

My breasts popped out and he lowered his mouth to latch onto a nipple. I arched my back, offering more of my chest to him. I moaned as pleasure shot from my nipple to my pussy, which ached with a need to feel him inside me.

As if he could read my thoughts, Cameron pushed my skirt up, bunching it up around my waist. He brought his big hand to my panties and groaned at how wet I was. As if that was the deciding factor, he stood up with me and carried me upstairs.

"I want to fuck you on the bed where we won't be accidentally interrupted," he said.

I was glad that he remembered Ethan even though once

he slept, he never woke up in the night. He had always been a deep sleeper, and now more than ever, I was grateful for it.

Cameron kicked the door shut with his leg and then deposited me gently on the bed. I shimmied out of my skirt and pulled it over my feet. Cameron undressed while staring at me as if it was the first time we were having sex.

My eyes locked on his cock bobbing up when he pulled down his boxer briefs. I could swear saliva was dripping down the sides of my mouth. He got on the bed, folded my legs and got in between my knees. He spread them open and stared down at my panties which were stuck to my folds.

"Fuck," he hissed and then pulled my panties to the side and stared down at my soaking wet pussy. He grabbed the hem and pulled them down.

In a kneeling position, Cameron lined up the head of his cock at the entrance to my pussy and dragged it over my slit, spreading my wetness over the rest of me. I moaned for him and raised my hips for more.

He did this several times before he plunged his cock into my waiting, aching pussy. I let out a loud cry, raising my hips rhythmically to meet every thrust. Our gazes met in a lusty stare before Cameron brought his mouth down to kiss me.

I panted as the beginnings of an orgasm formed in my core, spinning me until I exploded. I wrapped my legs tightly around Cameron's waist while he continued pumping, chasing his own release.

"Fuck Savannah," he moaned once before his hot cream rushed into me, filling me with heat and liquid.

17

Savannah

I didn't have to be told that the law firm I'd just walked into was too expensive for me. My heels were swallowed by the thick royal blue carpet as I entered the reception area.

The walls were glass from floor to ceiling with a view of the town that was breathtaking. On one side was a fancy looking waiting area that reminded me of Cameron's living space. I made my way to the reception desk that was manned by three ladies.

One looked up at me and smiled in an impersonal manner, that made me want to fidget. I thought about my savings which were almost nonexistent. I was definitely in the wrong place.

"Hello. How can I help you?" she said.

It took a second to make up my mind. "Sorry, I think I came to the wrong address," I said and fled.

There was no way I would afford the consultation fees, let alone the final total. No. I had to find a lawyer I could afford. There had to be a few cheap ones who were good as well.

For a second, I was tempted to call my sister. Her and my brother-in-law owned their own law firm and they'd be more than happy to help me with Ethan's case. I squared my shoulders. When I moved to Paradise, I'd made up my mind to be independent and not to depend on my family. I was not going to go to them for help.

I found a coffee shop and entered. My tummy growled with hunger as the scent of coffee and baked goodies wafted up my nose. I'd left home early for the drive to Helena and I'd not had time to eat breakfast.

As soon as I placed my order, I fished out my phone and went online to search for Lawyer listings in Helena. I found a few, who looked as though they were within my budget. I got a pen and notebook from my purse and noted the names, addresses and numbers.

The server brought my coffee and croissant. As I ate, my mind drifted to Cameron and I wondered what he was doing. I knew he was at work, but he rarely spoke about his job which made it difficult to visualize his day.

I snapped back to the present with the realization that I thought about Cameron more and more when we were not together. It was easy to fall for him. He was everything that any woman would want in a man. Gentle, a hell of a good lover, protective, I could go on and on.

The only problem was one. We had gotten married for convenience. A favor to me and we had no feelings for each other. When our marriage had served its purpose, we would part ways and everyone would go on with their lives.

A pang came over me at the thought of never seeing Cameron again. I shook my head free of those thoughts and told myself to stop being silly. Adulting meant coming to terms with the reality of things, one of which was that Cameron and I were temporary.

I took a last bite of my croissant. I'd been so lost in thought that I'd eaten the whole thing without tasting it. I washed it down with coffee and took my phone to start making calls. The first was to a law firm called Alert Consulting. The phone was picked up on the second ring.

I introduced myself and asked for an appointment the same day. She told me in her chirpy voice that Mr. Davis could not see me as all his slots were filled up. Disappointed but hopeful, I made the next call and I got the same response.

I tried pleading my case but the woman who I spoke to was probably used to it. No amount of begging was going to secure me an appointment.

My third call proved lucky. Sally, as she introduced herself, got me an appointment with a Mr. Parks for ten o'clock. Relieved, I drank the rest of my coffee unhurriedly, knowing that I had half an hour and the law offices were a five-minute walk away.

In the same way I'd deduced that the lawyer's fees would be too expensive for me at Clark and Clark, the law firm that Cameron had sent me to, I knew that Mr. Park's law firm was affordable. First it was in a somewhat dingy part of town and secondly, it was clearly a one-man operation, manned by Sally in a tiny reception area.

"Hey," she said with a wide smile when I entered. The click of my heels on the faded tiles had announced my arrival before I physically appeared. "You must be Savannah Elliott."

"I am," I said with a smile.

"Mr. Park is waiting for you," Sally said and stood up.

She went to a door on one side of the wall, and after a sharp knock, she held it open for me.

The man who stood up to greet me wore an ill-fitting gray suit and he wore a serious expression that gave me hope that he knew his stuff.

"Jim's the name," he said.

I smiled. "Savannah."

His gaze dropped to my chest and back to my face so fast that I thought I must have imagined it.

"Please sit down." He indicated the visitor's chair and went around to his side of the desk. "How can I help you?"

I cleared my throat and told him my issue with Finn, beginning with our failed marriage. I hesitated, weighing whether to tell him that my marriage to Cameron was not real but I figured the less people who knew, the better. I was pleased to note that Jim took notes as I spoke.

When I was done he asked me a few questions then had me fill a form with my personal details. Then he told me about the law and custody cases but he used too much legal jargon for me to understand what he was saying. Before I knew it, he was done and winding up our appointment.

"Have Sally give you my card in case you need to get in touch with me. Email is the best way," he said, while moving towards the door. "Sally will give you your invoice as well."

I expected to feel relieved that my case was now in the hands of a professional, but all I felt was anxiety. Jim had not reassured me that my case was airtight and no one was going to take my son away from me. I got nightmares at night, imagining that Ethan was under the care of Finn and Nancy.

Later, as I drove back to Paradise, misery clung to me. It felt like a wasted day even though I'd secured myself a lawyer I could afford. I got back to town in time for my shift.

The first thing I did was go into the manager's office to let her know that I was going to be moving on to another job.

"No one stays in this job," she moaned.

I laughed. "Honestly, it's a fun job but I've gotten a chance to work in a beauty salon and it's been my dream."

"Cutting Edge?" she asked.

I nodded. "Yes."

"I'll be seeing you there then," she said. "It's a good thing to follow your dreams, Savannah. If that doesn't work out or for some reason or you don't like it, you can always come back to us. We'd love to have you in any position."

We hugged. I loved Paradise. Everyone felt like a friend even when you hadn't known each other for long. My deliveries for the day were within twenty miles and I finished early, coinciding with Heather's shift.

I had time before picking up Ethan and we went for coffee at Joe's. I told her about my visit to Helena.

"You're a proud fool," Heather said. "Cameron knew you couldn't afford his law firm but he sent you there, knowing that he would pay for it. Don't refuse help when it's offered, Savannah."

I took a sip of my coffee. "I can't. He's already done enough for us. It's not fair to use him."

Heather spluttered and almost spilled her coffee. Her gorgeous green eyes widened. "Are you serious? The man is your legal husband. How is letting him help you using him? Cameron's not a fool. He hasn't gotten where he is in life because of luck."

She was making sense but on this one, I knew I was right. Ours wasn't a real marriage and even if it was, Ethan and my woes with his father were my responsibility.

"I can't," I said to Heather and then because I didn't want

to debate this any more, I told her about starting to work at Cutting Edge. "I'm so excited."

"Yaaay, that means I might get all the good deals," she said and we both laughed. "This is a good season for you, Savannah. Embrace and enjoy it. Cutting Edge will be a wonderful place to work."

"Thanks," I said smiling. Maybe Heather was right. My time to be happy and to achieve has come. All my life, I'd felt like a muddled mess. Aunt May had changed all that by leaving me her cottage and her van, giving me a fresh start in Paradise.

Cameron had kept the good luck ball rolling by offering to marry me. Then the job at Cutting Edge. It felt as if I was exactly where I should have been at that point in my life. The only thing that marred it was Finn. I never told Cameron that Finn had promised he was going to win custody of Ethan. His confidence had shaken me.

Heather made me laugh when she told me about a blind date which a friend had arranged for her.

"He kept suggesting that we go back to his place," Heather said. "Ugh. I hate it when a man thinks that he can get into your panties after a couple of dates."

I laughed. "I have no idea."

She raised an eyebrow.

"I've never been on a date with anyone else apart from Finn," I admitted. "We dated in high school and got married right after."

"What about Cameron?" she said.

My face heated up. "We didn't date. I got stuck at his place during a storm, had sex and more sex and then he offered to marry me." I giggled as soon as that summary was out of my mouth.

"Oh wow, you really are innocent when it comes to

men," Heather said. "And I thought I was Mother Teresa. You dress sexy and it's easy to conclude that—"

"That I'm a whore," I said in a dry tone.

Heather grinned. "I wouldn't word it so strongly. But I've never thought of you like that but I never imagined you were that inexperienced either."

I laughed, loving her honesty, which was what had brought us close together. "I love to look and feel sexy," I said. "I always have."

"I've taken a leaf from you too," Heather said. "I'm always in high heels these days and next, I want to upgrade my clothes. I want to feel and look sexy too."

"Good for you," I told her. It was odd that someone admired me and wanted to emulate me. It had never happened in all my life. I loved Paradise and its people.

18

Cameron

I rolled to Savannah's side and found it empty. She had already left to take Ethan to school. It was rare for her to leave without waking me up with a kiss or a hug. But she had been weird the last couple of days. Something was clearly on her mind and I'd tried to get it out of her to no avail.

Yawning, I roused myself and pushed myself to a sitting position. My body still ached from the previous day's activities at work. We had lost a young tourist, a twelve year old boy.

He reminded me of Ethan and I'd worked like a mad man searching my designated part of the park. It had been near the cold, icy lake and I'd waded through it just to be sure that he had not fallen in accidentally. Highly unlikely since the lake was not deep but you never ruled anything out in search and rescue.

He'd eventually been found by one of the other park rangers on duty, crouched and frightened in one of the numerous caves in the park. Relief had surged through me as I imagined it had been Savannah and Ethan going through that trauma.

I headed to the bathroom to freshen myself up. As I brushed my teeth, I mused over the thing that was bugging Savannah. I'd tried to give her space hoping she would get comfortable enough to confide in me. I was worried as she seemed to be growing withdrawn every day and it was driving me insane. I wanted my Savannah back and I didn't know how to do it.

My way was asking directly which I'd done several times. Clearly that wasn't working. I dressed and made the bed then went to Ethan's room and did the same. I tidied up some toys and flung the windows open for some fresh air.

Downstairs, the scent of coffee perfumed the air and I gratefully poured myself a cup, saying a silent thank you for Savannah. My mind turned to the day's planned activities. I had a plan for getting the information from Savannah, after which I'd head to the cottage.

I needed to order paint from the hardware but before that I wanted to do a thorough inspection of the cottage and see what was needed. I loved outdoor work and I was looking forward to the next few weeks. I couldn't wait to show Savannah when it was all done, to see her reaction. Thinking about that made me grin like an idiot.

The sound of her minivan came as I was finishing my coffee, reminding me of the small car I wanted to get her. I wanted to make her life as comfortable as possible and while the minivan had been okay for deliveries, now that she would be working at the salon, she needed something smaller and more reliable.

Knowing Savannah, she was going to say no, unless it was already bought and hers. I couldn't wait to surprise her.

I'd never derived pleasure from gifting another person with material things as I was to Savannah. She deserved so much more.

While I waited for her to enter the house, I made her coffee, just the way she liked it. The front door opened and the familiar sound of high heels clicking the floor lifted my heart. Savannah appeared and when she saw me sitting at the island a smile came over her features.

The smile did not quite reach her eyes. "Morning husband," she said, coming to where I was to kiss me. Her lips were soft and deliciously cold against mine.

"Morning wife." Anyone listening to us would find it difficult to believe we were not a real husband and wife. I found it difficult to be realistic about our relationship.

I'd started to get used to having Savannah and Ethan in my life. I loved Ethan's noises when he was home and when he wasn't the house became too quiet. God help me but I'd also gotten used to having a soft, warm body in my bed and I couldn't fathom how it would be without Savannah in it.

"How was Ethan this morning?" I asked as I handed her the coffee I made for her.

"Thanks," she said and took a sip. "Good, he was looking forward to playing with Jeff. He forgot they were not friends yesterday."

I laughed.

A shadow came over Savannah's features but it quickly disappeared.

"Are you sure you're okay to pick him up later?" she said.

"Yes, of course," I said. "I'll be at the cottage and don't worry. I'm very punctual."

"I know," she said.

"Hey, I need you to be honest with me. I know something's been bugging you. What is it?"

She put on an innocent expression and stared at me over the rim of her mug. "I have no idea what you're talking about."

I let it pass and waited patiently for Savannah to finish her coffee. When she was done, I carried the mug to the sink, then returned to where Savannah sat. I lifted her easily from the stool to the island, ignoring her surprised expression.

"I guess we're going to have to do this the hard way," I said and without giving her a chance to talk, I pushed up her dress and spread her legs.

A giggle escaped her lips. I loved that Savannah was always up for whatever I had in mind, especially if it was sensual.

"What are you doing?" she said.

"Just want to make you feel good." I skimmed over her thighs, taking my time until I got to her apex.

Savannah laughed. "At this time of morning? Here? What if someone sees us?"

"No one will see us and nobody comes here without telling us beforehand. And if they do, you're my wife. We have every right to do what we want in the privacy of our house." I ran a thumb over her now wet panties.

A moan escaped her mouth. I'd only just begun. I couldn't wait to taste her but not just yet. Savannah didn't know it, but it was going to be a long morning for her.

She slid further down the counter, giving me better access to her pussy. Using both thumbs I pressed the front of her pussy and she raised her hips, demanding for more. I loved the musky scent of her arousal and I bent down to inhale it.

I placed my palms on her inner thighs and spread her further, then I licked her over the material of her panties.

The caveman in me demanded that I tear the panties off her and eat her pussy with abandon but that wasn't the plan. I used my tongue, mouth and teeth on her.

"Oh God Cameron, that feels so good," she said, throwing her head back. "Take off my panties. I need to feel you."

"Not just yet babe," I said but I did compromise by pulling them to one side.

I hissed at the sight of her pussy glistening with her arousal. I took one swipe and swallowed Savannah's wetness. She tasted of candy and honey. Her whimpering filled the kitchen.

I teased her with my tongue, flicking it over her clit in feather light movements, knowing what she wanted was friction.

"More. I need more," she panted and raised her hips to pull down her panties herself. Kicking them to the floor, Savannah repositioned herself on the counter, folded her legs at the knees and threw them apart.

I groaned, unable to control myself at the sight of her pinkness spread before me. I inhaled deeply and returned to my task, flicking my tongue over her sensitive parts and even pushing it inside but barely.

I could feel the frustration building in her. I drew back but kept my hands on her thighs. "Tell me, what's been eating at you?"

She raised her head and stared at me in disbelief. "Are you serious right now? Can we talk about that later? Fuck Cameron, I need your mouth on me, not have it talking."

I chuckled, enjoying her reaction. "I want my mouth on you too but I've been worried sick about you. It's kind of hard to concentrate on pleasuring you when I keep wondering what the problem is."

"I told you, there's nothing. I'm okay."

She wasn't quite there yet. I lowered my head and blew into her folds and then licked her clit with the tip of my tongue. I teased her until I sensed that she was on the verge of coming, then drew back.

"Don't stop," Savannah said. "I'm so close."

I almost gave in but knowing what was bothering my wife was important and if sex was my only weapon, then so be it. It didn't help that my cock was throbbing painfully and demanding to be released from the confines of my pants. I pushed away the image of lining my cock at her soaked entrance and slowly penetrating her.

"I know you Savannah and I can tell when something is bothering you, so don't bother to deny it."

She raised her head again and looked at me with blazing, wild eyes. "I'll tell you but I need you to make me come first."

I was tempted but I managed to hang on to my self-control. I rubbed her clit lightly with my thumb. "My cock is so hard for you right now. You love it when I'm inside you, don't you?"

She breathed hard and fast. "I love your big cock inside me." Her eyes glazed over. "Let me see it."

I kept one hand on her thigh and with the other, I drew my cock from my pants. It looked obscenely huge in my fist. I pulled Savannah to the edge of the counter and moved the head of my cock to her entrance. She kept her eyes on it as it pushed through her pretty folds.

It took every ounce of self-control I had not to ram my cock in. Instead, I pushed it in as far as the head, salivating at the sight of her pussy lips stretched around my cock. Savannah shifted further to the edge, greedy for more. I moved back. Her eyes shot to my face.

"You make me so hard," I said.

"Fuck me Cameron," she said.

"I will, as soon as you tell me what the problem is," I said, gritting my teeth. I wanted to push my cock in so badly. Needed to hear her moan and dig her nails into my back.

"I can't believe you're using sex as a weapon," Savannah said. "Two can play that game." She did something with her muscles and her pussy clenched on the head of my cock tightly.

With a growl I became undone. I grabbed her thighs and slowly pushed my cock in, her walls clamping down on me. "Fuck," I hissed.

A smile of triumph came over her lips but it disappeared as soon as I bottomed out. She bit on her lower lip. "That feels so good Cameron."

A sudden need to have her on the bed came over me. I slipped my hands under her ass and lifted her off the counter, keeping my cock buried deep inside her pussy. I kissed her deeply before moving towards the stairs. She bounced as we walked, making it seem as though I was slowly thrusting into her.

We fell on the bed with Savannah on top of me. She flattened her palms over my chest and raised herself off my cock. I rocked upwards, following her rhythm as she rode me.

In teasing Savannah, I had taken myself to a near breaking point as well, and my orgasm came fast and quick. I held off long enough for Savannah to orgasm, then with a roar, I busted into her, filling her with my seed.

I couldn't fucking believe I'd not gone through with the plan. I fell on the bed next to Savannah, disappointed in myself.

"I never saw your lawyer," Savannah said quietly. She rolled onto her back and stared at the ceiling.

It took a moment to come out of the self-blame fog I was in and to understand what she had said. I sat up and stared down at her. "Why?"

She swung her gaze to mine. "Because I couldn't afford it. I wanted to go for someone I could afford."

I had so much to say about that but it wasn't fair to say it. First of all, you paid for what you got.

"I got this lawyer and even paid a deposit but I can never get hold of him and he's not replying to my emails. He picked up my call once and told me to be patient that he's working on things," Savannah said.

My fists curled up as anger came over me. What was wrong with people? How could you take advantage of a vulnerable mother like Savannah? Unfortunately, such bastards were a dime a dozen. I was sure he would keep stringing Savannah along, perhaps ask for more money.

"I can make another appointment for you, if you like," I said.

"Yes please," Savannah said in a small voice.

"No problem." Relief surged through me.

19

Savannah

It felt odd to be walking down the aisle shopping for groceries for my own household. I felt carefree and for the first time, I wasn't in a mad rush to finish shopping.

Ethan was safe with Cameron. I'd left him playing on the living room floor, while Cameron was stretched out on the couch, working on his laptop. It tugged at my heart how domestic we had become and at the same time, it pained me to remember, one day, it would all come to an end.

The three of us fit so well together that you would think we had always lived together. Ethan had taken to Cameron and they did a lot of boy stuff together. Ethan's favorite was walking and playing in the woods. I loved that Cameron took those opportunities to teach him about keeping himself safe.

When I got everything I needed, I pushed the cart to Heather's checkout counter. She grinned when she saw me.

"Hey you," she said. "I bet that feels amazing."

I laughed. "It does. How are you?"

"Good," she said as she passed my items through the scanning machine. She paused, looked around to check that no one could hear her, then leaned forward. "It's a good thing you left. There's word that the store has been sold."

"Oh no," I said, speaking in a whisper. "What does Lillian say?"

Heather shook her head. "She's tightlipped but you can tell, she's worried."

"Maybe it's a sign that you should go back to school," I said to her softly. Heather had started working right after high school, impatient as young people usually were to start earning her own money.

Later was when she realized that the longer you stayed in school, the more money you earned. She had saved a tidy sum with the intention of going to college except she kept putting it off with more excuses than sand in the desert.

"I don't know," she said, a look of fear in her eyes.

My heart ached for her. I knew the fear that came with wanting to jump off the cliff and follow your dreams and how it held you back. "You can do it Heather."

"It's easy for you to say that. You never feel scared. You just do stuff without giving it a second thought."

"I wasn't always this way. I told you about Finn. I knew I shouldn't be with him but I still stayed. Fear held me back but I promised myself I would never live that way again. You can do it too."

Heather gave me a shaky smile. "I'll seriously think about it."

Someone came with their cart behind me bringing our conversation to a stop. On the way back home, I mused over how much my life had changed since moving to Paradise. I felt purposeful for the first time in years and I believed that I was capable of being a good mother to Ethan.

But it wasn't all me. I'd gotten a nudge in the right direction from people who cared about me until I'd reached the point of having confidence in myself and my abilities. I hoped Heather would take a leap of faith and believe in herself.

I never ceased to enjoy the drive to and from home. I loved the view of the mountains and the woods. Every moment, I expected to see a deer leap to the road but it never happened. I never stopped hoping and Ethan asked me every day whether I'd seen a deer.

As I turned into the driveway, a familiar looking silver BMW came into view. My breath hitched when it dawned on me who it belonged to. My brother-in-law, Sam. With my heart pounding rapidly in my chest, I carried the groceries to the house, wrestling with the front door, before I got it open.

What in God's name was Sam doing here unless I was mistaken and that was not his car. But his had a distinct shade of silver that was not common. The house was oddly quiet. There was no one in the living room.

"Cameron? Ethan?" I called out. Silence met my words. Puzzled, I carried my shopping to the kitchen and deposited it on the counter. If Cameron and Ethan were not in the house, they were out in the woods. But what about Sam or whoever the visitor was?

I flung the back door open and stepped out. I cut across the backyard but before I got to the woods, voices wafted towards me. The next moment, Ethan and Liam came running down the path, their laughter filling the air.

"Mom! You're back," Ethan yelled. "Liam is here with

Uncle Sam and Aunt Ivy." He threw himself at me and gave me a quick hug.

I reached for Liam and pulled him to me. "Hey you! What a nice surprise. When did you guys get here and where are your mom and dad?"

"They're coming with Cameron," Ethan said, bouncing on his heels.

Why had they come without letting me know first? I searched my mind for how my sister could have gotten my address but she was a lawyer and they had all sorts of ways of finding out stuff.

Cameron appeared first. He smiled at me and I let out a breath I hadn't known I'd been holding. Everything was fine. No one was sick or worse. He came and kissed me lightly on the mouth.

"Savannah," Ivy cried out, her face flushed from the walk. "You never said..." We hugged. "You live in a paradise," she continued as she drew back to give Sam and I room to hug. "Everything is beautiful and Cameron was so gracious about us showing up without warning."

"You are family," Cameron said.

I shot him a grateful look. Our marriage was not real and entertaining my family had not been part of the deal. We made our way back to the house. Inside, the boys raced upstairs with Ethan eager to show his cousin his room. My heart expanded to painful proportions at the joy in my son's voice.

We had never had much in life, even when I'd been married to Finn. Ethan had always been the one doing the admiring. It warmed my heart to see him having something exciting to share with his cousin. I owed Cameron so much. There was no way I was ever going to repay him.

"I was just about to make lunch," I said.

"I'll help," Ivy said.

The men went to the living room while Ivy and I stayed in the kitchen.

"Would you believe it if I told you that we were in the neighborhood and just decided to pop in?" she asked with a cheeky grin.

"No," I said, fighting down my irritation. It hurt that she couldn't just ask me what she wanted to know instead of sneaking up on me.

"I didn't think you would," Ivy said. "I was worried about you. We all are. Mom said she has texted you about taking your husband for a visit but you always claim to be busy."

"I am busy," I told her. Not entirely the truth but it was hard to show off your new husband to your parents and family when your marriage wasn't real. It was easier to stay away.

"I knew if I told you I wanted to come, you would have found a way to brush me off."

Ivy was probably right. I felt bad for pushing my family away but they were so judgmental. So quick to form the opinion that I'd fucked up. I just didn't want to deal with that.

"I'll take Cameron to visit," I said.

"You don't need to sound so enthusiastic about it," Ivy said.

I'd removed everything I needed to cook from the fridge. I faced Ivy with one hand on my waist. "You guys are always criticizing and I'm kind of tired of being the family fuck up. You're all so perfect and I can't compete with that." My chest ached as the words that I'd longed to say for so long left my mouth.

Ivy's eyes widened. "How can you say that? We love you

and just want you to find your path. Nobody intends to make you feel like you're a mess."

Guilt came over me when I remembered Rebecca's reaction when I told her that I was married. She had been cool about it so it wasn't fair to say that they all criticized me. My mom had been predictably upset but as usual, she had shown her anger and disapproval without saying much.

"Anyway, I think you made a wonderful choice. Cameron told us how he fell in love with you at first sight when you scolded him for rudeness in the woods," Ivy said, then sighed. "That's so romantic."

I didn't know what to say. Cameron had twisted that story to make it look cute. How I wished it was true that he had fallen in love with me at first glance. It had been more of a fall in irritation at first sight.

"Was it the same for you?" Ivy asked. "Did you fall in love with him at the same time?"

God. I forgot how romantic Ivy was which was at odds with her character considering she was known as a cut throat lawyer. "No, mine came a little slower."

"Look at that smile," Ivy said, looking at me.

I stopped smiling and busied myself with stirring the contents of the pot. Could I be—? No. I wasn't in love with Cameron. I liked him a lot and I was intensely attracted to him, but love? I thought of the way the world became a brighter place when he simply walked into a room.

Or the way seeing him smile made me smile without knowing the reason why. Fear came over me. I couldn't let myself fall in love with Cameron. It could only end in heartbreak and I was done with getting hurt over a man.

20

Savannah

The sign on the door of Cutting Edge said that the salon was closed but that came as no surprise since it was before opening hours. I pushed the door open and when it gave way, I stepped in.

"Wow," was my first impression of the interior of Cutting Edge. I loved the arched blue shapes around the salon and the classy oak paneling.

"Hi," a white blond woman said, emerging from the inside. She smiled. "Sorry, we won't be open for another half hour."

"I'm not a customer," I said. "My name is Savannah—"

"Oh yes of course," she exclaimed and then came to where I stood and offered a pretty manicured hand. "Cassie told me to expect you. Silly me, it must have slipped from my mind. My name is Daisy, I'm the receptionist."

I took her hand. "It's a pleasure to meet you."

She went around to the reception desk. "Cassie left some paperwork for you to fill out. Here it is and here's a pen."

I grabbed the stack of papers and sat down in the waiting area to fill them out. They were standard stuff you filled out when starting a new job. Cassie walked in as I was filling out the forms.

"Hi Savannah," she said cheerfully and winked. "Glad you made it. I was afraid that brother of mine would distract you."

I laughed. "He's at work."

She exchanged pleasantries with Daisy then she said to her. "I didn't tell you but Savannah is my sister-in-law. She's married to Cameron."

"Oh," Daisy said. "I met Cameron when he came to see you." She turned to me. "You'll love it here. Everyone is so friendly."

Daisy hadn't lied. Four other women of varying ages came in to work, each of them introducing themselves and being super helpful. I was assigned to Paula, a dark haired talkative woman. She was the best person to learn from as she explained everything she was doing. We started off by cleaning and tidying her station, then her first client came in for a trim.

Cutting Edge was even more popular than I'd originally thought. Every stylist had appointments back to back. I had thought Cassie was being nice when she said they needed another employee.

At eleven, we got sandwiches and coffee from Joe's and sat down to eat when work allowed. I stayed until it was time to pick Ethan up from school. Though tired, I felt exhilarated, and I could easily have put in a twelve-hour shift. It hadn't felt like work at all and I'd enjoyed chatting with the clients.

∾

I GOT to the school a bit early and I took that time to call my mother. I wanted to take Cameron to meet her and my dad. Cameron wanted to as well. The sooner I did it, the faster it would be out of my mind.

She picked up her phone in her usual brisk tone. My stomach muscles tightened. It happened every time I spoke to my mother. If you met the two of us, you would question how a woman as polished as my mother had ended up with me as a daughter.

I wasn't putting myself down either. Our differences were glaring. She was an architect for goodness's sake and until recently, I worked in a grocery store doing their deliveries.

"Hello Savannah," she said. "How is Ethan? Has he adapted to his new school?"

She never asked how I was. "He's fine and he loves his school," I said, bracing myself to ask if we could arrange for lunch.

She beat me to it. "Ivy told me you want to bring your new husband to meet us. That's fine. We'll make it a family lunch. We haven't had one of those in a while. How does this Saturday sound?"

"I'll check if Cameron is working and I'll let you know," I said.

"Let me know on time," she said.

My mother was a stickler for time and schedules. I loved schedules as well but she took it to another level. We said goodbye and it felt as though a weight had been lifted off me.

Ethan came to the van and as usual, it felt like a lovable hurricane as he spoke nonstop about his day. Cameron texted me to say that he would be late as they still had a search and rescue going on. After my concentration was crap and even Ethan complained I wasn't listening to him.

I knew Cameron's job as a park ranger could be dangerous but I'd never felt as worried as I did. He hadn't said anything alarming but I couldn't stop worrying. Ethan tried to negotiate his way into staying up to wait for Cameron. It was sweet and scary the way he had become attached to him.

Cameron came home at eleven with his uniform so filthy you couldn't tell what the original color had been. Other than that and looking exhausted, he looked fine.

"How was your first day at work?" Cameron asked even before he shut the front door.

"Very good, I'll tell you all about it after you've showered. What about you? Are you okay?"

He smiled. "I'm good. We lost a man who stupidly decided to venture into the caves alone. We should have left him there overnight but he had a wife and kids." He shook his head. "We always have those."

"I was worried," I admitted as I followed him upstairs. For reasons I couldn't explain, I wanted to be near him.

He stopped on the last stair and turned to look at me. "Don't ever worry about me. I take good care of myself. I don't do stupid things."

"Good," I said.

Something intense passed between us before Cameron turned away and headed to our bedroom. I followed him in.

"You look like you could do with a bath rather than a shower," I said. "Do you want me to fill it for you?"

"Yes please," he said.

I went to our bedroom and proceeded to fill the bathtub with water. I felt so relieved and stupidly happy to have Cameron home. Was that a sign of love? All I knew was that

I'd never been as happy as I had been since Cameron and I got married.

It was as if my brain could not grasp the concept of a marriage of convenience. The bathroom door opened and Cameron walked in completely naked. He really was gorgeous. My eyes moved over his sculpted chest down to his flat six pack, and then to his enormous cock.

I could never get used to how well-endowed Cameron was. It didn't help matters that his cock was semi hard. I let out a giggle. "Are you always aroused?"

"When I'm around you," he said as he sank into the water. He let out appreciative noises. "This feels so good. It would be even better with you in it."

I grinned. "I was hoping you would ask." I stripped off my shorts and shirt and went in after Cameron. The water was perfectly warm. I grabbed a bottle of shampoo and knelt between his legs. I poured a dollop on my hand and leaned forward to rub it on his hair.

"Tell me about your day?" Cameron reached out to touch my nipples. I ignored the shots of electricity that moved from my breasts to my pussy. I massaged his scalp.

"Your sister is a wonderful human being," I said, remembering how welcoming Cassie had been. Cameron wanted to hear everything from the moment I'd gotten there in the morning.

I lost track of what I was saying as desire raged through me. Clearly, I wasn't cut out for multitasking. I managed to rinse off the soap on Cameron's head.

A moan left my mouth. "You're distracting me."

Cameron chuckled. "You distract me all the time."

I moved away to reach for the washcloth. After dousing it with body wash, I rubbed it over Cameron's chest and shoulders. I loved how powerfully muscular he was. He made me feel safe, as though nothing bad could happen to me.

"My mom invited us for lunch next Saturday," I said.

"I'd love to go. I want to meet your family," Cameron said in the simple way he had of stating things. He simplified life.

"Thanks," I said, momentarily overcome by emotion. I stopped what I was doing. "They'd love to meet you too. You were a hit with Ivy and Sam."

Cameron laughed. "I want to be a hit with you." He cupped my cheek and stared into my eyes as though he meant what he was saying.

I had to shake my head to bring myself back to earth. Cameron had taken to flirting with me, saying things that he did not mean. It felt good to hear them but I had to constantly remind myself that it meant nothing.

I washed Cameron from head to toe, ignoring his jutting cock. When I was done, I rinsed him and then stepped out of the tub. Cameron stared at me as if I had hurt him which made me giggle.

He gestured at his erect, massive cock. "You're just going to go and leave me like this?"

"I've never told you this but I hate bathtub sex," I said, grabbing a towel. "I'll be waiting between the sheets," I added as enticingly as I could. I blew Cameron a kiss and left the bathroom.

I wiped myself dry and as I'd promised Cameron, I entered the bed. The sheets felt cool against my skin. I squeezed my legs together in an effort to control the ache between my legs.

A minute later, Cameron emerged from the bathroom, led by his erection. I giggled and pulled the sheets up to my face.

"You're the cause of this," he said and without preamble, he entered the bed and pulled me to him.

"I'm going to make you feel better," I said.

"Yeah," Cameron said, cupping my cheeks.

"Like this," I murmured, bringing my lips to his. I loved the taste of him and how he took charge of every situation. He slipped his tongue into my mouth and circled my tongue before engaging it into a dance.

Cameron's hand glided over my body before settling on my ass. "Have I told you today, how beautiful you are?"

I smiled. "Yes, but I'm not averse to hearing it again."

"You're a very beautiful woman," he murmured, staring at me like he was speaking from the heart.

At that moment, I realized how much I wanted us to be real. Cameron was the perfect partner. He complimented me multiple times a day making me feel like the sexiest woman he had ever met.

Except I knew it wasn't true. The shadows of sorrow in Cameron's eyes had reduced but they hadn't left. His late wife was the one topic we never spoke about. I'd tried asking him once but his reaction had spoken louder than words. An angry look had come over his features and he had brushed away my question.

Understandably so. Amanda had been the love of his life. Still I wondered how he had been as a loving husband. Cameron was perfect as far as I was concerned and we were not in love. How then was he, when he was in love? I guess I would never find out.

He peppered kisses on my collar bone and sunk lower, trailing kisses downwards, until he was weighing my breasts in his hands. He bit a nipple to the point of pleasure and pain, doing it over and over again, until I begged him to move to the other.

Cameron worked on my nipples until the ache moved to my pussy. "I want you to fuck me," I moan, giving his head a nudge downwards.

He groans. "Have I ever told you how much I love a woman who knows what she wants. It's so sexy."

"Mmmmm." A memory comes to my mind of Finn telling me to shut up during sex and he doesn't want to have a whore for a wife. I shut down the memory. Finn had no place in my present perfect life.

Cameron knelt between my legs and gripping his cock, he rubbed it up and down my folds before plunging it in. I let out a cry and stared down at where our bodies met.

"You feel so good," I said to him.

Cameron met my gaze with his smoldering one. "So do you. Perfect." He moved in and out in a slow, precise rhythm that had me gasping for him.

I raised my hips to meet his every thrust. "Faster," I gasped.

He shifted and raised my legs, holding each up on his waist, then he continued thrusting. His cock went deeper than it ever had, hitting foreign exotic spots, and I whimpered as my orgasm raced towards me.

"Cameron," I cried, my voice getting hoarse.

"Come for me Savannah. I want this tight pussy coming hard on my dick," he commanded.

The orgasm hit me at full force, sending my body into spasms that continued to rock me even as Cameron grunted his release. He lowered my legs back to the bed and covering my body, he kissed me slowly and leisurely.

21

Cameron

"Would you please zip me up?" Savannah said, turning around.

"My pleasure." I meant every word. Savannah had become my dose of happiness. Doing anything for her, no matter how big or small, brought me joy. I stepped behind her and before pulling up the zipper, I kissed her bare back, inhaling her female scent as if it would be the last time.

Savannah giggled as hot air tickled her back. "Can I ask you something?" she said and when I said yes, she continued. "Does it bother you when I wear stuff like this?"

"I love it when you dress sexy and you always do. It makes me anticipate each day, to see what you'll wear."

Savannah looked at me over her shoulder. "Really?"

I pulled up the zipper as slowly as I could to savor the moment. Her dress was black and white, coming to a stop above her knees and hugging her curves perfectly. "You dress beautifully."

She turned around, looped her hands around my neck and hugged me.

Hugging her back, I said, "What's this for? Not that I'm complaining."

"For being the kind of man you are," Savannah said.

I smiled but inside, I was frowning. When she said stuff like that, it incensed me to imagine what that shithole of a man had said to her when they were married. Savannah was a queen and she deserved to be treated like one.

She stepped away and I continued dressing.

"Hey, I got an email from the lawyers yesterday," Savannah said after a moment. "They were just updating me. Apparently, they've already sent emails to Finn and to his lawyer, advising them any correspondence should be sent to them, not me."

"Good."

"I can't tell you how good it feels to have lawyers who are actually doing something," she said.

"I'm glad you're happy." With my lawyers working on Ethan's custody case, I wasn't worried. A bad lawyer, on the other hand, could make you lose an airtight case.

An hour later, Savannah and Ethan were singing tunelessly on the drive to Rogers. I laughed more than I ever had as their voices grew louder and louder.

"You know this one Cameron," Savannah said, then belted out the first words of the popular pop song, 'Whose waiting for me'. I joined in, throwing my voice which hadn't sang in years, out there.

"You have a really loud voice Cameron," Ethan said when the song was over.

We sang until Ethan fell asleep. Warmth filled my chest as it dawned on me that I was truly happy. In the past, it was either anger or despondence. It felt good to be human again and to feel normal human emotions. I threw Savannah a sideways smile of gratitude.

She thought I was the one who had helped her but in reality, she was the one who had saved me from a life of misery.

"We're almost there," she said to me and directed me off the highway.

Soon we were in the suburbs, and then on a quiet, fancy street that was clearly the wealthy area. Savannah had never mentioned what her parents did, other than to say she didn't get along with them. I was curious to meet them as I didn't understand how you could not get along with Savannah.

I slowed down as per Savannah's directions and pulled into a driveway with several cars already parked. I turned off the engine and looked up at the mansion set back from the road and surrounded by a lush green lawn. Clearly, Savannah's parents were wealthy, so why hadn't they helped out their daughter when she had been struggling.

There was a lot about Savannah I didn't know. We got out of the truck and Ethan shot off towards the front door.

"This is my old childhood home," Savannah said with a nervous smile.

"You grew up stylish," I commented.

"Better humble and loving, than stylish and cold," she said and went after Ethan without explaining what she meant.

I followed them enjoying the views of the immaculate landscaping. Ethan couldn't stay still as he waited for the door to be answered. His impatience made me smile. He clearly loved his grandparents, which was a good sign.

The door opened moments later and a uniformed maid appeared. Her face lit up when she saw Savannah.

"Savannah, hi," she said, keeping her voice down. She

touched Savannah's arm and then quickly hugged Ethan who was trying to wiggle past her. "And you. My, you've become a big boy."

"Hi Bella," Savannah said and leaned forward to kiss the woman on the cheek. She turned to me. "Bella raised me and my sisters. Bella, this is my husband, Cameron."

She turned her smile towards me and if she was surprised at the sudden appearance of a husband, she didn't show it. "It's a pleasure to meet you, sir."

"Call me Cameron," I said.

She stepped to one side and showed us in and as they walked together, Savannah slipped an arm around Bella's waist. She was clearly special to my wife. It was odd to think that and a shot of guilt went through me. I hadn't felt guilty in a long time and it took me by surprise.

"Everyone is in the family room," Bella said, stopping in front of a wide entryway.

I could hear chatter from the inside and gesturing at me, Savannah led the way in. Everyone stood up when we entered and my eyes were immediately drawn to Savannah's parents who stood together with Ethan standing between them.

Everyone apart from Ivy and Sam stared at me with open curiosity. Understandably so. Sam stepped forward and we man hugged each other, then Ivy followed with a hug.

I waited for Savannah to greet everyone, then she came back to stand by my side to introduce me to everyone.

"This is our oldest sister, Rebecca and her husband Michael," Savannah said.

Rebecca was an older, more serious version of Savannah, going by her solemn expression and formal dress code.

"It's a pleasure to meet you," I said to her with a shake of her hand.

Michael's face broke into a smile and I found myself liking him instantly. Like Sam, he was clearly a friendly guy.

"Welcome to the family," he said, shaking my hand vigorously.

"Thanks man," I said.

Then it was the parents turn and I could feel Savannah's tension flowing off her. I wished I could hold her close and tell her to stop stressing. As much as we all loved our families, ultimately, it was about us and our happiness. The rest were sideshows and after Finn, I was pretty sure I was a big improvement.

"Cameron, this is my father, George Hayes."

We shook hands solemnly and I could tell, he didn't know what to make of me just yet.

"My mother, Mary Hayes," Savannah said.

She gave me a smile, which I took as a win. Ethan took off in search of his cousin and the rest of us sat around making small talk. The interest was on me, which I'd expected and I was happy to answer the subtle and not so subtle questions directed my way.

Mrs. Lee did most of the talking and started by asking me directly what I did. I told them about my job as a park ranger and mentioned that I'd previously worked in investments.

Mr. Lee spoke up then. Turned out that he was an investment banker and that broke the ice as we talked about a shared passion. I realized later, over dinner, that I was actually having a good time. I loved talking about investments. You never knew when a tip could come your way.

Savannah's brother-in-law's were big investors and we had a great time, discussing our investments. We sort of excluded the ladies as they were not interested but they seemed to be having their own good time as I caught the words pregnant from Rebecca and the smile that appeared on her husband's face.

Over coffee, Mrs. Lee turned to me and asked me a question that I hadn't been expecting.

"This is not your first marriage, is it?" she asked even though I could tell from her expression she already knew the answer.

I had nothing to hide. "No, it's not. I lost Amanda five years ago after six years of marriage. She died in a car accident." As my late wife's name left my mouth, it dawned on me that I hadn't mentioned her in a long time. I had started to forget about her.

"Oh," Mrs. Lee said. Clearly, that piece of information was news. She probably assumed that Amanda and I had divorced.

My throat and lungs suddenly felt sore. I'd made a promise to never forget Amanda and now I was already breaking that promise. I hadn't visited her grave in weeks, something I used to do on a daily basis. I wracked my brain for what had made me stop. The answer came soon after. I pushed my first wife out of my mind a few weeks after I started sleeping with Savannah.

Lunch was a feast, laid out carefully on the dining table but I'd lost my appetite. All I could think about was Amanda. How would it make her feel to know that meeting another woman had made me push her out of my mind?

Amanda had been the love of my life and I could never love another woman after her. Savannah, who was seated on my left side, nudged me under the table.

"Are you okay?" she asked in a whisper.

Everyone else was engrossed in a debate.

I nodded. "I'm okay."

"You're not. Was it the mention of Amanda?" Savannah said, a worried look on her face. "I never told her. I don't know where she got that information from."

"It's fine." I looked away. My guilt was twofold. One for forgetting about my first wife and second for putting that worried look on Savannah's face. I didn't deserve her. Even as a fake wife, although there was nothing fake about the way we lived.

I forced myself back into the present but was immediately distracted when Rebecca mentioned Sam and Ivy's law firm. I turned a questioning glance at Savannah and she nodded, instantly understanding my question.

There was so much about her family that I did not understand. If her sister and brother in law were lawyers, why had Savannah not consulted them? Don't get me wrong, I was glad that she had gone with my lawyers as they were one of the best. But I couldn't help but wonder why?

22

Cameron

I loved her. I had fucking fallen in love with Savannah. That was the reason why I'd stopped thinking about Amanda and visiting her grave. I gripped the steering wheel tighter. I'd done the very thing I'd promised myself I wouldn't do. I had fallen in love with my fake wife.

Anger coursed through me. Why had I allowed my feelings to get involved? My intentions had been noble when I offered to marry Savannah. I'd wanted to provide for her and Ethan a safe haven from her ex. When did my feelings for her grow?

One way or another, I had to rectify that. I had to push my feelings to a back burner and focus on being what I'd promised to be—a protector.

"You're very quiet," Savannah said an hour into the ride back home.

"I'm okay."

"You never talk about Amanda," she said softly.

I checked on Ethan over the rearview mirror and saw that he was asleep. Ignoring the pain slicing across my chest, I thought of an answer. "I already told you what happened. I guess there's nothing else to say." I couldn't help the defensive tone that crept into my voice.

"You must have loved her very much," Savannah said.

"Yes." I still do.

She let out a nervous laugh. "It's silly but sometimes I feel jealous of her."

I stopped breathing. Why would Savannah be jealous of a dead woman? "Why?"

"She was married to a wonderful man. She experienced love. I've never had that," Savannah said.

I clenched my teeth tightly together. There was no way I was going to admit that I loved her. That had not been our deal and even though there was a chance that our marriage could work, I didn't want it. Amanda had been enough for me. I'd made a promise to myself. The love we had shared would carry me through the rest of my life until the day I left this world and joined her.

"You have something that she would have given anything to have," I said.

"What?"

I glanced at the rearview mirror again. "Ethan. We had tried for years to get pregnant until we finally went the IVF route. It took three tries for Amanda to conceive. When she died, she was seven months pregnant. They tried to save our daughter and failed." My heart felt as if it was bleeding inside my chest.

"Oh my God," Savannah said. "I didn't know that she was pregnant. Oh God." She was silent for a moment. "I'm so sorry Cameron."

I nodded. "Me too. She would have been almost five years old." I'd wondered for years how she would have looked. Probably taken after her mother, a blond haired little girl with long curly hair. It still hurt to picture her.

Savannah didn't know what to say after that and we were quiet for the rest of the drive. When we got home, I didn't enter the house. Instead, I made sure Savannah and Ethan were safely inside, then I took off for the woods.

My destination was my wife and daughter's grave. They had been buried together in the same casket and it had given me comfort to know they were together.

It was easier to access the grave site from the main road as I'd picked out the edge of my property as a grave site. I walked instead, enjoying the evening breeze and the absence of thought in my mind.

As I got l closer, Amanda took up more and more of my head space. Her image was as clear in my mind as the last time I'd seen her alive. But she didn't feel like someone I'd been close to. She had moved further from my heart. I tried to bring back the strong emotions I usually had when I thought of Amanda but nothing came.

I walked faster. I would feel it when I got to where we had laid her to rest. Weeds had sprouted from neglect and I set about pulling them out. Anger gripped me and I couldn't tell you what the fuck was eating me.

Life was so fucking unfair. Why did Amanda have to die so young? Why had our daughter not survived? Something that I had never done, happened. Tears filled my eyes, blinding me. Then, something burst from me and I sobbed like a three-year-old child.

I hadn't cried when the car rolled over the safety railing, nor did I cried when I saw Amanda's mangled body as it was pulled from the wreck. I hadn't shed a single tear at the funeral either or any time after that. Until now.

I was helpless to stop the flood. Every part of me hurt as I cried for my dead wife and child. I knelt on the grave and pounded the ground. The pain came with as much force as it had come then but there was one difference. I had wanted to go to them then.

Not anymore. I cried until there were no more tears to cry. I got up and continued pulling out weeds, everything in me numb. I lost track of time but memories of Amanda's smiling face filled my mind. The pain slowly ebbed away. I made a promise to Amanda.

"I'm not going to forget you my love," I said but even as I whispered the words, I felt like the world's greatest liar. I'd already started to forget her. She did not occupy my thoughts for twenty-four hours as she had.

To be honest, that had happened even before Savannah and Ethan had come into my life. I just hadn't realized it.

"Do you regret marrying me?" Savannah asked me when we were in bed.

We'd had dinner and after relaxing a little, catching up with the news, Savannah and I had opted for an early night in readiness for the work day. We'd both been quiet and subdued over dinner but thank God for Ethan.

He saved the evening by keeping the conversation going.

Savannah turned to face me by lying on her back.

"No. Why would you think that?" I said. I hated that she had to ask that question but I knew I was the cause of it.

"You've been so detached today," she said. "You were fine

when we were driving to Rogers but on the way back you were different."

I cleared my throat. The first thing I needed Savannah to understand was that I never did things that I regretted. If I made a commitment to do something, I followed it through, no matter what.

"I've told you before Savannah and I'll tell you again. I entered into this with a clear mind and I'd do it again for you and Ethan, no questions asked."

Her features visibly relaxed. "I just thought maybe—"

"Don't ever think that. Helping you and Ethan has given me a purpose in life." I hesitated as I searched for the right words. "It was tough and my life felt empty. You and Ethan changed that." Emotion choked me and I couldn't speak again without exposing my biggest secret.

"Thank you." She moved closer until her nipples were touching my chest.

My cock stirred. I'd never been aroused as easily by another woman as I was with Savannah. Guilt struck me as soon as that thought formed. Did that mean that sex hadn't been great with Amanda?

I scraped my hand through my hair. My mind was fucking me up. Making me think it wasn't possible to have had great sex with two women. Everything about my life with Amanda had been perfect but the truth was I couldn't remember how our sex life had been.

The memories had faded with the passing of the years and to be brutally honest, I was happy about that. I didn't want to constantly compare two women between the sheets. It wasn't fair, especially to Savannah.

"When you do that thing of running your hands through your hair, it means that you're fretting over something," Savannah said.

I laughed at her perception. It had been so long since I had been close enough to someone for them to read my gestures, I'd forgotten how special it made a person feel.

"The only thing on my mind right now is you," I said to her, running a finger down the valley between her breasts.

She shivered.

"I used to think you shivered when you were cold but now I know better. You shiver when you're aroused. When you are aching for me to fuck you."

She let out a sexy laugh. "And here I thought I was subtle."

"Don't ever be subtle with me," I told her while trailing my finger over her nipples. "You don't need to be. Anything you need, just ask."

"I like that," she said, drawing circles on my chest.

My cock jerked beneath my boxer briefs, making Savannah's eyes widen. I cupped her breasts over the silky material of her lingerie. I loved how her breasts filled my hands and I could never get enough of playing with them. I smoothed one strap off her shoulders and did the same with the other.

Pushing the fabric further down to expose her luscious breasts, I lowered my head to take an already aroused nipple into my mouth. I brushed my thumb over the other one before I shifted my mouth to it. I took my time ravishing Savannah, kissing her skin and inhaling her sweet feminine scents.

Before too long, I was firmly between her legs, gently spreading them open. My cock pulsed with need at the sight of her wet pussy begging for my tongue or cock. Desperate to taste her, I opted for tongue. I caressed her folds with my flattened tongue.

Savannah gripped my head tightly and let out a series of

moans that sounded as though she was running out of air. I liked her like that. It made me know I was doing the right thing.

I pushed my tongue deep inside and fucked her with it. Savannah rocked against my tongue and whimpered. I rubbed her clit with my thumb, keeping it up until she exploded on my tongue.

Her orgasm violently shook her whole body and only when she went still did I withdraw my tongue. I kissed her on the mouth and then got up to pull down my boxers. I was surprised that my erection had not torn a hole through them.

Instead of getting back on the bed, I angled Savannah to face the edge of the bed. I grabbed her legs and drew them around my waist. Guiding my throbbing length to her entrance, I pushed my dick in until my balls slapped against her ass.

Pulling out, I plunged back in, burying my cock to the hilt.

"Please Cameron," Savannah whispered as I fucked her deeply. My pleasure mounted but I was not ready to come yet.

"Let's make this last," I said to her, rubbing the length of my cock against her clit.

Savannah whimpered. "Oh God."

We moved faster and when I felt my orgasm coming too close, I slowed down, taking my time pulling out and thrusting back in. I distracted myself by looking at Savannah. Her gaze was on me and pretty lips were half parted. Not much help for distraction.

"I want to come, Cameron," she said. "I want to come on your big cock."

I growled. There was something about Savannah

speaking dirty that shattered my control. Like a beast, I grabbed her thighs and using them as an anchor, I fucked her like a mad man.

Our cries filled the room and at the back of my mind I worried that we might wake Ethan up. Except that I couldn't bring myself to stop. We had the perfect release, bucking and thrashing together as we orgasmed at the same time.

23

Savannah

I was learning so much working at Cutting Edge and even though Cassie was my sister-in-law, it wasn't awkward. What was a little uncomfortable was the first time I saw Cameron's mom working the reception.

Nobody had mentioned she worked there two days a week. Cassie later confided to me that it was to keep her busy and she liked it. Said it kept her from feeling too lonely at home.

When I walked into work, Mrs. Elliott was already behind the reception desk sipping a mug of coffee. "Morning Savannah," she said happily.

I liked that she was clearly a morning person like me. I wasn't really a morning person. I was an all-day person. I never got dips of energy like other people. That was one of the reasons I loved working in the salon.

"I have some good news for you," she said, leaning closer even though there was no one around. "You're getting your own clients today. I couldn't wait for you to come in to tell you."

I stared at her. "I can't. I'm not ready." On a practical level, I knew I could but on an emotional level, I had no confidence in myself.

"If there's one person who knows and loves her job, it's my daughter. If she says you're ready, she's right and you are ready."

My heart hammered in my chest and I threw a glance at the door and contemplated fleeing. Mrs. Elliott followed my gaze and laughed.

"And the three of us are going out to lunch to celebrate," she said.

It didn't seem as though I had a say in the matter. I was glad I had half an hour to myself before my first client arrived. I tidied up my work station although I'd cleaned up before leaving the previous evening.

I even had time for a cup of coffee and by nine, the salon was already buzzing with activity. My first appointment was to color hair. Easy peasy. Everyone shot me encouraging smiles and winks as they passed my station.

By the time lunchtime rolled around, it felt as if I'd done it for years. Working with Paula for more than a month had sharpened my skills and she said even though I'd studied for only six months, I had a natural skill, which had boosted my confidence to no end.

Cassie, Mrs. Elliott and I left the restaurant together.

"We won't go to just any old restaurant," Cassie said. "We'll drive to Rosetta's."

Rosetta's was a trendy new Italian restaurant with a dinner reservation list as long as my arm. Everyone wanted to try it out. Cameron and I had agreed to give it a few weeks and wait for the buzz to die down.

It was on the edge of town, set in its own gardens and outdoor space. The worst of spring had passed but it was chilly and both Cassie and I insisted we sit indoors. I'd already started feeling protective over Cameron's mom even though she wasn't really my mother-in-law.

The hostess showed us to a table at the far end which was a lot quieter. As we perused the menus, I asked myself several times what the hell I was doing having lunch with Cameron's sister and mom. To make it worse, I couldn't text Cameron for support as he was at work, and there was usually no good cell phone coverage.

I felt like an even bigger fraud when a friend of the family, a woman about Mrs. Elliott's age stopped by the table to say hello.

"This is my daughter-in-law, Savannah," Mrs. Elliott said proudly. "She's our Cameron's wife."

The other woman's eyes widened. "Oh. Congratulations my dear," she said to me and turned to Mrs. Elliott. "Don't tell me there was a wedding that I never got to know about."

Mrs. Elliott laughed and handled the awkward question like a pro. "They did the Vegas thing. I hear it's the thing to do now if you don't want a fuss, and Savannah and Cameron did not."

By the time she was done with the lengthy explanation, her friend was already nodding along as if eloping was the normal way of doing things.

She left and the server brought us food and drink menus. We gave our orders and when the server left, Cassie placed her hands on the table. That's when I noticed the gleaming diamond on her finger.

I stared at her and then the ring. "Are you engaged?" Cameron had never mentioned that his sister was seriously seeing someone. I'd never seen a sign of any man at the salon.

"Yes!" Cassie said. "I've had this ring all day today and the only person who noticed was mom."

"I'm so sorry," I said. "I can't believe I didn't see that. It's so beautiful."

Mrs. Elliott patted my arm. "You were too stressed to notice anything today." She chuckled. "All the feedback we got from your clients was glowing. Well done."

"I knew you could do it," Cassie added happily.

"Thanks for the confidence and the opportunity." Cassie could have said no when Cameron asked her if I could apprentice at her salon. She had gone a step further and offered me a job.

I would be forever grateful to her for her kindness.

"I followed my gut instincts and they've never let me down," she said with a grin.

The server brought our drinks and poured the water into glasses. I took a sip of mine and glanced at Cassie's diamond again. "Enough about me. Congratulations! Who is he? Have I met him at the salon?"

Cassie laughed. "No. He's a well-kept secret. His name is Patrick Perkins and he lives and works in Southden."

Southden was the nearest town to Paradise and about the same size if not larger than our town. A lot of people drove to Southden to shop or for dinner if they wanted a larger variety than what Paradise had to offer.

Cassie looked so animated when she talked about Patrick. A longing came over me. How awesome to have permission to fall in love with the person you were with. When you got married for any other reason other than love, you gave up the right to fall in love with that person.

That didn't stop the heart though.

"I want us to be as happy and as in love as you and Cameron obviously are," Cassie continued.

"We are not that open with our feelings," I said with a self-conscious laugh.

"Are you kidding me?" Cassie said. "Have you seen the way my brother looks at you?"

"How?" I asked.

"As if you're his favorite dessert," she said and shot a glance at her mother. "Sorry Mom but Savannah asked."

We all laughed but inside, my heart was shrinking. What Cassie had described was a man who found his wife physically attractive. That had always been the case between us but Cameron's feelings hadn't grown like mine had.

"I'm so happy to see my son living and happy again," Mrs. Elliott said. "We thought we had lost him forever but now he's slowly coming back to us." She got a handkerchief from her bag and dabbed at her eyes. "Thank you Savannah."

Guilt rose up my throat. Cameron had such a great family. I felt like an asshole for lying to them and being someone I was not. I inhaled deeply and reminded myself that I'd done it for Ethan. That didn't wipe off the guilt but it did ease it the tiniest bit.

"Patrick's family is throwing us an engagement party," Cassie continued.

"That's going to be fun," I said.

Cassie's eyes narrowed. "Wait. It just crossed my mind that we never celebrated you and Cameron's wedding."

I grimaced internally. "That's because we wanted it that way. I'm happy for you and I'm sure that Cameron will be just as happy."

"I have an idea," Cassie cried out. "Please say yes."

I laughed. "I'd have to know the question first."

Before Cassie could talk, two servers came bearing our food. The tantalizing scent of pasta dripping with sauces wafted up my nose. I loved Italian food, and Mexican, and Chineses... in other words, I loved all types of food.

"Looks delicious," Mrs. Elliott said, eyeing the steam rising from her piping hot food.

Cassie was the only one not impressed by the food. She was waiting impatiently for my attention.

"You were going to ask something," I said to her.

"Yes," she said, her eyes gleaming with excitement.

I was intrigued.

"Savannah, will you please be my bridesmaid?" She asked.

My eyes widened so much, I thought they would pop out from my face. "Bridesmaid? Are you serious?" I was married to her brother and Cassie was my employer but that had happened in a very short time span. We didn't know each other.

"It would mean so much to me," Cassie continued. "Plus, what better way to welcome you to the family."

A nervous laugh escaped my lips as I frantically thought of ways to get out of it. Cassie was sweet and the nicest person that I'd ever met but I didn't want her to hate her wedding pictures years later when she saw my face in her lineup. By which time, Cameron and I would have divorced.

"You're special to my brother and therefore special to me," Cassie said.

I shifted my glance to Mrs. Elliott to see if I could get help from that end.

She flashed me a warm smile. "I think it would be beautiful. A real family affair."

They were going to hate me the day they realized that Cameron and I were not a real couple. I wanted to disappear from the restaurant. They were nice people and they did not deserve to be lied to. I couldn't count the number of times I'd had that thought since arriving at the restaurant.

"Of course. I would love to and I'm so honored," I said weakly.

Cassie beamed. "Thanks so much. I wasn't sure you were going to say yes."

I didn't want to ask her why or talk about me at all. I let out a sigh of relief when the conversation shifted to when they hoped to have the wedding.

Later in the evening when Cameron got home, it was the first thing I told him. Ethan was upstairs in his room showering and I was in the kitchen cooking dinner.

Cameron strolled into the kitchen wearing his ranger's uniform. Pinpricks of excitement ran up my spine. I hadn't known this about myself but I loved a man in uniform.

"Hey handsome," I said, walking into his arms.

"Hey," he said, lowering his head to kiss the sensitive parts of my neck. "I texted you earlier and you didn't respond."

"Sorry, I haven't looked at my phone in hours. What did you need?" When we texted each other or called, it was because we needed the other to run an errand or do something related to the house.

"Nothing. Just missed you," he said and moved to the coffee machine to pour himself a cup of coffee.

He missed me? I wanted to believe so badly that he had missed me because I missed Cameron at all hours of the day.

"I missed you too," I said casually, not wanting to come out so heavy. "I had lunch with your mom and sister."

"Nice," Cameron said, leaning on the counter to face me.

"Did you know that your sister was seeing someone?" I asked him.

He looked at me shamefaced. "I know very little about my siblings' lives."

My chest squeezed as I imagined the kind of pain that Cameron had gone through when he lost Amanda. The kind of pain that made it impossible to be around other people.

"She's engaged," I told him. "To a man called Patrick Perkins and he lives in Southden."

Cameron shook his head. "Never heard of him."

"Anyway," I said quickly, wanting to wipe off the sad look from his face. "His family is throwing an engagement party for Cassie and Patrick so we'll get to meet him then."

Cameron's handsome face frowned. "Shouldn't that be the bride's family's responsibility?"

I'd thought so at the time.

Cameron reached into his pocket and pulled out his phone. I took that opportunity to check on the meatloaf from the oven. Cameron spoke to his sister and when he was done, he had a satisfied look on his face that made me smile.

"We're having the engagement party here," he said then smiled sheepishly. "I've never thrown a party before. Will you help?"

I laughed. "I'm your sister's bridesmaid. Of course, I will."

"Cassie told me. I'm glad you said yes," he said.

My laughter disappeared. "I feel like an impostor."

He closed the distance between us and slipped his hands around my waist. "Don't. You're my wife and that's all that counts. The rest of it is no one's business but our own."

All tension left my body. Cameron had a way of making

me feel better with just a few words. I went on tip toe and touched my lips to his. Cameron tightened his hold on me, pulling me against his hard body.

He captured my lower lip and gave it a nibble.

"Yuck," Ethan said from behind us.

We laughingly pulled apart.

24

Cameron

I kept an eye on Ethan as I chopped firewood in the clearing. We hadn't finished the pile in the back but for me, working with my hands was my way of relaxing. The rest of my relaxation methods involved my wife who was at that moment meeting with an event planner.

We had decided to hire one rather than have Savannah run around when she had to work as well and take care of Ethan too. It was frightening the way I missed her when we were not together. I'd started to have this stupid nightmare where Savannah told me she was ready for us to divorce.

I had woken up in a cold sweat then surged with relief when I saw Savannah lying down next to me. I was becoming a fucking wreck. I bent to drag a log and did not see Ethan in my line of vision. He'd been arranging his own small pile of chopped wood.

Maybe he had gotten bored and had gone back to playing in the trees.

"Ethan," I called and waited to see his impish face

emerge from behind one of the massive redwood trees. I forced down the rising panic. I'd taught Ethan the dangers of wandering off by himself in the woods and he had listened carefully.

He couldn't be very far. "Ethan," I called over and over again, moving further from the clearing. My heartbeat raced to a near explosion. Ethan had wandered off. I broke out into a cold sweat. How long ago had he disappeared? I wanted to punch myself.

Why hadn't I been paying closer attention to him? He was probably lost and scared wherever he was. But he couldn't be far. I raced around in circles after trying and failing to locate a trail. I was getting nowhere. I stopped and forced myself to think.

Ethan was fascinated by the stream that bordered my land and the neighbor's land on the western side. He had asked me that very morning whether we could go and I'd told him we'd go the following weekend.

He could be anywhere but the stream was a good start. I moved as fast as I could, moving away from the path and cutting across the vegetation and trees. I wasn't a deeply religious person but I prayed. I pushed away the image of Savannah's face.

Oh God, please let him be safe and sound.

He could be bitten by mosquitoes. What a stupid thought. I brushed tree branches from my face as I half walked, half ran. Mosquitoes were the least of what could happen to a little boy out in the woods alone. But I was going to find him. I was a park ranger and finding lost people was my job.

My phone vibrated in my pocket. I was about to ignore it, then it hit me that it could be Savannah. I slowed down and with a trembling hand, I fished it out from my pocket.

Savannah's name flashed across the screen. I swiped to answer.

"I'm standing in the clearing and my boys are nowhere to be seen," she said.

I swallowed hard. "Savannah, I lost Ethan." It pained me to say the words but I couldn't lie to her. I had failed her so badly. She had entrusted the most precious person she loved in this world to me and he had gotten lost under my watch.

"What do you mean, lost?" she asked in a voice laced with panic.

"I was chopping wood and when I looked up, he wasn't there," I explained. "But I'll find him. I have an idea where he could be."

"Oh my God, Cameron, what if something has happened to him?" Savannah said, her voice breaking at the end.

"There are no wild animals in the woods, Savannah," I said firmly. "I'll bring him home safely."

"Where are you? I have to come," she said, crying into the phone.

It broke my heart but like I'd told Savannah, I was going to find him. "No, that will just take up more precious time. Savannah, go home and wait for us. I won't come back without him." I meant it. It didn't matter whether it took hours or days. I wasn't returning home without Ethan.

"Okay." I could tell that she was trying very hard to be brave. "Please bring my boy back home safely."

"I will. I promise."

"Should I call the police?" Savannah asked.

"If he's not where I think he is, I'll let you know and we can call for help." I disconnected the call and was about to pick up my earlier pace when my training kicked in.

Rushing through the woods was not a smart thing to do. If Ethan was calling out for help, I would not hear him with the racket I was causing with my boots. I slowed down and every few steps I shouted his name.

My progress felt excruciatingly slow. I lost all concept of time as I tuned all my senses to my surroundings. The stream was downhill as my boots crunched leaves noisily, I thought I had the voice of a child.

"Ethan, is that you?" I called, pausing to listen.

"Cameron," he shouted back.

Relief surged through me. Tears filled my eyes. "Where are you Ethan?"

"Near the river," he said.

I moved like a tornado until the stream became visible below me. That's when I saw him. He was seated on the ground looking up at me. As I got closer, I noticed the streaks of tears on his cheeks.

"Are you okay?" I asked bending to pick him up.

He burst into tears. I picked him up and held him to me, resisting the urge to hug him tightly. I didn't know if he was hurt and I was afraid to hurt him further.

"I got lost Cameron," he said in between sobs. "And then I fell and hurt my leg."

"You're safe now. It's okay," I said over and over again until his sobs subsided.

Ethan raised his head and looked at me. "I'm sorry I wandered off. I thought I'd be back quickly."

I didn't want to scold him but I needed him to understand how easy it was to get lost. "You should have waited until the following weekend for me to take you."

He became teary again. "I know. I'm sorry. I promise I'll never wander off again alone."

I kissed his forehead and reached for my phone. Savannah answered on the first ring.

"I have him and he's okay apart from his knee which is painful from a fall," I said, speaking quickly.

"Thank God," Savannah said, laughing and crying at the same time. "I'm waiting for you."

I moved as fast as I could, ensuring that the branches above us did not hurt Ethan. In ten minutes, we burst out of the woods and when Savannah saw us, she came running. She threw her arms around both of us and hugged us.

"You gave us a scare Ethan," she said, drawing back. "You know the rules. You're not allowed to go off into the woods alone."

"I know mom. I'm sorry."

"I'm sure Ethan has learned his lesson," I said, feeling sorry for him.

Ethan sniffed. "My leg hurts."

"It's not broken but we need to get it checked out," I told Savannah.

"I'll get the truck keys and meet you at the front," she said and took off on a run towards the house.

"Are we going to the hospital?" Ethan asked, lifting his head from my shoulder.

"Yes, but the doctor there is very nice. In fact, you've met him. He's my brother."

"Wow," Ethan exclaimed. "Will he let me touch his stethoscope?"

"I'm sure he will, if we ask very nicely." I needed to make sure that my brother was actually at work.

"Hey," Thomas said when he answered the call.

"Hey, thanks for picking up my call. I know you're busy," I said. It seems as if every time I contacted my siblings, it was to ask for a favor. I made a promise to myself to change that.

"Your family," he said.

I told him about Ethan hurting his knee and he assured me that most likely it was just a superficial wound.

"That was my brother Thomas," I explained to Savannah as she opened the back passenger door. "He's waiting for us at the hospital."

"Thanks," Savannah said.

We settled Ethan at the back and were soon on our way. The hospital was at least twenty minutes away but Ethan did not appear to be in any pain. He was telling his mother about his adventure in the woods. I smiled at the ending of the tale.

It didn't end with him seated down on the ground crying. No. He was on top of a several feet tall tree, waving his hands from the top.

Thomas was waiting for us when we arrived and he had a small wheelchair with him.

"This ride belongs to Ethan," he said in a deep voice, pretending he was speaking on a microphone.

Ethan giggled as I lowered him to the wheelchair.

"Thanks bro," I told Thomas as we followed him in.

"Thank you Thomas," Savannah said, sprinting to keep up.

Our destination was the ER. Thomas transferred Ethan from the wheelchair to the small examination bed and proceeded to poke around his leg. Ethan yelped once but he didn't cry.

"It's superficial," Thomas later told us. "I'll have someone clean it up and bandage it. It should be fine in a day or two."

We were done with the hospital in less than twenty

minutes. Ethan was tired and he slept the whole way home. I carried him from the truck to his bedroom and all the while, he did not stir.

Savannah and I stood at the doorway watching him sleep.

"I'm so sorry," I said, preparing myself to face her wrath.

"What for?" she asked me with a genuinely puzzled look on her face.

"For not being careful enough with Ethan in the woods."

She took my hand and led me away from Ethan's door. "Ethan is a six-year-old boy. This was bound to happen at one time or another. I'm hoping it will be a big lesson to him but I don't blame you. Do you know how many times I've lost him in a mall or the store?"

I couldn't believe that she wasn't angry. Gratitude flowed through me.

"I trust you with both our lives," she added.

Lacking words to express what I was feeling, I pulled her to me and held her tightly. I didn't know what I would do when Savannah decided to move on. One thing was for sure. It would come from her, not me.

25

Savannah

"You're not nervous about going to my mom's, are you?" Cameron asked me in a low voice, though Ethan was engrossed in watching a cartoon on an IPad.

"No, I was just thinking about the mediation meeting this coming week," I said. Finn's lawyer had communicated and as he had threatened, he wanted custody of Ethan.

Even though I knew the chance of him succeeding in taking Ethan away from me were almost nil, I still worried. Nothing was set in stone and that was my son we were talking about.

"You're sure you don't want me to go with you?" Cameron asked, glancing at me with concern written on his face.

Amanda had been a lucky woman to be married to Cameron. And to think I'd thought he was a grumpy horrible man when I met him. He was the opposite of that. He went beyond the normal ranges of kindness. If he asked me to marry him for real, or rather to make our marriage real, I'd say yes without hesitation.

"I'll be fine, thanks." The mediation meeting was something I needed to do alone. Besides, I didn't want to take up any more of Cameron's time. He was already doing a few repairs at the cottage for me.

"You said you bought paint from the hardware store," I said, changing the topic. "You haven't told me how much the cost was."

"Don't worry about it," Cameron said dismissively. "I haven't spent much and I'm enjoying myself."

He probably was too as he spent a lot of his off days at the cottage. "Okay but please don't spend too much."

"Stop worrying," he said. "And we're here. I wish one of my siblings had a child for Ethan to play with."

I laughed at the concern in Cameron's voice. "He's fine, besides, there's Jack who is just as fun as having a human playmate."

Cameron smiled as he brought the truck to a stop. "You're right about that."

"Can I get out mom?" Ethan asked as soon as the engine died down. "I want to play with Jack."

"Yes you can and be sure to knock first," I said, speaking to Ethan's back as he had already shot out of the truck.

Cameron and I followed him out at a more leisurely pace. I giggled at the memory of how nervous I had been that first day when I met Cameron's family. It had been awkward as hell but his mom and Cassie had been super friendly.

Thomas had been great too when we took care of Ethan at the hospital. I was looking forward to getting to know them even better. It didn't matter how long we'd be married for. He had assured me that he would never tell anyone that ours was a marriage of convenience so I needn't worry that they would hate me later.

I'd decided I was going to enjoy these relationships I was forming in Paradise because of Cameron. Ethan knocked once and turned the knob. Before I could shout at him to mind his manners, he was already inside.

Cameron laughed. "I love that kid."

I grinned. "Me too. I just hope he behaves himself in front of Patrick."

"Ethan always behaves himself, it doesn't matter whether there's anyone or not," Cameron said.

"He's a good kid." I knew how lucky I was.

Cassie was the one who had invited us for dinner to meet her fiancé. I was looking forward to meeting the man who had won the heart of such a special woman. In addition to being hard working, Cassie was a genuinely good human being and she treated all her employees like family.

"No point in knocking," Cameron said, twisting the door knob.

"Nope," I said.

He held the door for me and as I entered, I went on tip toe and kissed him lightly on the lips. I loved his reaction. His eyes widened and then the widest smile pulled at his lips.

"We should do that again," he said, following me in.

I laughed, glad that he hadn't thought it weird. I tried not to be physically affectionate with Cameron in public. It wasn't part of our deal and I didn't want him to become uncomfortable or regret helping me.

By the noise coming from the family, it sounded as though there were fifty people inside. I smiled even before entering. There was something so warm and wholesome to be in the midst of people who clearly cared for one another.

I couldn't imagine how hurt they had been when Cameron pushed them away.

Ethan flew past with Jack on his heels. I opened my mouth to speak then promptly shut it. As Cameron would have said, let the boy enjoy himself. Everyone was present and I noticed the sandy haired gentleman as soon as I stepped into the room.

Thomas was the nearest to me and we hugged warmly.

"Thanks so much for everything," I said to him. He had come a day later to check on Ethan's knee, going over the call of duty.

"I'm glad I could help," he said warmly. Close up, Thomas's resemblance to Cameron was more pronounced. "You and Ethan are family."

I hugged Asher next, who was warmer than the last time. Then I moved to Mrs. Elliott who greeted me with genuine joy in her voice. Cassie was next and then she held her fiancé's hand, looking at him with love shining from her eyes.

A stab of longing went through me. I felt that longing more and more, especially when I saw a couple in love.

"Patrick, this is Savannah, my sister-in-law," Cassie said.

He shook my hand. "It's nice to meet you, Savannah," he said with a friendly smile. "Cassie talks about you a lot."

"She's my favorite sister-in-law," Cassie quipped.

"The only sister-in-law," I commented in a dry tone and everyone laughed. "It's nice to meet you too." I couldn't say that Cassie talked about him because she didn't. Cassie came across as social and she was, but she was also very private.

"This is my brother Cameron," Cassie continued.

The two men shook hands. Ethan chose that moment to come running into the family room, holding on to Jack's neck. Cameron grabbed his hand and tugged him gently to his side, then draped an arm around Ethan's shoulders.

"And this is our son, Ethan."

Warmth spread from my core to the rest of my body. Ethan looked up and beamed at Cameron. I could see he liked being referred to as Cameron's son.

"Hi," Patrick said.

"Hi," Ethan said.

Ten minutes later, as we all trooped to the dining room, I couldn't stop thinking about Cameron calling Ethan 'son'. It wasn't just that either, it was the obvious affection for Ethan in his voice as he said it.

Ethan was used to constant criticism from his dad. I never forgot the day Finn said that children should be raised with a bit of fear. That had stuck with me and returned to the surface when Finn intimidated Ethan by shouting in his face.

All our little boy had wanted was to experience fatherly love. Cameron had shown him more love in the few months we had been married than Finn had in all of Ethan's life.

"Can I help?" I ask, following Mrs. Elliott and Cassie to the kitchen.

"Sure. Everything's ready, we just need to bring it to the table," Mrs. Elliott said.

"How's the party planning going?" Cassie asked when we got to the kitchen.

"Good, I'm having fun picking themes and colors," I said. Planning the party had become a nice distraction from the worries over the custody case.

"Are you sure it's not too much?" Cassie said. "When Cameron insisted on hosting the engagement party, I knew all the work would fall on you."

I laughed. "I'm enjoying it actually. I promise."

She seemed satisfied. "Please let me know when it becomes too much. Patrick and I have compiled a list of the people we want to invite. I'll give it to you later."

We ferried dishes of food from the kitchen to the dining room. Cassie and her mom had outdone themselves preparing dinner. I wasn't the greatest cook. Cameron cooked dinner most nights and I cleaned up. I made a mental note to ask Mrs. Elliott to give me a few cooking classes.

"Your father would have been so proud of all of you," Mrs. Elliott said, growing suddenly emotional. She looked around the table and then focused on me and then Patrick. "He would have loved to meet you."

"I would have loved to meet him," I said sincerely.

Under the table, Cameron rested his hand on my thigh and then gently squeezed it. Shots of electricity shot up my leg. My body interpreted everything that Cameron did as a turn on, even in the midst of company.

"He would be proud of you too Mom," Cassie said. "You've done a good job with us."

Mrs. Elliott turned her gaze to Cameron and an awkward moment followed. Then it was as if Cameron and his mother were the only ones at the table.

"Mom, it wasn't your fault," Cameron said softly. "That was all me and I handled it the only way I knew how to. The only way I could."

She nodded. "Don't disappear again, okay?"

"I won't," Cameron said. "In any case, Ethan and Savannah won't let me. They love this place a lot more than I do."

"It's the people," I said.

"We love you too," Mrs. Elliott. "I love how quickly our family is growing. Now if these sons of mine would make their mother proud and find good girls to marry, my happiness would be complete."

"You're going to wait for a long while Mom," Asher said.

The heavy emotions in the room dissipated and as we ate, we stuck to light topics. Asher regaled us with tales from his job. Being a firefighter sounded like constant action.

Patrick was a talker as well and he didn't seem to mind being asked questions about himself and his family.

"They're really looking forward to coming down and meeting the whole family," he said, then said to Cameron. "Thank you for hosting the engagement party."

"You are welcome. Savannah and I are happy to do it," Cameron said, flashing me a loving smile.

Either he was a very good actor or... I didn't want to go down that road. I knew it would lead to disappointment and pain. Still, I couldn't push it out of my mind. What if he had feelings for me too?

No. If he did, Cameron would have already said something. He was that kind of a man. At the beginning, he had clearly told me he was done with love. A man did not say those kinds of things unless he meant it.

It was a fun evening but we left immediately after dinner Ethan had already started to doze.

"Patrick seems like a good person," I said to Cameron as we drove back home.

"I thought so too. I feel bad that I know so little about my family," Cameron said.

I reached across and squeezed his thigh. "You have time to rectify that."

He looked at me and smiled. My heart did somersaults in my chest. I wanted to see that smile for the rest of my life.

26

Cameron

J oy filled me at the sight of our front garden milling with people working hard to prepare for the day ahead. A white tent covered half of the garden and from my bedroom window, I could make out Savannah speaking with the event planner.

Ethan appeared from one end and together with his new friend, they were pulling his toy wagon and having a great time. The other boy who was about his age was the event planner's son. I grinned as I watched Ethan. Gratitude filled me as I watched him being a kid. Thank God I could provide for him a safe place to be a child.

The memory of the day he got lost popped into my mind and my heart squeezed. Since then, we'd gone back to the woods several times and to be sure, he had learned his lesson. He kept close to me and he asked all sorts of questions about being in the woods.

Ethan's physical safety was not the issue. It was his own father. The mediation meeting had not gone well as Finn insisted on getting full custody. Obviously no court was going to grant him that but the thought of it kept Savannah up at night.

There was another meeting next week. Hopefully Finn would be reasonable about his demands. Meanwhile, everything in me demanded that I look out for my wife. Except I couldn't and I fucking hated feeling helpless.

Ethan and his friend disappeared from view and my gaze swung back to Savannah. As though sensing I was staring at her, she looked up at our window but she couldn't see me as our windows were one way. Then she moved out of my line of view.

She was so beautiful and so giving of herself. I'd insisted on holding the engagement party but it was Savannah who had done all the work. What did I know about themes and colors?

The door to our bedroom clicked. I looked down to ensure that the towel around my waist was secure. I looked over my shoulder as the door swung open.

"I could feel you looking down at me from up here," Savannah said as she locked the door behind her. "Sneaky."

I laughed. "How now? I was enjoying the view from up here."

She came and stood behind me and slipped her hands around my neck. "Do you want company in enjoying the view?" She pressed her breasts against my back and dropped one hand to cup my cock.

I was completely naked as I'd been about to get dressed after taking a shower. Savannah turned me around to face her and then tugged at the towel until it fell off. My cock pointed straight out, already hard just from her light touch.

Savannah giggled. "If something happened and that

window became opaque, the whole world would see your ass."

"Hardly the whole world," I said. "Just the event planner."

She dropped to her knees and wrapped her hands around my cock. "You're so big," she said and brushed the tip with her lips.

My breath audibly hitched in my throat. I loved what Savannah was doing with her lips and fingers. Her touch was feather light and anticipation was killing me.

"I'm not sure whether we have time for this," Savannah said and then licked my precum.

I could have laughed if I wasn't so aroused. "That's called teasing Savannah, and you don't want to be labeled a tease."

"We have guests in two hours," she continued, seemingly not caring that her husband would label her a tease. "Maybe we can continue this later, when they leave?" said the woman who was on her knees playing with my cock.

"Don't you dare," I growled.

She laughed as she moved her hand up and down my length. More. I needed more. I rocked my hips in time to her strokes. She adjusted her position and swirled her tongue over my tip. I groaned softly and resisted the urge to grip the back of her head.

She parted her lips and I slid my dick into her mouth. Savannah took every inch of my huge cock into her mouth, little moans escaping her lips. She did something new with her throat, something she had never done before.

"Fuck Savannah, where did you learn that?" I asked with a twinge of jealousy. Not that I thought she was seeing anyone but the thought of another man in her past having enjoyed such attention...

"I like to read erotic stuff," she said, pulling my cock out for a moment. "And you are my guinea pig."

"Anytime," I said, groaning as she took my cock into her mouth again. She held it in place with one hand and moved up and down, making slurping noises as she did so.

She worked me into a frenzy with her mouth and tongue. Unable to keep my hands to myself, I grabbed a handful of her hair and held her in place. A need to make her completely mine came over me. It was something that had been building and now as she sucked my cock, it grew like a monster.

Savannah was mine on paper. I wanted her to be wholly mine. I wanted to claim her body and her heart.

"I want you to be mine, Savannah," I growled as my orgasm grew like a rising crescendo.

She made a sound which could have meant anything. My balls tightened and in the next moment, I thundered into Savannah's mouth like a storm. For a second, I felt guilty for not giving her a warning then I remembered what she had said, nothing gave her satisfaction like swallowing my cum. How lucky could a man get?

EACH TIME OUR EYES MET, Savannah and I exchanged a secret smile. We were at the same table together with Ivy, Sam and my mom and Thomas.

Asher was the emcee and he was doing a great job keeping everyone entertained. We had come to the introductions part and he was introducing Patrick and my sister. They stood up but it was clear they only had eyes for each other.

Amanda and I didn't have an engagement party. I tried

to recall our wedding and whether we had been as in love as Patrick and Cassie were. Instead of seeing Amanda on our wedding day, an image of Savannah and I getting married popped into my mind.

Guilt swept through me. I had already replaced Amanda in my mind, I just didn't want to admit it. Patrick gestured to a boy a little older than Ethan and introduced him as his son, Josh. That surprised me. My sister was going to be a stepmom. I briefly wondered what had happened to Josh's mom.

It was our turn to introduce ourselves. It felt good and disloyal at the same time, to introduce Savannah and Ethan as my family.

I'm sorry Amanda.

After the introductions, the bar was open and people were free to mill around and get to know each other. I got a glass of chardonnay for Savannah and handed it to her.

"Thanks," she said, flashing me a smile that made my heart beat like a teenager's. She was in her element, socializing and making everyone feel welcome. Unlike me, Savannah was a social butterfly. She loved being amongst people.

It pained me when I remembered the things she had told me about her marriage. How Finn had called her an attention seeker when they went out for family or friends events. All because she loved socializing. What was it that made a man like Finn so insecure that all he could do was criticize his wife when she shone? I didn't fucking get it. And how did the criticism make him feel better?

"Hey, think you could spare a minute out of staring at your wife and chat with your sister," Cassie said, grabbing my arm.

I laughed. "You're one to talk. You should have seen the

way you were looking at Patrick? Do you want me to describe it to you?"

Cassie burst out laughing as she propelled me towards the bar. "Please don't. I have a feeling it's not PG rated."

At the makeshift bar, I asked for a beer while Cassie asked for a double shot or bourbon. I raised my eyebrow at her when the bar man turned around to prepare our drinks.

"I need Dutch courage," she said. "I've been in a state of panic since we introduced ourselves."

"Why is that? Did you just find out what Patrick's last name is?" I teased trying to ease the look of terror on her face.

It worked. She laughed. "That's the stupidest thing you've ever said." A pensive expression replaced the laughter. "You know, I'd forgotten what a good listener you were. Out of all my brothers, you were my favorite Cameron. Still are to be honest. I could always talk to you about anything."

"I'm sorry." I didn't know what else to say.

"It's okay," Cassie said. "As Mom said, what matters is that you are back with us again."

The bar man placed our drinks on the counter and we both reached for them at the same time. Cassie tossed back her bourbon on ice and finished it in one gulp. She set the glass back on the bar and immediately asked for another.

I sipped my beer and observed her.

She met my gaze. "I'm scared, Cameron. I'm going to be a stepmom. What the heck do I know about mothering? I've been tempted to ask Savannah for some advice the last couple of weeks but I couldn't work up the courage."

"Savannah's easy. You should know that by now," I said. I'd never seen my sister so nervous about something. She was the most composed person I knew. "I don't get it though.

There's nothing difficult about being a stepparent. I'm doing it with Ethan."

Cassie took a sip of her drink. "I should be talking to you actually. I'm feeling the pressure of responsibility."

"You shouldn't. Kids bring more joy than worry. You're naturally good with people. A couple of months from now, you'll tell me how silly you were to worry," I said, giving her a reassuring smile. "What sort of a kid is Josh?" He and Ethan had already become friends and that to me spoke volumes about his character.

"He's a really nice kid. He lived with his mother until recently when she decided to get married. She wanted a fresh start to her new family so she dumped him at his father's place without warning."

I folded my fists. What was wrong with these people? Why did they sire children if they couldn't take care of them? "Poor kid."

"Yeah, he's been through a lot. Patrick had tried to get custody but it didn't work. Hopefully now Josh will have a more stable home life," Cassie said.

"He will with both of you in his life. Kids don't need much. Just love and knowing they're loved," I said. Ethan had blossomed ever since he and his mother moved in with me.

I hadn't done anything special but I hadn't made Ethan feel insecure and not enough, as his father had constantly done.

Cassie inhaled deeply and loudly. "Okay, I can do this."

I nodded. "You can." I had missed my friendship with my sister. Why had I pushed her away? Of all people, she's the one person who could have been there for me. Helped me navigate my grief.

"You look so deep in thought. Are you thinking about Amanda?" Cassie asked softly.

"Not really," I said. "I was thinking how much easier my journey would have been if I had allowed you to be there for me."

"That's the past. Let's dump it there. This is now."

I loved Cassie for that.

27

Savannah

I woke up to a pounding heartbeat and it took me a few seconds to realize the reason why. The custody meeting. Why couldn't Finn and Nancy leave us alone? Have their own child and leave my Ethan alone. I rolled onto my back and stared at the ceiling.

What if the unimaginable happened and he won custody of Ethan? Pain spread across my chest. I couldn't live without my boy. It wasn't just that either. Finn was a terrible father. Instead of building Ethan up, he slowly destroyed his self-esteem. I knew very little about Nancy but I'd not been impressed with the little I'd seen of her.

She treated me like the scum of the earth, shooting daggers at me, and I understood it was probably due to what Finn had told her. Still, what did that say about her intelligence? There were two sides to every story. I turned to lie on my side and stared at the wall.

The bed shifted on Cameron's side and he moved until he was spooning me.

"You're not asleep, are you?" he said, his voice husky from sleep.

"No," I admitted, resting my hand over his strong one.

"Everything's going to be fine," Cameron said. "You're an awesome mother Savannah. Ethan belongs with you and that's where he'll stay."

I smiled in the semi-darkness and felt my tension ebbing away with Cameron's reassuring words. We talked until my alarm went off, then it was time to get up and start the day. We had fallen into a routine where one person used the shower while the other straightened our room.

My phone vibrated as I returned from the shower. I tapped on the screen to read the message.

"How sweet," I said to Cameron. "It's Cassie. She's thanking us for the engagement party and she says it was perfect."

Cameron smiled. "It was. I can't remember the last time I had so much fun."

"Or went to a party," I teased him.

"That too."

The party had been a welcome distraction, else I'd have worried about the mediation meeting all weekend. I texted 'You're welcome' to Cassie then went to Cameron and slipped my hands around his waist.

His eyes dipped to my breasts barely covered by the towel. I loved the effect I had on my husband. He raised his gaze to my face, a tender expression on his features. A look I had never seen before. My heart rate kicked up a notch. Cameron opened his mouth to speak.

At that very moment, my phone vibrated on the night table, the noise jarring and loud.

Cameron smiled and stepped back, the moment broken. Disappointment filled me. Cameron had been about to say something important. Something momentous that would have changed our relationship, maybe taken it to the next level.

Either that or I was getting desperate. I hated to imagine it was the latter. I turned to pick up my phone without a lot of enthusiasm. It was a thumbs up emoji from Cassie. Our moment had been interrupted because of a fucking thumbs up emoji. Not Cassie's fault, just the timing.

I turned back to Cameron. He was on his way to the bathroom.

I was being stupid, I told myself. If it had been something important, Cameron would have said it, phone interruption or not. I exhaled and told myself to let it go.

I woke Ethan up and got him ready for school.

"You're being weird mom," Ethan commented when I stared at him for too long.

I loved that the three of us started the day together and ended it by having dinner together. Over breakfast, Cameron was not his usual calm self. He kept glancing at his phone. It made me even more nervous than I already was.

Before he finished his breakfast, he excused himself by saying something about checking on the minivan. It dawned on me then why he had been so restless. He was worried about my safety driving to Helena alone.

Cameron did not trust the minivan despite my reassuring him it was a sturdy vehicle and it had never given me mechanical problems. It felt good to have someone care about my welfare.

He returned ten minutes later by which time Ethan and I were done and the dishes washed.

"Ready?" Cameron said with eyes that sparkled and gleamed.

"Yes." I narrowed my eyes at him. He was up to something.

I helped Ethan with his backpack and we made for the front door. Cameron held the door open and Ethan stepped out.

"Wow!" he exclaimed.

I followed him out and ground to a halt at the sight of a brand new shiny blue Kia Sportage.

"That's your mom's new car," Cameron said.

"Wow," Ethan exclaimed again.

"What do you mean?" I asked Cameron.

"I got it for you," he said, walking towards the vehicle. Ethan took off and zipped past, stopping only when he got to the car. "Come and see it up close. I wasn't sure about the color. I hope you like it."

My feet moved of their own accord. I was sure that my eyes were close to popping out of their sockets. A car! Cameron had bought me a car. I walked around it admiring its shiny exterior.

It was so tempting to say yes but it wouldn't be right. I wasn't Cameron's real wife. Accepting such an expensive gift from him was wrong. He came and stood behind me and wrapped his hands around my waist.

"Can I get in?" Ethan asked.

"Yes," Cameron said with a laugh. "That's your ride to school this morning."

"Yes!" Ethan shouted and pulled the door open. I cringed and fought down the urge to ask him to be careful.

"Well, what do you think?" Cameron said. "You haven't said a word."

"It's a beautiful car Cameron," I said, turning around to face him. "But it's not right to accept such an expensive gift from you. It wouldn't be fair."

His features became inscrutable. "Why don't you let me worry about what's fair or not? And you and Ethan are my family now. Tomorrow doesn't matter."

I was too choked up to speak.

Cameron opened the driver's door and handed me the keys. "Here you go. Enjoy your ride to school and to Helena."

I wiped off the tears falling down my cheeks with the back of my hand. Instead of entering the car, I hugged Cameron and murmured thank you over and over again.

I entered the car and took a few seconds to admire the interior and inhale the scent of leather and newness. "This is the first new car I've ever driven and owned."

"The start of many," Cameron said, bringing fresh tears to my eyes.

I STAGGERED out of the building and onto the street, barely holding it together. My heart pounded hard against my chest and it felt as if my life was spiraling out of control. I hurried to the parking area, desperate to get away.

I walked around the car park for a couple of minutes unable to find the minivan while all along, the events of the meeting played in my head like a video. Finn and Nancy were going to take Ethan on Saturday afternoon and bring him back on Sunday.

Panic rose up my chest. I couldn't let them have him. The thought of not knowing how Ethan was faring pushed me over the edge. A man starting his car jolted me back to the present. I had no idea how many times I had walked around the parking lot.

My gaze fell on a shiny KIA. That's when it hit me. That

was my car. The one that Cameron had gifted me that very morning. I hurried to it and fished out my keys. Only when I was in the privacy of the car did I allow the tears to fall.

With trembling fingers, I pulled out my phone and called Cameron, even though I knew the network was terrible in the park. To my relief, he picked up on the first ring.

"Hey, how did it go?" he asked.

Instead of answering, I burst into tears. Cameron whispered soothing sounds into the phone and waited until I got myself under control again. I told him how Finn had insisted it was his turn now to have a chance to get to know his son and that he wanted full custody.

He had also questioned the stability of our marriage since he had never heard me mention a fiancé or boyfriend. After a lot of back and forth arguments and accusations, my lawyer, a wonderful gentleman with a calm demeanor, had advised me to agree to the every other week visitations on a six month trial basis.

"I'm sure he knows what he's doing," Cameron said.

"How can I let Ethan go knowing what a terrible father Finn is?" I said, tears filling my eyes.

"He's a terrible father but he would never physically harm Ethan," Cameron said. "He has never hurt him, has he?"

"No," I said. "He just uses words to hurt and Ethan is scared of him," I said.

"We'll have prepared him," Cameron said. "Ethan will take his cue from us. If we appear panicked or scared, he'll feel the same way. If we're calm and confident, he'll be the same way."

The more he spoke, the more my panic dissipated and letting go of my boy for a night seemed doable. We finished talking and after reassuring Cameron that I was good to drive, we disconnected the call.

As soon as I disconnected the call, my phone rang. This time, it was Heather. She was a real friend and kept abreast of everything going on with my life.

"Hey," I said after I swiped to answer.

"Hi," Heather said. "How did the meeting go?"

I let out a sigh. "Finn and Nancy will have Ethan for the weekend." I couldn't believe how calm and accepting I sounded.

"Oh my God, I'm sorry Savannah," Heather said, sounding horrified. "I know how worried you were about something like that happening."

"Yeah. My lawyer said it was best if I cooperate at this stage and that at the end, it will work in my favor."

"Bastard," Heather hissed into the phone. "How are you not screaming and cursing? That's what I'd be doing."

I laughed. "I was a few minutes ago but Cameron talked me out of my panic."

Heather was silent for a few seconds. "I don't care what you say but there's something special between the two of you. All you need is one person to be brave enough to admit their feelings. You're perfect for each other."

"We've just become really good friends." The words sounded hollow even to my own ears. Which friends went at each other the way we did? We had sex countless times and we still tore each other's clothes off. Okay, maybe friends was pushing it. The correct word was attraction.

"Are you in love with him?" Heather asked softly.

I closed my eyes. I inhaled deeply and then opened my eyes. "Yes." I had no doubt about that. "But that could also be because he's become my knight in shining armor so many times."

"Bullshit," Heather said in a harsh voice. "The least you can do is to be honest with yourself."

"It doesn't matter though," I said just as harshly. "Cameron was very clear he would never fall in love with another woman. I can't live the rest of my life loving a man whose heart belonged to another. I just can't."

28

Cameron

The sound of a muffled sob woke me up from a deep slumber. At first, I thought I'd been dreaming but it came again, right from Savannah's side. I turned around to face her.

"Hey, are you crying?" I asked her, prying her hands away from her face. Her cheeks were wet. "What is it Savannah?"

"I'm scared of giving Finn my baby," she said. "What if he doesn't bring him back?"

I'd had the same fears myself but I wasn't going to admit that to Savannah. That bastard was capable of running off with Ethan but he would have to move to another planet for us not to find him.

I pushed away my fears, knowing the chances of Finn disappearing with Ethan were slim. He needed to be on his best behavior to even have a shot at getting full custody of Ethan.

"He's going to bring him back," I said. "He's not foolish

and I'm sure he knows if he's late by as much as half an hour, it will affect his custody case." I pulled Savannah into my arms and held her tightly.

Listening to her crying felt as though my own heart was breaking into tiny fucking pieces. I felt so damn helpless. I couldn't fall asleep again but I was glad Savannah did. Dawn found me still staring at the ceiling.

As I contemplated getting up to make myself a cup of coffee, a soft knock came on our door. I gently shifted away from Savannah then careful not to wake her up, I padded to the door and opened it.

"Cameron, I can't sleep," Ethan said, rubbing his eyes.

"It's okay," I said. "I'll stay with you until you can." It was too early for him to be up and his dad was not coming to pick him up until the afternoon.

I picked him up and immediately found the culprit of his inability to sleep. He had wet himself. In his room, I helped Ethan change into fresh pajamas, then changed his beddings.

"Thanks Cameron," he said sleepily.

I kissed his forehead. "Anytime buddy." I stayed with him until I was sure he was asleep then returned to our room to get dressed.

Savannah was sound asleep and I quietly dressed then grabbing my cell phone, I went downstairs to the kitchen. As I waited for the coffee to brew, I used my phone to research custody cases and what happened if one parent does not obey the custody agreement.

When Savannah came downstairs an hour later, breakfast was ready. I kissed and hugged her then urged her to eat something.

"I peeked in at Ethan," she said.

"Is he still asleep?" I asked as I poured coffee for her.

"Completely but his pajamas are different from the ones he wore last night," she said.

"Yeah, I helped him change. He had an accident," I carried Savannah's coffee to the island and set it in front of her.

"Thanks," she said, a worried expression on her face. "He hasn't done that in years. Poor kid. He must be anxious about going to sleep at Finn's house."

I hated what the whole situation was doing to Ethan and Savannah. On top of that, it was clear that Finn had no real interest in his son. If he was, where had he been all this time? Why now?

It was a long morning for all of us but mostly for Savannah. She followed Ethan wherever he went until I was forced to gently tell her that her anxiety was rubbing off on Ethan.

We barely ate any lunch. The only person who ate the burgers I'd grilled was Ethan but as the time drew nearer he had withdrawn and Savannah's anxiety had doubled.

"Go and get your bag" Savannah said to Ethan. He had packed a small backpack for his one night away.

As soon as he was out of the living room, Savannah's eyes filled with tears. "I don't know if I can do this," she said.

I went to her and knelt down in front of her. "Listen to me. Yes, you can. You're doing this for Ethan. For the future. Don't forget that you're not handing him over to a stranger. Finn is his father. He won't harm it."

She nodded and wiped off the tears from her eyes. "Will you check on Ethan? I don't want him to see me crying."

I kissed her lightly. "I will." I bounded up the stairs and went straight to Ethan's room. His door was slightly open and when I entered, I found him seated cross legged on the bed, hugging a teddy bear. When he saw me, he tossed it to the floor as if it had suddenly become dangerous.

I picked it up and sat down. "Are you okay buddy?"

He shook his head. "I don't want to go."

"It's only for one night and then tomorrow, Dad will bring you back," I said.

Tears filled his eyes. "Why do I have to go?"

I moved closer and took his hand. "Because he's your dad and guess what? He loves you and he wants to get to know you."

His lower lip trembled. "But mommy doesn't want me to go."

"Mommy wants you to spend time with your dad but she's going to miss you terribly. So will I. But your dad needs you too."

"He does?" Ethan asked.

I nodded. "You're his little boy and mine too and mom's. We all love you so much and we all want to be with you."

An unsure smile pulled at his lips. "Dad loves me too?"

"He does. Grown-ups are weird though." I made a face which made Ethan giggle. I felt as though I'd won a prize in a fair.

By the time we left his room, Ethan was in high spirits and he was telling me all the stuff he would tell his dad. Lucky bastard to have such a bright and sweet child. I hoped that something would open his eyes and he would see how special Ethan was.

"Mom," he said when he got to the living room. "Don't miss me too much. I'll be back before you know it."

Savannah flashed me a smile. "I'll try not to. And you try to have some fun, okay?"

He smiled and nodded. After that, things happened pretty fast. The sounds of a car screeching on the gravel announced Finn's arrival. Savannah and I exchanged a look, then we all trooped out of the house.

Finn got out of his car wearing the stupid smirk that tempted me to wipe it off his face with a punch. It was mostly directed at Savannah and as hard as she tried to act like it didn't affect her, it did. More so when he helped Ethan into the car and when he shut the door, he smirked at her as if to mock the distress he knew she had to be feeling.

Ethan waved until the car disappeared. Savannah buried her face into her hands and cried silently. I turned her around to face me and folded her into my arms. It hurt to see Ethan being driven off even though the driver was his father.

I could not imagine how much worse it was for Savannah.

The house felt empty when we returned, as if Ethan had taken with him all the energy in the house.

"This is going to be one long ass weekend," Savannah said, standing in the foyer with her hands on her hips.

"No it won't. We're going out for dinner tonight," I said.

She glanced at her watch. "Dinner is hours away."

"I've booked you an appointment at Cutting Edge to get your hair done as well as all the other things that ladies love. My sister is waiting for you."

She looked at me as if I'd just fallen from the skies. I grinned at her expression.

"You did all that for me?" Savannah asked, close to tears.

"It's nothing. Now go on and get ready. I'll drop you off and then pick you up later, when you are done."

She reached for my hand and gave it a squeeze before heading up the stairs. I sat in the living room with my laptop while Savannah got ready. Every time I found myself worrying over Ethan, I kicked away that thought and reminded myself Finn was his father.

It didn't stop the worrying from trying to take over my mind every few minutes. Savannah returned downstairs wearing sexy yoga pants and a top that revealed a bit of her stomach. A groan escaped my lips when my eyes fell on the exposed skin of her belly.

She laughed. "You're the most easily aroused man I know."

I shut my laptop and put it away. "That's because you're the sexiest woman I know." I meant it too. A glance from Savannah was enough to make my cock hard, like it was now. "Come and sit on me for a second."

She narrowed her eyes. "Do I look like I'm eight years old?"

A laugh broke out of me. "What if I promise to keep my hands to myself?"

"Okay," she said, her eyes twinkling. She lowered her bag to the floor and then came and straddled me. "Remember your promise."

Her scent hit me first, surrounding me with female sweetness. She inched further up until she was sitting on my erect cock. Fuck. What the hell had I been thinking telling her \I would keep my hands to myself? I desperately needed to touch her.

I raised my gaze to hers. "What about a kiss?" I said, sounding as desperate as I felt.

Savannah draped her hands around my shoulders and kissed me. I hated that I couldn't touch her but a promise was a promise.

"I love how hard you are for me," she said and stood up. "I'll take care of that tonight, after dinner. But for now, I have an appointment."

"Fair enough." I was glad the distraction was working and she was looking forward to the appointment.

On the drive, Savannah was unusually quiet. "He's going to be okay and I bet he has a good time."

She flashed me a smile and said thank you. I wished I could do more but all our hands were tied. We had to wait for the law to take its course. At the beauty salon, we agreed she would text or call me when she was done and we would go for dinner after that.

Instead of going back home, I made a detour to the cottage. I had a bit more painting to do the following week, then it was just having it cleaned and it would be ready for the market.

I'd done a pretty good job with it. It looked nothing like it had when Savannah and Ethan had been living there. Already, an estate agent had come by asking if he could list the house for rent or sale. I had figured why not, as the rent would be extra income for Savannah.

I was working on installing the kitchen cabinets, after which the kitchen would be completely done. I couldn't wait to show Savannah the results of months of work. And hopefully, the house would have a tenant ready to occupy it. Savannah deserved all the good things in this world and if she let me, I would give them to her.

I stayed for three hours, then headed back home to get ready for dinner. As I showered, I couldn't help but wonder what Ethan was doing at that very moment. If he had been home, he would have been downstairs playing with his toys or watching TV.

I needed the distraction of dinner as badly as Savannah needed it.

If that bastard so much as laid a finger on him...

29

Savannah

"You can come in now," I shouted to Cassie. I adjusted my silver dress while I waited for Cassie's inspection.

I felt like a new woman after getting my hair done, and a spa treatment as well as my nails. The door swung in and when Cassie entered, her hand flew to her mouth.

"I knew you were smokin', but that dress takes sexy to a whole new level. My brother won't be able to keep his eyes or hands off you," she said.

I laughed. "Thanks. I was sort of hoping for that effect." I loved it when my husband hungrily followed me with his eyes and the dress I was wearing was the most daring I owned. It had a plunging neckline and it fit me like a glove.

"What are you guys celebrating?" Cassie asked.

"We're not celebrating. Cameron did all this to distract me from my ex taking Ethan for the weekend." While I hadn't forgotten my baby was not home, the separation wasn't as heart wrenching. I could do this.

"Oh," Cassie exclaimed. "Being away from Ethan must be tough."

Her surprise was genuine. She hadn't known anything about today and why Cameron had booked an afternoon of pampering for me. My heart melted at how protective and private Cameron was.

"It is, but Cameron has been awesome," I said. I was so lucky to have him by my side. I didn't know how my life would be when he was no longer in it. I shoved those thoughts away. It was not the time to think about that.

Cassie stepped closer and fussed with my dress around the shoulders. "We're sort of going to have the same situation," she said hesitantly as if she wasn't sure she wanted to talk about it.

She told me about Patrick's son, Jesse and how he had come to start living with his dad. My heart went out to Jesse. It was horrible to feel unwanted by your own parent. While Finn hadn't out rightly rejected Ethan, I'd seen the effect his constant criticism had on my little boy.

"I don't know how to be a mom," Cassie finally admitted, stepping back.

"There's nothing to it, honestly," I said. "All Josh needs from you is tons of love and acceptance. He just needs to feel as if he belongs somewhere. He needs to feel special. Cameron did it perfectly with Ethan."

Cassie's features relaxed as she smiled. "My brother does it so well, he makes it look easy."

"He does." I couldn't ask for a better father figure for Ethan and I know how lucky I am to have Cameron in my life.

I thought of all the things he had done for me and for us and guilt almost swallowed me whole. Every time I thought about that, it felt as if we were taking advantage of his good nature. Being a user was not a good feeling.

A knock came on Cassie's office door. Cassie called out for the person to enter. The door swung open and Cameron appeared, looking steaming hot in a casual black jacket over a button down white shirt. My husband cleaned up well.

"You look amazing," I said to him but clearly, he was not listening to me.

His eyes hungrily moved up and down my body several times until Cassie started to giggle. That snapped Cameron back to the present.

"I guess this is my cue to leave. Have fun at dinner guys," Cassie said, laughing as she shut the door behind her.

"You are so beautiful," Cameron said, his voice awestruck. "Must we go for dinner tonight?"

I laughed, pleased at his reaction. "Don't even think about it."

He checked that the door was shut and then moved to where I stood and slipped his hands around my waist, pulling me close. Enveloping me with his tantalizing male scent, he tilted his head and swooped in to kiss me. I let out a moan as his tongue found mine and slid hotly over each other.

God, I loved Cameron's kisses. My entire body came alive and I pressed myself to him, hungry for more friction. His large hands moved down to cup my ass over my dress.

Wetness spread to my panties and dampened my thighs. I was close to losing control. Throwing the whole evening to the wind and giving in to having sex in Cassie's office. That thought gave me the strength to gently push Cameron away when we came up for air.

"It's dinner time." I grabbed my purse.

"Let's hope we don't run into anyone on the way down,"

Cameron said, glancing down at the tent in front of his pants.

I laughed. "I'll stand in front of you."

We made it to the restaurant in time for our six o'clock reservation. Cameron held my hand as we walked through the revolving doors. As we waited to be shown to our table, my thoughts meandered to Ethan. Was he having dinner? Was he missing us?

The hostess showed us to our table and withdrew, saying a waiter would take our drinks order shortly.

"I'm sure that he's okay," Cameron said, reading my thoughts perfectly.

I nodded, trying to put on a brave face. "I hope that Finn doesn't scold him if he doesn't finish his dinner." Ethan was an okay eater but like most kids, he had his moments when he refused to finish his food. Finn's way of dealing with it had been to scold him which of course ended with Ethan throwing up the little dinner he had eaten.

Which would in turn get Finn even angrier. My heart clenched at the memory of a terrified Ethan looking up at his father and begging to be left alone. I gripped the sides of my chair, fighting the urge to get up and go get my child back.

"Don't torture yourself with such thoughts," Cameron said. "Remember he also needs Ethan to like living with him at this point so he's unlikely to do anything to upset him."

Cameron was right. He was probably going to try and charm Ethan. That relaxed me somewhat and when the waiter brought the drinks and food menu, I'd calmed down enough to place an order.

"Gorgeous evening dresses were designed for you," Cameron says. "You look enticing."

I smile, glad for the compliment. I was a bit of an exhibitionist, especially when it came to Cameron. He made me feel like the sexiest woman alive with his reactions and compliments.

"Thank you," I said and made a resolution to myself that I was going to enjoy the evening. There was nothing I could do about Ethan being with his dad, and as Cameron had pointed out, there was no point in torturing myself with worst-case-scenarios.

We sipped on our wine and chatted as we waited for the food. I could see why the restaurant was so popular. The ambience was perfect and slowly I felt myself relaxing and enjoying the evening.

As we ate, I caught the sight of a heavily pregnant woman walking across the restaurant, her husband or partner, gently holding her arm. I swung my gaze back to Cameron and saw he too was looking at the couple. When he looked at me, his face had an odd expression.

I want to have his babies. The thought shook me. What had driven me to think something as outrageous as that?

"Do you want to have another child or children in the future?" Cameron asked, as if he could read my thoughts.

"I don't know," I lied. "I've never given it much thought with all the drama in my life." That second part was true. When I'd still been married to Finn, the last thing on my mind had been another child.

He hadn't wanted another child either, so that had fallen to the back burner. Even if he had, I doubt I'd have agreed to do it. It hadn't taken long to realize marrying Finn had been a mistake and I wasn't going to bring another child into an unhappy marriage.

"You're a wonderful mother," Cameron said, his eyes boring into mine. "If I ever wanted a child, I'd want you to be its mother."

I inhaled a sharp breath. I didn't know how to take that declaration but somehow I knew what he meant. He and I got along perfectly. It's as though we were two parts of a missing puzzle that had been finally brought together.

The only thing lacking was love. At least from his end. If he hadn't loved his late wife so much, maybe we would have had a chance. I pushed away the thought. It was unhelpful and fell firmly in the category of things I could not control.

I cocked my head to one side and held his gaze. "I would want you to be my baby's father too."

We continued eating and moved on to other topics of conversation. Cameron talked about work, something he had started doing more often. I was fascinated by the stuff he did all day. His work, like mine, never got boring.

I was in awe of the stuff park rangers did. Conducting tours but the stuff that fascinated me the most was the search and rescue. It reminded me of how quickly Cameron had found Ethan the day he disappeared in the woods. His quick thinking and action had saved my son.

After dinner, we lingered in the restaurant as I finished off the last of the wine and Cameron drank water. When we left, I was slightly tipsy and definitely feeling sexy and I couldn't wait to get my husband home.

We went straight upstairs to our room without turning on the lights. We were both breathing heavily and it wasn't from running. As soon as the door shut, Cameron pulled me into his arms and kissed me deeply, as if continuing from the episode in his sister's office.

I had other things in mind though. After a moment, I dropped to my knees and opened Cameron's zipper and pulled out his incredibly erect cock. I fisted it marveling at his size. Inching forward, I licked off the wetness gathered at the tip, swallowing the mixture of salt and sweetness.

Cameron groaned deeply as I took him into my mouth, taking as much of his cock as I could.

"Fuck," Cameron hissed, the words sounding as if he was choking. I couldn't see his face from my angle but I could easily imagine the look of tortured ecstasy drawn across his face.

I sucked his dick, making sure that each time, the tip hit the back of my throat. I moved faster as I felt his orgasm drawing closer and just as I thought he was about to come, Cameron pulled his cock out of my mouth

I looked up at him with a pout. Without saying a word, Cameron pulled me to my feet and holding me close kissed me, the taste of him still in my mouth. I felt like I could combust.

I knew why he had pulled out of me. His own pleasure came secondary to mine and no matter how close he came, Cameron had never once come before me. He was selfless and he had taught me how sweet and great sex could be.

I let my hands roam over his chest and shoulders as he did the same to me, caressing my back and my ass. His erection pressing against my thigh, causing a tingling sensation up and down my legs.

"You make me so fucking hard," Cameron said.

I shivered as he moved his mouth to my neck.

"I love this dress but it's gotta come off," he said, cupping my breasts over the material of my dress.

I moaned. "Oh God Cameron." My nipples ached with the need to have his hands on my bare skin.

30

Cameron

God, I loved her! The strength of my emotions for her almost knocked me off my feet. I wanted to tell her so badly that I loved her. That I would wait patiently for her love, even if it took all my life.

Her nipples were hard and pointed in the material of her dress. I reached for the thin straps and pushed them off her shoulders, then I pulled her dress down to her waist.

I inhaled sharply at the sight of her full breasts, barely contained in a lacy black bra. I trailed a finger over the swollen tops and then used my tongue to do the same. I loved the softness of Savannah's skin. She held my head down, guiding me to her nipple.

I pulled down the cups of her bra, releasing her breasts for my pleasure. Like a man starved, I grabbed both her breasts, taking one of her nipples into my mouth. I sucked on it and then swirled my tongue over it.

"Oh God, yes," Savannah moaned. She arched her back, offering more of herself to me.

I took it all, greedily moving from one nipple to another. I had made a silent vow in the restaurant that tonight, I would do everything I could to keep her mind from worrying about Ethan.

I was going to ravish her and exhaust her, so by the time her head hit the pillow, she would be too tired to do anything but sleep.

"I want you on the bed," I said, gently moving her forward.

She got on the bed with me closely following her. I pushed up her dress to her waist and pulled down her panties. I spread her legs and arranged myself between them.

"You're completely soaked," I said, my voice echoing with wonder.

"You do that to me Cameron," Savannah said.

I went at her pussy like a caveman, licking and sucking as if it was my first and last time. Savannah tasted like heaven and I couldn't get enough of her. I fucked her with my tongue and my fingers until she begged me to allow her to come. I loved that she thought I held that much power over her body.

"Come for me," I commanded and captured her clit and sucked on it.

She let out a long scream of my name as an orgasm ripped through her. She gripped my head tightly and rode the orgasm until it finally ebbed away.

"That was epic," she said as I licked her dry, being careful with her now sensitive parts.

My cock ached as I moved up to lay by her side. After a moment, Savannah turned to me with a mischievous look in her eyes.

"Remove your pants," she said. "I want that big cock to fill me up until I can't breathe."

My cock twitched in my pants as if it had understood her words. "Don't you need a moment to recover?" I asked while I did as she asked.

"Nope, not me," she said and straddled me.

"Take off the dress," I said.

Without taking her eyes off my face, she raised her dress and pulled it over her head, leaving her gorgeously naked. She went on her knees and inched forward until her pussy was poised over my cock. I wrapped my hand around the base of it, holding it ready for her.

She took her time though, as if there was no rush.

"Savannah." My voice held a tone of warning.

She laughed softly. "Relax ranger. We have all night. Besides, you're the one whose emotions are always under control."

What was she talking about? "I have no control in your presence, Savannah." She could tell me to crawl across the room and I'd do it. She had that much power over me and I loved it.

Her features softened. "Really?"

I nodded. My cock jerked with impatience and we both laughed. Savannah lowered herself until my tip was touching her folds. I hissed out a breath. Her eyes glazed over as she made herself move back and forth across my length, like a saw.

Her wetness coated my cock, covering it with her juices.

"I'm going to explode," I said, my voice rough with arousal.

"No, you won't," Savannah said but in the next moment, she lowered herself onto my cock, moving slowly and deliberately.

She placed her hands on my chest using me as leverage. I moved my hand out of the way as she sat on me, her ass touching my aching balls.

"How does that feel?" Savannah asked me.

"Like heaven," I said, meaning every word. I could happily stay with my cock buried in her for the rest of my life.

My gaze fell on her breasts as she lifted herself up and then slammed back down on my cock. Fuck. Me. She was the epitome of womanhood. Savannah was the perfect woman, inside and outside. Her body was made for me. She was all the things I loved in a woman and hadn't known.

With my cock buried deeply inside her, Savannah leaned forward, brushing her breasts against my chest and kissed me hard on my mouth. I opened my mouth and for the next several minutes, we kissed while I softly rocked upwards, fucking her from below.

My hands moved to her ass and holding her cheeks firmly, I raised her up and down my length. Our breathing grew more labored as we edged nearer to orgasm. Savannah straightened and returned her palms to my chest.

Moving my hands to her hips, we fell into a fast, deep rhythm and in minutes, Savannah's moans deepened and I knew she was seconds from coming. I was right. Her nails dug into my chest and then her whole body fell apart, becoming like a rag doll.

I chased my orgasm, pounding hard into her until streams of cum jetted out of the tip of my cock, filling her with my seed.

~

"YOU KEPT YOUR PROMISE," Savannah said sleepily the following morning. She rolled over and draped her arm around me.

"It was an easy promise to keep." We'd had sex half the night and when we finally fell asleep, it was from sheer, sweet exhaustion. I pulled Savannah closer and planted a kiss at the top of her head.

She was silent for a moment before she spoke again. "I hope he slept well."

I hope he didn't cry himself to sleep. I was pretty sure that was what was both in our minds. Finn was returning Ethan at noon. "We'll find out soon enough. Just a couple more hours to go and our boy is home."

"Yes," she said and buried her face in my chest.

"I'm so proud of you for handling this so well. I know how hard it was," I said. She had given in to the lawyer's advice without a fight and allowed Ethan to spend a night with his dad.

"That's because I trust you," Savannah said. "You said it will be okay in the end and I believe you."

I inhaled sharply. Her words made me want to declare my love there and then. I grinded my teeth and clenched my jaw tight. I wasn't going to break our agreement because I couldn't control my emotions.

Knowing Savannah, she would probably say she loved me too if I confessed my love, but we'd both know it was a different kind of love she was talking about. The friendship kind of love. Not this searing, all-encompassing love that turned me into a fucking mess.

We got up soon after and headed downstairs for coffee.

"I don't know how I would have gone through yesterday and last night without you Cameron. Thank you," she said as we sat across each other on the island.

"I'm glad I could help." I wanted to do more than that. I wanted to protect her and Ethan for the rest of my life. Except that was a role I had not been invited to take. Savannah deserved to be with someone she loved and not in a one sided relationship. If I loved her as much as I claimed to, I would sacrifice everything for her happiness and that sacrifice meant letting her go.

The morning hours dragged by as we found ways to keep ourselves occupied and not keep glancing at the clock. Eventually noon rolled around, and Savannah and I waited for Ethan at the front of the house.

"He's late," Savannah said at five minutes past twelve.

"Let's give it a bit more time. Maybe there's traffic," I said, ignoring the tension rolling off me.

Everyone had watched child abduction cases where one parent took off with the child and seemingly disappeared from the face of the earth. I fervently hoped that Finn was not that type of person. He was a coward from the little I'd seen of him. Cowards did not take risks, even stupid ones.

Savannah took my hand then let it go and paced. If that bastard did not bring Ethan back, I was going to hunt him down wherever he was. I would not rest until Ethan was home.

Before I could work myself up to a frenzy the sound of a car coming down our driveway sounded. Relief surged through me when Finn's white Sedan appeared in the drive.

"Thank God," Savannah said over and over again.

We both went to the car when it came to a stop. I opened the passenger seat and Ethan flew out, straight into his mother's arms. I reached for Ethan's bag inside the car, stared at the back of Finn's head and banged the door shut. I ruffled Ethan's hair as he and his mother clung to each other.

Finn did not get out of the car or say a word. He gunned the car and moments later, he was speeding away.

"I missed you, mommy," Ethan said, his voice sounding like he was close to tears.

"Not as much as I missed you," Savannah said.

"I missed you too Ethan," I said in a voice that sounded as if it belonged to a stranger.

He came to me and threw himself against me in a hug. I held him tightly and over his head, Savannah and I exchanged worried glances. I shepherded my family into the house. *A temporary family*, a voice inside of me reminded me.

"How was it?" Savannah asked Ethan, pulling him nearer to her on the couch.

"Fine," Ethan said. "But I don't like Nancy very much. She wanted me to call her mom but I refused and she got mad."

My insides clenched. I was sure Savannah was feeling a lot worse but you couldn't tell from looking at her. She patted his head.

"Did you have a good time though?" she asked.

"It was okay. Dad got me pizza and ice cream for dinner yesterday. It was nice," Ethan said and Savannah and I exchanged a look of relief. He was okay.

Later that night, after we'd tucked Ethan into bed, and we were in our own bed, Savannah swung a worried gaze at me.

"I don't know if I can do this again," she said, a frightened look on her face. "I don't want to give those people my child."

I felt exactly the same way. "It's only Sunday. We have two more weeks before we have to do it again. Let's wait and see how it goes."

"I'm telling you Cameron, I can't do it," she said, her voice rising.

I pulled her to me and kissed her. Hard. She inhaled sharply and as I deepened the kiss, her muscles relaxed, her body softening against mine. "Right now you're here with me and Ethan is home in his own bed. He's safe. Let's not worry about anything tonight."

31

Savannah

I slid my car into a street parking spot in front of the bridal store and turned the ignition key. I sat for a few seconds admiring the interior of my car. I still hadn't gotten used to being the owner of a brand new car.

It still didn't sit well with me that Cameron had gifted it to me for no other reason than I was his wife. A fake wife at that. I walked around feeling as if I was taking advantage of his good nature, and that feeling was growing stronger and stronger.

I'd brought so much baggage into his life and still, he kept giving and giving. I hated feeling like a user. My phone vibrated from my handbag and I reached for it on the front passenger seat.

Heather's name flashed across the screen and my lips pulled into a smile as I answered the call.

"Hey you," I said.

"Hi," Heather said in the slightly breathless way she had of speaking. "Have you reached Southden?"

"Just got here," I said and while throwing a glance at the bridal store, I inhaled deeply. "This is madness," I told Heather, glad to have someone to voice my thoughts to. "I have no business being in Cassie's wedding."

"I beg to differ. You're an awesome person Savannah. She wants you in her wedding for that reason."

I rolled my eyes. "She wants me as a bridesmaid because I'm her brother's wife."

"She's gotten to know you and she confides in you a lot now. I highly doubt she tells you her deepest fears and secrets because you're her brother's wife."

"But that makes it worse. Imagine if she knew our marriage is not based on actual feelings."

Heather made a weird noise that sounded as if it had come from her nose. "Again, I beg to differ. I've never met two people more in love and perfect for each other." She let out a sigh.

I loved Heather like a sister but I didn't always take her word for something. She was a terrible romantic and she saw love where none existed. She had made up her mind a long time ago that Cameron and I were in love.

"Anyway, go and have fun trying on dresses," she said. "You could even try on a wedding dress for you and Cameron's fifth anniversary."

I laughed. Our days together were numbered. Cameron's goodness had a limit. He would get tired of being the giver and I would understand it completely. Because of him, I was getting the best legal help anyone could hope for. Because of him, my son had learnt that not all men were bullies like his father.

Because of Cameron, my belief in love had been restored. I was capable of falling in love again and somewhere in the future, the love of my life was waiting for me.

The moment that thought formed, an image of Cameron's gorgeous face filled my mind.

Heather and I said goodbye and I grabbed my handbag and got out of the car. A minute later, I was walking through the glass doors of the bridal store.

"Savannah," Cassie called out from across the room where she stood with Susie, a stylist at the salon and Cassie's very good friend, and another woman, going through a rack of clothes.

Smiling to hide the nervousness I was feeling, I joined them. "Hi."

Cassie hugged me and then introduced me to the other woman. "This is my sister-in-law, Savannah. And this is my maid of honor, Amy. She lives in Helena and we've been friends since college."

Amy and I exchanged smiles.

"I'm not late, am I?" I said.

"Not at all," Cassie said and then showed me a few dresses they had zeroed in on but they weren't quite right.

I joined them and started on one end of a new rack brimming with clothes. As I sifted through them, it reminded me of my wedding ceremony a few months ago. It seemed so long ago that Cameron and I had gotten married. I can't believe that I agreed to marry a stranger.

But I was in a bad place with Finn wanting to take Ethan away from me. I could never repay Cameron for what he had done for us.

"So, Cassie tells me you're newly married as well," Amy said, coming to help me with my rack.

I smiled at her but inside, I was groaning. I hated talking about my marriage to Cameron. "Yes, Cameron and I have only been married for a couple of months."

"I've always dreamed of getting married but my life

seems to be that movie, 'always a bridesmaid'," she said and made a face.

I laughed. "Love happens when you least expect it." She was pretty with long blond locks that cascaded down her back. I was surprised no one had snagged her yet and she didn't sound like she had a boyfriend either.

"I hope so," she said and then held up a gorgeous strappy satin dress with a long slit on the side.

"I love that!" I exclaimed, already imagining Cameron's reaction when he saw me in that dress. I could see him groaning sexily as he came towards me, his eyes roving up and down my body.

"I love it too," Amy said.

Cassie and Susie heard our excitement and came to look at the dress. We all loved it and asked the attendant to bring out three of the same dresses in our sizes.

For the next hour, we all tried on several dresses but none came close to the satin one and eventually we settled on it. Cassie insisted on buying us lunch after we were done with shopping.

The store attendant directed us to a cozy café a few shops down the street.

"I'm so happy we're done," Cassie said after we'd given our orders. "I thought we'd have to make several trips before we found the perfect dress."

"We did that with my cousin's wedding last year," Amy said. "I love her but she was a nightmare bride."

We laughed as she regaled us with tales of her cousin's outrageous demands during the preparations for the wedding.

"Did you have a big wedding?" Amy asked me.

"No, Cameron and I eloped," I said, trying to make it

sound romantic as opposed to a quick ceremony whose intention had been to help me keep my son.

"They only told us after the fact," Cassie said and then clasped her hands together. "That was just like Cameron, and you two are perfect for each other."

Amy's eyes misted. "That's the most romantic thing I've ever heard. You didn't need anyone else to make your wedding ceremony special."

I felt like a complete fraud as I sat there smiling as if it had happened exactly as Amy had described it.

MY PHONE VIBRATED WITH A MESSAGE. It was from Cameron letting me know he was waiting for me downstairs. He had finished the repairs at the cottage and we had agreed to meet at lunch time so I could see the new look.

"Tell Cameron to call his mother," Mrs. Elliott said from the reception desk.

"I will," I said and waved goodbye. Cameron's mom was the perfect mother-in-law. She treated me with respect while also showing me she was there for me if I ever needed anything.

I'll admit that I did keep her at arm's length but that was expected considering my marriage to Cameron had a time limit. Had we been a real married couple, I would not have fumbled for excuses when she invited me to her house. I felt guilty each time I did so but I told myself it was for the best.

Cameron was leaning against his truck and when he saw me, he smiled. My heart skipped a beat. My husband was hot. Not for the first time, I wished we were a regular couple, who had met, fallen in love and then gotten married.

"Hey beautiful," Cameron said, pulling off his

sunglasses. I loved how his smile reached his eyes and lit up his whole face. As if seeing me was the best thing that had happened to him all day.

"Hi," I said, walking straight into his arms.

Anyone watching us hugging and kissing would not believe it if we told them we were not a real couple. Cameron slipped his tongue into my mouth, not caring that we were standing in front of a busy street.

When we drew back, my skin flamed with arousal and my panties were damp. For a full minute there, I'd forgotten where we were.

"I should pick you up more often if this is the kind of hello I'll get," Cameron said.

I laughed. "You were the one who kissed me first," I said.

Laughing along, he took my hand and walked me to the passenger side and opened the door for me. As the door slammed shut, sadness engulfed me. I'd had this horrible feeling that we were nearing the end.

It didn't make any sense but I couldn't shake it off. I was quiet on the way to the cottage and Cameron noticed it.

"Are you okay? You're not usually this quiet," he said, a note of concern in his voice.

"I'm fine, just excited to see what you've done." Truth be told, I was apprehensive as well. Cameron had been working on the cottage for weeks even though some weeks he only managed one day.

I expected him to bill me for the amount he had spent. When I asked, he kept putting it off or changing the topic. Part of my apprehension came from the fact I was worried about the amount I would need to repay him. I hope it's manageable and he remembered to keep it simple.

Cameron smiled mysteriously in response. I noticed the change in the exterior of the cottage from quite a distance. It stood out from the rest of the houses on the street and when we got closer, I couldn't believe how gorgeous and inviting it looked.

"It looks so new," I said. "It's a wonder what a coat of paint will do." When I got out of the truck and went closer, I saw that it wasn't just a coat of paint.

He'd replaced the roof, redone the patio and put in a new flooring. Horror and awe came over me. Already, without stepping into the cottage, Cameron had gone over my budget. Nausea rose up my throat as I followed Cameron in.

Nothing was familiar about the small foyer. The carpet was stripped and the wood below buffed and stained. I went numb as I entered the living room. It looked a lot larger and brighter.

The walls had been painted a gorgeous warm mahogany color and like the foyer, the rugs had been thrown out and the woodwork stained. It looked nothing like it had before. The worst of it was Cameron had put in new furniture, brand new sofas and couches as well as a coffee table.

The ceiling had gotten a fresh coat of paint as well. The kitchen was flooded with sunlight. I had no idea what Cameron had done with the windows but somehow they brought more light in.

I looked at everything with dismay while attempting to keep a neutral expression on my face. How was I ever going to repay all the money back that Cameron had spent?

"Well, what do you think?" Cameron said.

"It's beautiful. It looks like a brand new house," I said, still unable to believe what I was seeing.

"An agent came by and she's already found a tenant for you. You can start earning rental income immediately," Cameron said.

I was drowning in guilt as I stared at Cameron. Why was he doing all this for me? I was his wife only by name. Had it been done out of love it would have been different but Cameron was doing it out of the goodness of his heart and it wasn't right. First the car, then paying my legal fees and now this... it wasn't right, unless...

I took a step closer to him and stared into his eyes. My heart pounded hard in my chest. "Why Cameron?"

He stared back at me quizzically.

"Why do all this for me?" My heart felt like it was bleeding as I waited for his answer. Suddenly, all I wanted him to say was that he loved me. That he did all the things he did for me because he loved me.

"Because you're my wife and you deserve it."

My heart shrunk. That was what I had been afraid of. He was doing it out of a sense of duty, not because he loved me. I was a fool. Cameron had told me from the very beginning. He could never love another woman.

Even without love, Cameron was the perfect husband. But I didn't want to play second fiddle. I wanted it all.

32

Cameron

Savannah stirred way earlier than she usually woke up but I had expected this. Two weeks had gone by too fast and it was the Saturday that Finn came to pick up Ethan.

I didn't feel as confident when I turned around to gather Savannah into my arms. Things had been weird between us since I took Savannah to the cottage. She had been happy with how the cottage had turned out but since then, the atmosphere between us had been off.

It had been so long since Amanda that I'd forgotten how to deal with such things. I'd asked her a few times but she insisted she was okay. I couldn't resort to tormenting her sexually like the other time as she had forbidden me from ever dong that again.

All I could do was wait and hope she would confide in me soon. I kissed her gently on her sweet, soft lips and relaxed when she responded. I inhaled her scents of sleep and let my hands roam her naked body. Savannah raised a leg and draped it across my thighs.

I slid my hand between her legs and was met by a stream of her arousal. I caressed her folds and then shifted and guided my cock to her welcoming heat. I pushed into her wet sheath and groaned into her mouth as I sunk into her.

"So good," Savannah moaned, rocking her hips in time to my thrusts.

I moved faster and faster, and before I knew it, Savannah was digging her nails into my shoulders and whimpering my name as she came.

"Fuck yes," I cried as my orgasm followed and I shot hot cum deep inside her body.

I held her close as the aftershocks of our orgasms left our bodies. We did not speak but we didn't need to. That was the thing with Savannah and I. When we made love, we were in perfect sync with one another. We communicated without words.

I would miss this the most when our marriage ended, which I had absolutely no doubt about. Savannah deserved to be in a marriage based on love not convenience.

Her breathing grew heavier as she drifted to sleep. I found myself drifting too and the next time I woke up, the sun was streaming into our room and Savannah was already awake. I rubbed sleep off my eyes and after stretching, I headed straight to the shower.

It was going to be a long day, first waiting for Finn to come and then worrying when he left with Ethan. I sure hope to God the lawyers knew what they were doing because I didn't know how long Savannah could do it for.

The scent of frying bacon met me as I entered the kitchen. Savannah and Ethan were at the table having breakfast. My entire mood lifted when they turned to me and smiled. We had become a real family without trying. It had happened naturally.

"Good morning, early risers," I said, kissing Ethan's forehead.

Savannah met my gaze as I lowered my head to kiss her and a blush covered her cheeks. I winked at her knowing she was remembering our early morning sex session that had acted like a sleeping pill and lured us back to sleep.

"We just woke up Cameron," Ethan said. He was surprisingly cheerful considering he was spending the weekend with his father. That pleased me and made some of my anxiety dissipate.

"We left some bacon for you," Savannah said. "Your plate is in the microwave."

I warmed the bacon and the pancakes, poured myself a mug of coffee and joined them at the table when my breakfast warmed up. Savannah shot me a sad glance and I knew she was thinking of the moment when Finn would come for Ethan.

We chatted over breakfast, taking care not to veer to our plans for the day. After breakfast, I cleaned up while Ethan and Savannah went up to his room to pack for his night out.

Twelve found us hanging around the living room listening for Finn's car. I glanced at my watch discreetly every few minutes. The clock hit one o'clock and he still hadn't come.

Needing something to do, I went to the kitchen and made for us all chicken sandwiches from the leftover grilled chicken from the previous night's dinner. I brought it to the living room and we all dug in.

Savannah texted me to ask if it was a good idea to call the lawyer. I replied why not? There was nothing to lose.

She returned to the table a few minutes later but she

looked calmer which made me assume she had gotten a hold of him.

"Dad's late, isn't he?" Ethan asked when we finished lunch.

Savannah nodded. "Yes, but maybe there was traffic somewhere."

As if on cue, Savannah's phone rang and she grabbed it. She glanced at the screen and nodded at me. It was Finn. She answered the call and left the room. A few seconds later, her raised voice could be heard from the living room.

I couldn't hear the full sentences but I caught a few words.

"Disappoint him..."

"Selfish..."

I'd heard enough. Ethan wore a petrified look.

"Want to go for a walk in the woods?"

He nodded vigorously. We left through the front door. I had my cell phone with me. Savannah could reach me if she wanted to but I had to get Ethan out of the house. He didn't need to hear his parents yelling at each other.

Ethan shared a love for nature and as soon as we ventured into the woods, our pace slowed down.

"Look, a brown squirrel with its babies," Ethan said.

I followed his pointing finger and saw the squirrel and two tiny ones as they disappeared into the thicket.

"Wow!" Ethan said. "Do you think that's a mommy squirrel or a daddy squirrel?"

"A daddy squirrel for sure. He was too big to be a mommy squirrel," I said.

We stood staring at the bush where they had disappeared through.

"My dad doesn't love me," Ethan said in a small voice.

Air stalled in my lungs. "Why do you say that son?" I asked him.

He shrugged and didn't say anything else. My heart went out to him. He looked so small and so alone. I dropped to my knees so that we were at eye level.

"Listen to me Ethan. You are loved by so many people, including your dad. Grownups are sometimes not very good at showing their love but your dad loves you. I know that for sure."

He nodded solemnly then asked, "Do you love me?"

"Do you even need to ask?" I said and he cracked a smile. "I love you Ethan and I'd do anything for you."

I could have punched the air with glee when the sad expression left his eyes.

"Can someone have two daddies?" Ethan continued.

I had an idea where this was going. "Yes. Several kids are lucky enough to have two dads."

"Can you be my dad?"

My heart felt like it was splitting into two. How did you tell a child that his mother was not in love with you and one day, you would no longer be a family? I couldn't break his heart at that moment.

"Yes, of course," I said, worrying what Savannah would say.

A wide grin split Ethan's face. I found myself grinning back. It didn't matter even if Savannah got mad. Seeing Ethan smiling was worth it. We took our time in the woods and by the time we returned to the house, Ethan had forgotten about his father coming for him.

Savannah gave him some milk and cake and when he was done eating, he asked to go upstairs and play in his room.

"What happened?" I asked Savannah when I heard Ethan's door closing.

She let out a sigh. "Apparently Nancy doesn't want Ethan this weekend. She said he was too much work and that I've spoiled him."

My anger rose. "What? Ethan is the most grounded kid I know and it's not just me saying so. Everybody says so."

Savannah smiled the slightest bit. "I love how fierce you become when it comes to protecting Ethan. I wish his father was like that."

I feel the same way about you.

It would have been so easy to say the words but I knew the effect it would have on Savannah. She would have felt obliged to say something along the lines of caring about me too. It would have broken my heart. I wanted Savannah to have genuine feelings for me, not feeling obligated to be nice.

"The good news is I did as the lawyer advised and recorded the call. He also said he had hoped for this outcome. Most people underestimate how much work is involved with taking care of a child," Savannah said.

"I don't find it hard taking care of Ethan. He's six years old and he can do most stuff by himself. He's fun and really good company."

Savannah patted my arm. "You have a big heart and you're an awesome human being."

Those were the words you didn't want to hear coming out of the woman you loved. You wanted words like hot, sexy, love, can't live without you... not awesome and big heart.

I put on a fucking brave smile. "Thanks. You're great too and a fantastic mom."

That night as we got ready for bed, Savannah was more

relaxed than I'd seen her in weeks. It was a good opportunity to figure out what had been going on with her in the last couple of days.

"I'm happy to see you like this," I said as we entered bed.

Savannah pulled up the duvet to her chin and turned to face me. "Like how?"

"Happy. Relaxed."

She grew solemn. "Yeah. It's been a weird few days."

"I know. What caused it, apart from Ethan leaving for the weekend?" I asked.

She shifted her gaze away from my face. Suddenly, the duvet pattern captured Savannah's interest. She took so long to respond, I gave up hope that she would say anything.

"I don't like that you spend so much of your money on me and Ethan," she finally said. "It's not right."

I resisted the urge to sigh. Money was money. I had plenty of it and it kept increasing as it happened with good investments. What else was I going to spend it on and I loved knowing I was making their lives easier.

"Money doesn't mean anything," I said, the truth of that statement slamming into me.

It didn't matter how much money I had. The one woman I wanted to love me didn't care about my money.

"I know it doesn't' and you're twisting the meaning of my words," Savannah said. "You know—"

I silenced her with a kiss. I didn't want to talk about money. Not then, not ever. The money I had was ours. All three of us.

33

Savannah

My phone rang as I was wiping the kitchen counters. It was Wednesday and I had an afternoon shift. Ethan was at school and Cameron had gone out for a walk in the woods. Maybe the walk would do him some good.

He had been morose the last couple of days and even telling him I had finally agreed to rent out the cottage had not cheered him up. It was unlike Cameron to be so low.

Apprehension grew in my belly when I saw who the caller was.

"Hi," I said, tightening my hold on the phone.

"Hello Savannah," Stan, my lawyer said. "I have some good news for you. Finn's lawyer got in touch. He's withdrawing the custody petition for now."

I covered my mouth, unable to believe my ears. "He what?"

"Yes," Stan said with a chuckle. "He's withdrawing it and

though he says that it's a temporary measure, I have a feeling we've heard the last of him."

Tears filled my eyes. "Oh God. The nightmare has finally ended. I can't tell you how grateful I am." I repeated this over and over again. I'd started getting anxious over the next visitation and now Stan was telling me I never had to give away my boy again?

When we ended the call, I stood in the kitchen crying tears of joy and relief. It had been so hard. My tears dried up and I filled a glass with water and gulped it down. I had to find Cameron and tell him everything that had happened.

I left the house and jogged across the back yard and headed down the path that went into the woods. I laughed as I ran. It was finally over. No more spending agonizing hours waiting for Finn to come for Ethan and no more feeling as though my heart was being shredded into pieces, watching his car drive off with my boy.

Cameron was not at the clearing where he chopped firewood. I hesitated before venturing deeper into the woods. I had an idea where he could be. I knew my way around the woods as I'd made it a mission since the day Ethan disappeared.

If Cameron was at his late wife's grave, that would explain his moroseness the last few days. He was missing his wife. It hurt to know I would never be enough for him but that was something I was going to have to come to terms with.

I loved the silence in the woods. The only sounds to be heard were of nature and those didn't count as noise. I knew where Amanda's grave was and after ten minutes of walking, I slowed down my step as I got nearer.

I heard Cameron before I saw him. Loud, heartbreaking sobs stood out from the normal sounds in the woods. My heart banged inside my chest as I edged closer to the clearing. That's when I saw him, kneeling by Amanda's grave, his head on the headstone.

From where I stood, I could see his shoulders heaving as violent sobs wracked his body. Seeing him like that, witnessing his pain, broke my heart. I'd never witnessed such pain in anyone, let alone in a man I was in love with.

I took a step back and then another until Cameron was out of view. Turning, I retraced my steps and left the woods, feeling as though I had left my heart at Amanda's grave. Sadness engulfed me and it took me twice as much time to walk back home.

Cameron had not been lying when he said he could never love another woman. His heart firmly belonged to Amanda. I was such a fool when it came to love. First I'd fallen in love with a narcissist, then as if that had not been a lesson in itself, I'd gone ahead and fallen in love with a man who had made it clear he wasn't interested in a real relationship.

Suddenly, I couldn't wait to part ways with Cameron. Being with him was becoming more painful than being without him.

THERE WAS nothing keeping us together and that realization had become like a growing wall between us. We never spoke about it but as the weeks went by, our general conversations reduced, as if we no longer had anything left to talk about.

The school holidays were drawing nearer and when Ivy called to ask if I could let Ethan go and stay with them for a week, an idea came to me.

Ethan was happy to go and spend part of the holidays

with his cousin which gave me more time at work and also to figure out my next steps. Left to Cameron, the status quo would remain but it wasn't fair to either of us. Both of us needed to go out there and live life. Find love.

"Enjoy yourself buddy," Cameron said to Ethan as he walked us to the car. I was driving Ethan to my sister's place after which I would return home, pack up and move my things to the guest room, then go to work.

I'd decided not to rip the bandage off all at once, rather, do it bit by bit. The first step was to move out of the master bedroom. Ivy and I weren't sure how long Ethan would be with them. We had decided to leave up to Ethan which worked out well for me as it gave me time to sort myself out.

"I will. I'll miss you, dad," Ethan said.

His words were like a knife stabbing me. He had taken to calling Cameron dad and I'd thought it sweet when Cameron told me about the conversation they'd had. Now, it hurt to hear it, knowing that soon, Cameron would not be in our lives.

I swallowed the lump in my throat. Conflicted feelings tore at me. Cameron said he was willing to be married to me for however long I wanted. Staying with him would give my son stability. But like our marriage so far, it was a selfish thought.

It was all about me and Ethan. I was tired of using Cameron and forever taking from him. I hated that feeling. That wasn't me. It wasn't just that either. The image of him crying by the grave was imprinted in my brain. It was a reminder of the special love he and Amanda had shared.

Something he and I could never have. I loved him. I'd fallen deeply in love with him. I wanted him to love me back. If I couldn't have that, then I didn't want any of him. I was greedy that way. Because of Cameron, I'd learnt I deserved love. I deserved to be loved wholly and completely and I was not going to give up until I found that special someone.

Ethan's hug to Cameron wasn't a desperate hug like the one he had given me when he was going off with Finn. This one was sweet and fast. A second later, he was inside the car.

"I'll see you in the evening," Cameron said and kissed me on the lips. My lips tingled in response. The chemistry between us had not changed. If anything it had grown stronger. If sex was a reflection of love, then our love for each other would have been out of this world.

The drive to Ivy's took less time than it usually did and by ten in the morning, we were there. Ethan tore off towards the house and I followed at a more leisurely pace, carrying his suitcase.

My sister was hugging Ethan in the foyer, then she directed him upstairs to Liam's room. She hugged and kissed me then took the suitcase from me. "I'll take that upstairs later. Got time for a cup of coffee?"

"Sure," I said, following her into the kitchen.

The relationship between me and my family has improved ever since I started working at the salon. I sort of understood now where they were coming from. It wasn't easy seeing someone you love seemingly wasting their life.

"Where's Sam?" I asked as I slid onto a stool.

"Work. I've said no to working on the weekends myself. I don't want to lose out on spending time with Liam. They grow up so fast." She poured the coffee into two mugs and set them on the island.

"Too fast," I agreed, sipping my coffee.

"How's it going at the salon?" Ivy asked.

"It's going well," I said with enthusiasm. Work was the one thing that was going super well. My clientele had grown and it felt good to have people book with me. I'd learnt so much. "Really well."

The only thing worrying me was whether Cassie would let me stay on when Cameron and I were no longer together. I'd been comforting myself that I could get another job with my new skills, but I didn't want to work elsewhere. I loved Cutting Edge and all my coworkers.

"I'm happy for you," Ivy said and then narrowed her eyes. "Why do you have bugs under your eyes? Aren't you sleeping?"

A sigh escaped my mouth. "Not very well," I admitted. I didn't have the energy to lie.

"Why, what's going on?" Ivy said, concern drawn on her face.

My shoulders slumped as I stared at her feeling utterly miserable. I hadn't planned on ever telling anyone about my marriage to Cameron, apart from Heather of course, but I found myself pouring my heart out to Ivy.

She listened with a neutral expression and if the tale shocked her, she did not show it. That was probably because of her job. She was used to putting on a poker face in court.

"That makes sense," she said. "I never understood how you married him so fast after the experience you had with Finn. Most people who are recently divorced would not jump into marriage so quickly again," she said.

"Yeah. Cameron is the nicest person I've ever met but he'll never fall in love with me," I said, misery coating my voice.

"You say he married you to help you out?" Ivy said.

"Yes," I said.

"You want to tell me he wasn't the least bit attracted to you?" Ivy said.

"Well, yes, we did have amazing chemistry, but you don't

go and propose to someone you're attracted to, do you?" I said.

"No, of course not," Ivy said. "Still I'm thinking you stirred something in him. Something he hadn't felt in a long time."

I shrugged. "I don't feel good about taking things from him."

"I wouldn't either," Ivy agreed. "Have you told him how you feel?"

I raised an eyebrow. "You mean tell him that I love him?" When Ivy nodded I continued. "Of course not. I don't want to look like a bigger idiot than I already am. He loves his wife."

"His wife is gone," Ivy said softly. "You are his wife now. Just because you saw him crying at his wife's grave doesn't mean he doesn't love you. It just means he's a man capable of deep love."

I didn't bother responding. It was difficult to convey into words what I saw that day. It left me in no doubt that Cameron could only ever love one woman.

"If I were you I'd tell him," Ivy said. She probably would too. Ivy was brave like that. Actually, so was Rebecca. I was the only one in my family who was a bit of a coward. I hated to look like a fool and because of that, a lot of times, I chose not to put myself out there.

"I'm not as brave as you and Rebecca," I mumbled.

"What are you talking about?" Ivy said. "You're the bravest of all of us. You've raised a wonderful boy all by yourself. You left your scumbag of a husband and started a new life in another town and made a life for yourself there. How many people do you know who can do that?"

I smiled. When she put it that way, maybe I wasn't the coward I thought I was.

34

Cameron

It was late when I got home and I was sure that Savannah was already asleep. I'd already eaten a sandwich on the way home and all I wanted to do was enter bed and fall asleep with my wife in my arms. I padded upstairs and opened the door softly so as not to wake Savannah.

As I stripped off my clothes, my eyes adjusted to the darkness and I saw the bed was flat. Savannah was not in bed. Where was she? Her car was parked outside so she had to be somewhere in the house. Puzzled, I turned on the lights. I went in search of her in the other bedrooms.

Maybe she had missed Ethan and gone to sleep in his room. She wasn't there. I found her in the guest room next to Ethan's room. She sat up and blinked her eyes when I turned the lights on. She had obviously been asleep and I felt bad for waking her up but I had to know.

"Hey," I said. "What's going on? Why are you sleeping here?"

A nervous look came over her features then it disappeared. "I wrote you a text message, didn't you see it?"

"No, I haven't looked at my phone in hours," I said, going to sit at the edge of the bed.

She attempted to smile and failed. "I think we've come to the end of this road."

I blinked rapidly, unable to understand what she was talking about. What fucking road? I hadn't known we were on a road. "You're going to have to be a lot clearer than that."

She twisted her hands together. "I mean us. This marriage. It's served its purpose. There's no reason to be together anymore."

I felt like I was going to be fucking sick. I didn't see that coming. "We agreed there's no rush to divorce or separate."

"I know but it was foolish of us to think that would work. It's not fair to either of us to be in a fake marriage," she said.

"What about Ethan?" I was desperate and clawing at anything that would keep Savannah with me.

You can't go. I love Ethan. I love you. I'm in love with you.

"It makes me sad that he's already attached to you but I think in the long run, it will be for the best."

I paced the guestroom unable to think beyond the fact that our marriage was over. I stopped and looked at Savannah. "What changed? You seemed happy with the way we were?"

Guilt flashed across her eyes but it was gone in the next second. "It doesn't matter."

It does to me, I wanted to scream but it wasn't fair on her. She didn't love me and she didn't want to hurt my feelings by saying it. I wasn't going to make her say it.

"You don't have to leave," I said to her. "Until you're sure and comfortable."

"Thanks," she said and rubbed a hand over her face. I

saw then how stressed she was and all my protective feelings floated to the surface. Except from this moment I didn't have the right to be protective over her anymore.

"The cottage has a tenant," I pointed out gently.

"I know but I'm thinking of renting somewhere closer to the salon."

She had figured everything out.

"There's no rush though, is there?" I hated how pathetic I sounded.

"No," she said softly. "Thank you for everything you have done for me. I'll never be able to repay you."

"I didn't do it so you could repay me," I said, moving towards the door. It felt as if my life was over a second time.

I paused at the door and contemplated baring my heart to her. Telling her I couldn't live without her. That I needed her for my life to make sense. I couldn't. She deserved better.

I SPOTTED my sister as soon as I strolled into Joe's coffee house. I gave my order at the counter and joined her at the table. She had called me and insisted we have coffee even though the last thing I wanted to do was to socialize.

As soon as I'd disconnected the call, my brother, Asher, had called me inviting me for a drink. Apparently it was something my brothers had done for years and they had decided to include me. My first question had been whether he had spoken to Cassie but he hadn't. It was a coincidence that my siblings were asking me out at the same time.

"Hi," I said, bending to kiss Cassie on the cheek.

"Hey stranger," she said.

I sat down opposite her and attempted a smile. "What

do you mean, stranger? We spoke on the phone... when?" I wracked my brain but I couldn't remember the last time Cassie and I had spoken.

"See," she said triumphantly and took a sip of her coffee.

"Sorry," I mumbled. I'd promised my sister we would not grow apart again. It seemed as if I'd already started drifting away again.

"It's fine, you're here now," she said. "To be honest, I've been super busy as well. Who knew planning a wedding involved so much work."

The waitress brought my coffee and I thanked her.

"So," Cassie said conversationally. "How are things with Savannah?"

My antennae went up. "Good, why do you ask?" I said just as coolly.

"She seems so low these days and when I ask her, she says that everything's fine and yet it's not. Savannah is the most cheerful and fun person to be around. She's changed so much. Something is bugging her and she won't say what. I thought I would ask you."

I looked out the window and froze when I spotted Savannah's form. When she turned, I saw it wasn't Savannah. Her face did not even resemble Savannah's. She only looked like her from the back.

"Is everything okay? She told me that her ex had dropped the custody case," Cassie said.

"Yes and there's no reason for us to be married anymore." As soon as the words were out, I realized my mistake. I'd let the cat out of the fucking bag.

"What do you mean, there's no reason for you to be married anymore?" Cassie asked with a puzzled expression on her face.

I tried to think of a logical explanation for that statement but came up with nothing. The truth would have to do. I knew Cassie and she wasn't going to drop it until I told her.

"I proposed to Savannah to help her keep Ethan," I said and told her about Finn wanting full custody.

Her eyes widened as I spoke.

"Wow," she said when I was done. "I knew something was odd about the speed at which you'd gotten married. It was so unlike you, but the kindness is totally you."

"Yeah, that's what I am. Kind." I couldn't keep the bitterness from my voice especially when I remembered Savannah had used the same word to describe me.

"I don't understand why you're so upset. You wanted to help Savannah keep Ethan and you've succeeded. What's the problem?" Cassie asked.

"She wants us to separate," I said to Cassie.

She shook her head. "And?"

Was my sister stupid. "You want me to spell it out for you?"

"I want you to say it," Cassie said in a commanding voice. I'd forgotten her bossy side.

"I feel sorry for Patrick," I said.

She waved an impatient hand. "Don't worry about Patrick, he'll be fine. We're talking about you. Why don't you want Savannah to move out?"

"Because I love her," I said harshly.

Cassie threw her head back and laughed.

"I don't see what's funny about that," I mumbled.

"Of course you don't," she said. "But you've finally admitted to loving Savannah. You can't live without her and that has come as a shock to you."

"You're not helping."

"Okay fine. Have you told her all this?"

"No. I don't want her to feel obligated to stay with me," I said. "I know she's eager to go on with her life and I want to set her free."

"Let me tell you one thing brother. No woman is going to stay with you because of a sense of obligation. None."

Savannah would. Cassie didn't know her like I did.

"Take a risk and tell her how you feel," Cassie said. "What do you have to lose?"

"I'll think about it."

You would not think that Savannah and I lived in the same house. We had become like roommates and communicated through sticky notes on the fridge. I missed her but seeing her was more painful. When we did bump into each other, we were polite just as roommates were.

It left me wanting to punch the wall.

That evening, I made dinner and then went out for a walk in the woods. I'd given a lot of thought to what Cassie had said but I wasn't convinced that baring my feelings was the right thing to say.

When I returned to the house, Savannah was home. A desperate urge to see her came over me. She wasn't in the kitchen and refusing to overthink it, I bounded up the stairs in search of her. We were still friends, weren't we? And friends talked to each other, asking after each other's welfare.

I went to her room and knocked on the door. No answer. I pushed the door open and stepped in at the same time as the door to the adjoining door opened. She was startled to see me.

"I knocked but you didn't hear," I said quickly.

"It's fine. I was taking a shower."

She looked so fucking gorgeous in a towel that stopped

above her knees and her skin glowing. I felt as if I hadn't held or touched her in years.

"Cameron—"

"Savannah—"

We spoke at the same time and then laughed. I entered the room and Savannah walked closer to me. She was so close I could smell the scent of her shower gel. My gaze rippled over the swell of her breasts and all I could think about was sucking her nipples. God, I miss her.

Under my scrutiny, her nipples swelled under her towel. My breathing grew heavier. Savannah took another step towards me and as if in slow motion, her towel fell off. She gave a cry and made to reach for it.

"Don't," I said.

She raised her gaze to me and let the towel fall to the floor. A groan left my mouth as I went to her and covered her breasts with my hands. They felt so full and so perfect.

I lowered my head and greedily took a nipple into my mouth. Savannah whimpered loudly and forked her fingers through my hair. My cock went crazy in my pants, jerking wildly and demanding to be set free. I ignored it. My priority was to taste Savannah. I'd almost forgotten how she tasted.

I showered attention on her nipples then kissed her belly, inhaling her skin as I moved downwards. I parted her legs and flattening my tongue, I swiped her folds from top to bottom. Fuck, she tasted good.

"Oh God, Cameron," she cried.

I went crazy. There was no rhythm or rhyme to what I was doing. I ate her pussy with abandon, using my tongue, lips and fingers. I ate her like a man who had not been near a woman in decades and I felt that way.

When she came, she gripped my head tight and screamed my name over and over again.

35

Savannah

"Oh yes. More." I couldn't believe those words were coming from my mouth. I should have been telling Cameron to stop. Our relationship and the perks that came with it were over. We had no business having sex.

But I couldn't stop him. Not with the delightful things he was doing to my body with his mouth and tongue. Not when I desperately wanted to have his cock fill me up and relieve the throbbing ache in my pussy. It felt like a matter of life and death.

"Fuck me Cameron," I said, unable to wait any longer.

"Get on your knees," he commanded in that voice that drove me crazy.

I crawled onto the bed, my ass in the air and with his hands on my hips I peaked over my shoulder. Cameron draped half his body over mine and seared my lips with a kiss. Reaching around me he pinched each nipple with his hands and ground his steel hard cock against my ass.

"Fuck me. Right now." I'd never been so needy for him.

He pinched my nipples one last time and the next thing I felt was his hands spreading me open. When he pushed his cock in, I cried out from sheer pleasure. I'd missed this. How was I going to go on without Cameron? A sob broke out from me but luckily it was drowned out by the sounds of his balls smacking my ass.

Cameron pulled out and then slammed into me.

I moaned and fisted the covers. Then Cameron went still but I could hear his rugged breathing.

"What changed Savannah? You were happy. I was happy," he said, his voice thick with emotion.

I should have known better than attempting to have a conversation while having sex but I needed his cock to move. If answering his question would get him to fuck me again, it was a small price to pay.

"You love Amanda," I said at the same time as he thrust into me. "Oh God. Oh God."

"I'll always love her, she was my wife," Cameron said harshly, resting one hand on my ass cheek.

His cock surged, expanding me more. Exquisite. I fought to remember what Cameron had said.

"I know but there's a difference between loving someone and being in love with them. You'll always be in love with Amanda. You have no space for another woman." Tears filled my eyes. I had no idea what I was feeling. I was a hot mess.

Cameron positioned his hands on the borderlines of my ass and thighs and spread me wider. When he plunged into me, it felt as if his cock touched my cervix.

"What gave you that idea?" he said, breaking through the haze of lust that surrounded me.

"I saw you at her grave, crying." I was ashamed as I said

the words. That had been a deeply personal moment that I had no business witnessing.

He let out a guttural sound before speaking. "I was crying because I had broken my promise to her."

When he moved, his movements became sharp stabs of his cock. I breathed in and out through my mouth.

"I'd made a promise to Amanda that I would never love another woman and I broke that promise when I fell in love with you."

He slammed into me so hard, all rational thought was wiped from my mind. It took a full minute and a series of smaller thrusts before what Cameron had said sunk in.

"You're in love with me?" I asked, looking over my shoulder.

He went still, his cock hard and buried deep inside me.

"Cameron?" I prodded.

He sighed. "Yes but I don't want your sympathy or feelings of obligation to reciprocate."

I was torn between keeping his cock inside me and turning over to see his face. I moved forward, sliding off his cock and turned to lie on my back.

"Why did you do that?" Cameron said with a scowl. He wrapped a hand around the base of his cock and brought it to my entrance. I raised my hips as he eased it in.

"That feels so good," I said and wrapped my legs around his thighs holding him captive so he wouldn't move. I locked eyes with him. "Repeat what you said."

"Why did—"

"Before that," I snapped, trying my best to ignore the need to thrust.

"I'm in love with you Savannah and I want you and Elliott in my life forever. But—"

Joy spread through me. I put a finger to his lips. "No buts. I love you too Cameron."

His eyes widened and a look of disbelief came over his features. "You're not just saying it to make me happy?"

"What? Of course not. I would never do that. I love you Cameron but I didn't think you had it in you to love another woman."

"I loved you from the very beginning," Cameron said.

"Why didn't you tell me?" I asked him.

"I didn't want you to stay with me out of gratitude or obligation," Cameron said.

"We're such idiots, both of us," I said happily.

He started rocking slowly. I loosened the hold of my legs and raised my mouth to his. I caressed his face as his kiss consumed me. I couldn't believe what had just happened.

"I love everything about you Savannah," Cameron said moments later, as he drew back and raised my legs to his shoulders.

"I love everything about you too Cameron," I said.

"Ready for the ride of your life?" he asked with a smirk.

"I've been ready," I said.

He fucked me hard and fast, his gaze shifting from my bouncing breasts to my face. I felt like the sexiest woman alive, and I could have placed a bet that to Cameron, I was.

I almost giggled as I caught the look on Cameron's face as he walked the bride down the aisle, his gaze on me. He looked like he wanted to throw me over his shoulder and carry me off somewhere private and fuck me until morning.

Cassie whispered something in his ear and giggled. I had a pretty good idea of what she said. I couldn't take my eyes off Cameron either. He looked amazing in a black tux and white shirt, matching with the groom.

He and Cassie hugged and then he went to sit next to his mom and Ethan. He and Ethan high fived as he sat down. My boys. My family. I loved them so damn much that it hurt. I couldn't believe for once in my life, my dreams had come true. My life was perfect.

I was married to the love of my life and I no longer had to worry about my ex taking away my son. It turned out that Nancy didn't like children very much which suited me just fine.

Cassie and Patrick exchanged their vows, reminding me of when Cameron and I had done the same. It felt as though we spent the entire morning stealing glances at each other.

Patrick's best man gave a touching speech about him finding the perfect woman for him. Afterwards, they had their first dance. As it was coming to an end, I felt a hand on my arm.

"Mrs. Elliott, would you like to dance?"

I smiled up at Cameron as I took his hand. "I thought you'd never ask."

On the dance floor, Cameron held me close and positioned his mouth next to my ear.

"Savannah Elliott, do you take this man, Cameron Elliott, to be your lawfully wedded husband?"

A giggle broke out of me. "Yes I do." I grew solemn and pressed my face against his. "To love and to hold."

"Forever and ever," Cameron whispered back.

36

EPILOGUE

Savannah

I sat in what used to be Cassie's office, my gaze on the computer screen in front of me. My concentration was terrible, pulled between the row of pregnancy sticks on the desk and listening for the sound of Cameron's truck. Not that I had a chance of recognizing it from the office.

I couldn't believe it had happened for us. It had taken a full year of trying to finally fall pregnant. It had happened just in time. We had said if we didn't get pregnant in a year, we'd make an appointment with a specialist.

Ethan had gotten tired of asking for a baby sister or brother. I couldn't wait to see him taking on the role of big brother. The stick was the third one. When the first had turned positive, I had done a second and a third test. Luckily I kept several of them in my office.

I'd taken a naughty picture of myself and sent it to Cameron knowing it was the fastest way to lure him to my office. I wanted to tell him the news in person. It was a moment that would stay with us for a long time and I wanted it to be memorable.

Cameron had immediately texted, on my way.

I gave up on getting any work done. These days my work was more administrative though I kept a few clients on my roaster. Cassie had moved back to Helena and opened another branch of Cutting Edge. She had offered me a partnership but in the end, we had bought the salon off her.

I was now a firm believer in things working out as they should. Who would have thought that in a few short years, I would be the owner of a salon?

My phone vibrated with a message.

I'm here. Coming up.

Less than a minute later, the door swung open and Cameron entered, a visible bulge in the front of his pants. I hoped he hadn't met anyone on the way up. He turned the key, locking the door.

"On the desk. Show me what you sent me," Cameron said, his form imposing and demanding.

I got up and taking my time, walked to the desk and sat on it. I moved until I got into a comfortable position. I watched his face as I shamelessly spread my legs and pulled my dress up to my waist.

Cameron hissed as I leaned back to give him a better view. I pulled my panties to the side to give him a look at my soaking wet pussy.

"What got you so wet?" he asked.

"I was thinking about your cock stretching me... fucking me," I said with a moan.

I touched my folds and another moan escaped my mouth.

"Fuck," Cameron said, pulling down his zipper. His cock

was hard and huge. "Is that what you want? My cock in your sweet pussy?"

I loved it when Cameron talked dirty to me. "Yes please."

He came to me and pulled me to the edge of the desk. He reached for the hem of my panties and tugged. I raised my hips and the panties were off. Cameron held his cock against my pussy, then pushed it against my slit.

Slowly, it disappeared into my pussy, stretching me and filling me completely. Cameron gripped my hips and holding me in place, he thrust in and out with deep steady strokes. He let go of one hip and reached between us to strum my clit.

I moaned and whimpered at the intense sensations running through me. It didn't take long before my entire body was on fire and I was seeing stars. I urged Cameron to fill me with his seed as I came. He came with a groan and when we were done, we were both coated in sweat.

The bathroom in my office came in handy afterwards. We cleaned ourselves up and when we returned to the office, Cameron spotted the pregnancy test sticks.

"What are those?" he asked.

"That's the reason I called you over," I said, tingling with happiness. I took his hands and stared into his eyes. "We're pregnant Cameron. We did it."

His face lit up and the widest smile curled his lips. He shifted his glance from my face to my flat belly. Bending low, he planted a kiss on my belly.

"I'm so fucking happy," he said. "Ethan will be a big brother, can you believe it?"

I laughed.

He kissed me deeply. "You've brought sunshine into my life again. I love you, wife."

"I love you too, my darling husband."

The End

COMING NEXT - SAMPLE CHAPTERS

Chapter 1
Ella

"Mom," I interrupt, cutting off her rambling commentary about some historical documentary she's been watching. "We've been on this call for almost fifteen minutes and you keep talking about a documentary that you know very well I have no interest in, and worse you keep bursting into that nervous little laugh you make whenever you have something you want to say, but you don't know how the other person will take it. So come on. Out with it."

"I don't know what you mean, Ella," Mom says and laughs uneasily again. "What little laugh?"

"Umm, that one," I reply, rolling my eyes.

"Ok, ok, you got me," Mom mutters. "I just don't want to upset you, that's all."

So, I was right. Something is wrong. I knew it. My mom isn't the sort of person who calls just to chit chat. She calls when she has something to say and she just gets on with it. Unless it's something she doesn't want to say. I can feel the dread in my stomach sitting there like a hard ball. What is so bad that she can't tell me straight away?

"Is it grandma?" I ask in a small frightened voice.

"Oh God, no," Mom denies quickly and with such genuine horror that I relax a little bit. "Your grandma is healthier and probably more fit than the two of us put together."

"True," I agree, smiling weakly. I feel a lot better now that I know grandma is ok. "Just tell me what it is, Mom. There isn't too much worse than something bad happening to grandma."

"You're right, darling. It's actually not bad at all," Mom says in a fake happy voice. "Here goes." There is a pause and then...

"Your sister is getting married," she blurts out.

"What? Hayley is getting married?" I ask, quite shocked.

Hayley, my older sister, has made it absolutely and crystal clear she doesn't believe in marriage. In fact, she looks down her nose at people who need, as she puts it, ":a silly piece of paper from the Government to keep them together". She must have met someone damn special to have changed her mind.

"Fat chance of that," Mom says, making a snorting sound of disbelief. "No, Cassie is the one getting married." She clears her throat. "To Jeremy Barnet."

I have to admit I didn't see that one coming.

Whoa! I feel like I need to sit down, but instead, I lean forward, resting my elbows on the breakfast bar and look down at the delicate gray grains on the white marble top. It's like falling through the gray net.

Suddenly, I'm drawn back in time to the months before I moved away from my hometown, before I hurriedly trans-ferred to the San Francisco office. I see it all like a film reel of scenes, memories I don't want to recall ever again, but are waiting there in the background waiting for another chance to torment me.

I'm back at that office event. It was the last place I wanted to be, but the boss had insisted we all make an effort. So, there I was, bored out of my mind, clutching a glass of warm white wine, and longing for my cozy couch, my fluffy slippers and old pajamas.

"Champagne?" a male voice asks from above me.

I looked up to say, 'no thank you', but the words kind of stuck in my throat.

An extraordinarily handsome man wearing very tight black short shorts that left damn little to the imagination, a black bow tie, and... er nothing else, was standing next to me.

Okay!

He was also holding a tray of champagne flutes so I lifted a glass from his tray and he flashed me a big grin. His teeth were perfect, straight and super-white, and they really stood out against his tanned skin. I smiled back, he winked, then he turned away and disappeared into the crowd.

Kudos to whoever was in charge of hiring the wait staff, I thought amused, as I sipped the ice-cold bubbles.

When the event was finally over and I was on my way out I saw him again. He was dressed in jeans, a white t shirt, and a grey hoodie left open over the t-shirt. I think I preferred the bowtie, but it was cold outside... He smiled at me. Thinking he was being polite I let slip a cool smile in return. You could have knocked me down with a feather when he fell into step beside me and held out a white calling card.

"I know you're probably married or something, but just in case you're not, here's my number. I'm Jeremy by the way."

"I'm Ella and I'm definitely not married," I said, my fingers curling over his card. My voice sounded quite flirtatious so I must

have had a bit more of that deliciously cold champagne than I realized.

When he asked for my number, I gave it to him. He put it into his phone and promised to call me. I didn't really think he would, the guy looked like a hot male model and must have had women coming out of his ears, but to my great surprise, he did call.

We went on a date and before long, we were officially a couple.

Jeremy was nice. He was generally sweet and funny and we had a lot of fun together. And for a while it was good. I was getting jealous looks from old school friends, and most importantly, from my sisters. I guess I am that middle child cliché. Growing up, Hayley, my eldest sister was the clever one; Cassie, my youngest sister the beautiful one; and I was just the middle one, unremarkable and nondescript in Hayley's hand-me-downs. But now, I was the one with the dream career and a drop-dead gorgeous boyfriend.

I couldn't be overlooked now.

If I was honest though, I knew in my heart Jeremy and I were not going to turn into anything serious. For all his good points, Jeremy wasn't marriage material. At least not for me.

I found it hard to take him seriously. Not just because at thirty years old he had made a career choice that required him to be topless, but also because he sometimes acted like he was still nineteen.

For the life of me I couldn't imagine marrying him, starting a family with him, or growing old with him.

Still... we made a nice couple... for the moment.

Then one day, Cassie, called asking if she could come over for dinner that night. I said yes of course, although it was strange for Cassie to want to spend time with me. As Jeremy was coming to dinner anyway, I asked him to bring a friend. I didn't want Cassie to feel left out. I thought maybe we were finally going to bond and become close and I even started to imagine the four of us going on double dates, maybe even on vacation.

But Jeremy didn't bring a date for Cassie.

He arrived alone, claiming it had been too short notice. Cassie didn't seem to mind being the odd one out. In fact, by the time I served dessert I was starting to feel like I was the odd one out. The pair of them had been whispering and giggling half of the night, and I had to keep reminding myself that Jeremy was just being nice to my sister. After all, it was me who asked him to make sure we didn't make her feel unwelcome.

I put down my spoon having finished my dessert. "Anyone for anymore wine?" I asked, trying to keep my irritation from showing. I had to wait for them to finish giggling over some joke about a rap singer that completely went over my head. Then Cassie shook her head and Jeremy followed suite. I topped off my glass and suggested we finish the night.

"Actually Els, there's something I ... we ... wanted to talk to you about," Cassie said, her eyes sliding to Jeremy as she uttered with the word "we".

I stared at her confused. What could she possibly have to tell me that Jeremy was involved in too? I nodded for her to go on, unaware that my world was about to implode.

"I'm sorry Ella, you have to believe that. And you have to know I never meant to hurt you. What happened... well, it just happened. It wasn't planned or anything." She looked away from me. "Jeremy and I have been seeing each other."

"I ... What?" I blurted out, dumbfounded.

Cassie couldn't even look at me now and I turned my focus to Jeremy. He looked sheepish, but at least he is able to look back at me. "Is this true?"

He nodded guiltily. "Yes, it true. I'm so sorry Ella. I ... we ... we never wanted you to get hurt, but the heart wants what the heart wants right?"

I wanted to slap his childish face. Even Cassie had the decency to cringe at the cliched words. I took a deep breath. I was still shocked at the betrayal, but I had already decided I was not going to let them think for a second they had hurt me. I refused to give either of them that sort of power over me. I forced myself to laugh and after a second, the laughter isn't forced anymore, I was genuinely laughing.

"Els? Are you ok?" Cassie asked, after throwing a confused look at Jeremy.

Jeremy shrugged one shoulder, to indicate he had no idea what was going on with me. I got my laughter under control and shook my head in amazement at my situation.

"Sorry," I apologized. "I didn't mean to laugh. I just couldn't help it."

"Why? What could possibly be funny about this?" Cassie demanded. Just trust her to take that tone with me, when she just confessed to stealing my boyfriend.

"The fact that both of you think I'd be heartbroken over this. It's not like we were serious or anything and we never said we were exclusive. I mean I would have thought my own sister might have had a bit more class than this, but whatever." I shrugged. "I guess it's really ok. Mom and Dad always did teach us to pass our used toys onto the less fortunate."

I didn't really mean to be that much of an asshole, but the look on Cassie's face made me glad I said it. For once in her spoiled life, she looked taken aback. She was so used to getting what she wanted so easily that she had no awareness other people can be annoyed when what is theirs is taken away from them, even if they were about ready to cast them aside anyway.

"Now you're just being mean," Cassie flung at me.

She must have been trying to convince herself that her behavior wasn't the issue here. Suddenly I didn't want either of them in my home anymore.

"You're right. Jeremy and I were only ever going to be a fling. And to be honest, I think we would both agree that it had just about run its course."

Jeremy nodded his agreement.

"So good luck, Cassie. I genuinely hope you're both happy together." Then I stood and began to walk towards the front door.

"Ella? Are you ok?" my mom asks, and I'm brought back to the present, my mind still reeling with the past.

"Yes, yes, I'm fine," I answer automatically. "I'm a bit shocked though. I always thought Jeremy wasn't marriage material, but I also got the impression he didn't particularly want to give up his bachelor status either."

It's true. I never got the impression that Jeremy was about to propose to me, and I never got the impression that he would ever propose to anyone. He was too immature for that kind of commitment. And Cassie? I mean yes, she's a hopeless romantic, but at the same time, she's no fool and I didn't think she would rush into this either. Unless ... The truth hits me and I shake my head in wonder.

"Cassie's pregnant, isn't she?"

"Well now, that's not the only reason they're getting married. I'm sure they love each other," Mom says.

I have to bite my lip to stop myself from laughing. "Yes, yes, of course," I agree. "So, when is the wedding then? I would imagine it's going to be pretty soon if you don't want people to know she got pregnant outside of marriage."

"We don't care who knows," Mom snaps back, then she sighs loudly and goes on. "Oh, who am I trying to kid. It's in eight weeks' time."

"So, between Christmas and New Year's then?"

"Yes," my mom agrees. "Not the best timing but what can you do? Are you ok with all of this Ella?"

Does it matter if I'm not at this point? It's not going to change anything, is it?"

"Oh darling..."

"Actually, I'm fine Mom, honestly."

"Good, I'm glad to hear that. I'd hate for you to be hurt over this. You didn't really want him anyway, did you?"

"No, I didn't."

"So, you will be coming to the wedding, right?"

"Of course," I say slowly.

In truth, I would rather stick hot needles in my eyes. I already knew how this was going to go. Everyone will be whispering about poor old Ella who lost her boyfriend to her beautiful sister. I can already imagine the looks of pity they will throw at me.

"Great," Mom exclaims, sounding relieved and happy again. "I'll have Cassie send you an official invitation with all the details."

We say our goodbyes and end the call.

I'm fine. I don't care about Jeremy. Cassie is welcome to him. I didn't want to marry him then and I still don't want to now. So why then is there a part of me that is hurting so bad?

A feral growling sound rushed up my throat and I see a mist of red over my vision. I pick up a mug from the counter and hurl it at the nearest wall as hot tears sting my eyes. The mug smashes with a satisfying broken sound, the pieces tumbling to the ground. I angrily dash away my tears and go towards the mug, already annoyed at the mess and the unnecessary waste. I'm just glad it was empty. I pick up the pieces, wishing I could pick up the pieces of my heart that easily.

I go to the trash can and violently chuck the pieces in it.

Then I go to the sink, turn on the cold water and splash the cool water on my face. There. That's better.

I feel a brush against my leg and I look down and smile when I see my chubby, ginger fluff ball of a cat looking back up at me and meowing. I bend down and scratch behind his ears.

"Oh Merlin! Why am I even bothered?" I whisper. "It's not like I wish I was marrying Jeremy. I don't. I really don't. I'm just hurt they deceived me."

Merlin meows mournfully at me.

"If only I could understand you, you might turn out to have the answers," I murmur as I stroke his splendidly soft head.

He wanders off to his cushion and I go to the fridge and pull out half a bottle of white wine. I grab a large glass and fill it, using up all of the wine. I put the bottle on the side for recycling tomorrow and I take the glass of wine through the dining area into the living room.

I sink down into the cream leather couch and take a big gulp of the wine before I put it down on the coffee table and grab my laptop. A plan is starting to form and I already feel better as I fire up the laptop.

It's just hit me why I'm bothered about Cassie and Jeremy. It's because I can't stand the thought of being pitied by our friends, our family, and most of all by Cassie, who thinks she has somehow beaten me at the game of 'I already won the beauty prize now let's take everything else Ella has'.

I know what I need to do now. I need to go to the wedding, smile and laugh, and show the world I'm having the best time of my life, and then get the fuck out of there. Maybe I should ask at work if I can transfer to the Hong Kong office and make a fresh start altogether?

Yes, yes, that would be a nice, nice change, but I'm getting ahead of myself.

First the wedding. There is no way in hell I'm going to it as a single woman. I want a man on my arm. Preferably a hot, rich, successful man, or at the very least a hot man who can act like he's rich and successful.

I load Tinder and start working on my profile. The wedding is eight weeks away. That means I have maybe four to six weeks to find someone and convince them to come to this wedding and look as if he adores me. Four to six weeks to find a guy who will look good on my arm and stop me being an object of pity.

How hard can that be?

Chapter Two
Ella

I sit at the end of my bed. My makeup is done, my underwear is on, and I just need to finish pinning my hair up and put my dress on. I sigh as I tuck a loose strand of hair into my messy bun and pin it in place. I don't even really want to go to the party, but it's a work thing, I'm new there, and it looks really bad if you can't even be bothered to turn up for the Christmas party.

I'm not big on these events at the best of times if I'm honest, but I'm even less in the mood for a party today than I usually am. I have just over a week before the wedding and I haven't found anyone even close to suitable to take with me as my date.

It's not through lack of trying either. I've been on a string of disastrous dates over the last few weeks. Ones where the guy turns out to be twenty years older than his profile picture suggests, ones where their profile picture isn't even them. I've also been out with some guys who just wanted to hook up which was no use to me, and then there were a few genuine ones who I didn't click with enough to even pretend to play happy couples with. And honestly? I haven't met a single guy who could rival Jeremy in terms of looks and I refuse to turn up with someone who Cassie will triumphantly view as second best.

Does that make me shallow?

I'm thinking yes, it most probably does. Do I care? Nope. Not one bit. There's very little point in taking a date to avoid the pity party my family and friends will try to throw for me if the date is someone who will cause even more pity.

My hair is done and I stand up and walk to the full-length mirror. I turn this way and that to view it from all angles. I guess I'm happy with it. I move to my chest of drawers and start putting in a pair of earrings. As I'm fastening the second one, Merlin comes into the room and jumps up onto my bed.

"Well, hi there," I greet and get a meow in reply. "Do you think I might find my dream guy tonight, huh?"

Merlin doesn't even bother to meow at this and I can't help but laugh. Even my cat thinks I'm a lost cause. That's just great, isn't it.

"I know," I say. "I was crazy to think I would find what I was looking for without just giving in and paying for it. So, I guess that's the plan then. I'm now officially pathetic enough that I'm going to pay for an escort to be my date and the only friend I have to talk to about it is my cat."

Merlin gives me a haughty look before jumping down from the bed and stalking out of the room.

"Aww Merlin, I didn't mean it like that," I say laughing at his impeccable timing.

I actually feel a bit better about my situation now that

I've accepted the fact that I will need to suck it up and hire someone. It's probably a better idea anyway. With an actual date, something could go wrong. Knowing my luck, we could end up arguing or something. At least if I'm paying someone to act a role, I know how it will go. The last thing I need is unwanted surprises. I find that now I have a solution to my date problem, I can push this problem to the back of my mind for now and concentrate on my more immediate problem; what the hell am I going to wear to this party tonight?

I go to my closet and start flicking through the clothes there. I ignore the work clothes and my lounging-about casual clothes and focus solely on my nicer dresses. I have a few good choices after my string of dates, all of which I felt required something new to wear.

I instinctively reach for the black body con dress I wore last week for a dinner date. It's safe, the sort of dress that will allow me to blend into the background. I start to pull it off the hanger when my eyes catch the gold sequined dress I bought on a whim because it had a 75% discount tag hanging from it. It was so daring, so bold, so unapologetic even though it had been so severely marked down. I told myself I would definitely wear it. One day I would definitely dare myself into it.

Well, that day might be today. If there was ever a night to wear that kind of dress, it was for this Christmas party.

Slowly, I put my black dress back on the hanger and lay the gold dress on the bed. It lay beside the navy-blue dress I picked out earlier and already rejected in my mind. I run the material between my fingers. It shimmers like an Arabian dream. Dare I wear this? I don't know if I dare or not, but I convince myself that at the least I should try it on. It's not like anyone ever has to know I tried it on... if it looks silly on me.

I pull the dress on over my head, being careful not to wreck my hair. I get my arms in and pull it down and move over to the mirror. The dress ends mid-thigh showing more leg than I usually do. One of the joys of growing up with conservative parents – the constant reminders not to show too much leg, too much cleavage, too much anything.

Fuck it, I think to myself.

My legs look damned good and for once, I am going to show them off.

I nod in approval at myself but then I start to doubt myself. Is the dress too slutty? Do I look cheap? I tell myself "No" to both of these things. The dress isn't exactly neck high, but it's high enough that there's only a small peek of cleavage. And it's definitely does not look cheap. Even after the 75% discount it cost me a pretty penny. And it actually looks very good on me.

I realize today I don't want to wear my black dress and be in my comfort zone. I don't want to blend into the background. I am going to wear this dress and for once, I'm going to stand out. And I'm going to look good doing it. This will be my practice run for Cassie's wedding.

After I slip my feet into my high black heels, I spritz some perfume onto myself and I'm ready to go. I take one last look in the mirror. Am I really going to do this?

Yes, I am!

My cell phone dings and I glance down at the screen. There's a message telling me that my cab is here. I take a deep breath and pick the cell phone up and my purse and leave the bedroom. I feel goosebumps scurrying over my skin, excited by the fact that I'm stepping out of my comfort zone even if it is just for a stupid office party.

I go into the living room, grab my keys off the coffee table, and leave my apartment. I go downstairs, cross the lobby and exit the building.

Office party, here I come.

Chapter Three
Ella

The large conference room has been emptied out for the party. There's a bar at one end and a DJ booth at the other. The room has been decorated in festive red and green and there is a huge Christmas tree with winking fairy lights in the middle of the space. I have to admit that whoever undertook the decorating did a fine job. It's almost hard to remember this room is in our work building.

It actually feels like I'm in a ballroom of some fancy hotel.

I'm onto my third glass of wine and I'm starting to feel more than a little bit tipsy which is good because prior to feeling tipsy, I was feeling bored. I've been at this office for a couple of months now, but I barely know anyone. Obviously, I know who they are and they know who I am, and we exchange polite hellos, but that's about it. In the few weeks I've been here, I have made a total of zero friends.

I don't think I'm unlikeable and I certainly don't think that of my colleagues. I think my lack of friendship here stems from my arrival. I was more upset about Jeremy than I was willing to let on and because of that, I really didn't feel like socializing, let alone going out with a bunch of strangers and playing the getting to know you game, so whenever I was invited on staff nights out, I would always make out I had other plans. At some point, the invites stopped coming and by the time I felt ready to socialize again, the invites were long dead and I was too shy to ask if I could join them.

I decide then that my New Year's resolution will be to make some new friends. Maybe not with these people. It's probably too late with them. Also, I might be in Hong Kong in a few weeks. Maybe I'll join a class or a club. I want a group of loyal girlfriends like I see on the TV. Women, who you tell everything to, and who have your back no matter what. You meet for coffee and do lunch, and go on nights out on the town together. I want that.

I'm semi-aware I've wandered back to the bar and swapped my empty glass for another full one. I'm starting to feel more than a little bit drunk and I know I'm about to cross the line from tipsy to drunk. The sensible part of me says I should slow down, have a water next, but there's another part of me that's happy to be getting drunk and thinks fuck it. It's Christmas after all.

I take another big drink of my wine.

I find myself smiling as I catch the sight of Veronica dancing up a storm. She catches my eye and smiles back at me. Instead of looking away, I hold her gaze and she beckons to me. I hesitate only for a second. Then I make a conscious decision to stop worrying about what anyone else might think and just decide to enjoy myself. I walk towards Veronica. When I'm almost up to her, she takes my hand in hers and twirls me around.

I let her do it and laugh as I spin around in my gorgeous gold dress and insanely high heels.

As we dance together a few of the other girls from the office come and join us. Before I know it, I'm dancing and laughing with these women who I have treated as practically strangers but, in this moment, feel like friends.

We keep dancing and laughing as the lights flash and

the music pounds. I drink more wine and find that I am really, really, really pleased I came to the party after all. I'm enjoying myself so much I don't want the night to end.

I really do need to do this more often.

I excuse myself from the group and head out of the party room along the corridor. I open the door to the ladies' room and see that there is a line of at least six or seven women already waiting to use the facilities. I don't think my bladder can wait that long so I decide to go up to the second floor that is also part of our company's offices and use the bathroom there. The second floor is mostly for executives and the important types. They keep us riff raff on the ground and first floors. It's not like anyone is going to be up there now though, they are all either at the party or have begged off early and left.

I make my way to the elevators, aware that I'm actually a little unsteady on my feet. In fairness my super high heels probably don't help and I debate taking them off. I decide to wait until I'm back in the party to do it. I don't much like the idea of walking barefoot in a bathroom. Not even an executive one.

The elevator comes and I stumble into it and press the button for the second floor. I reach the second floor, still on my feet, and I get out of the elevator and go to the ladies' bathroom. I use the toilet, a relief in and of itself, then I come out of the stall and go to wash my hands at the sink. I've been humming to myself as I peed, but it's bothering me that I can't think what the song is. Without warning, as I wash my hands, it comes to me and I can't resist belting it out.

"I'm on the edge, the edge, the edge, the edge, the edge, the edge, the edge. I'm on the edge of glory, and I'm hanging in this moment with you. I'm on the edge with you," I sing.

I stop singing and laugh at my out of tune rendition of *The Edge of Glory*, noting that I probably got the words wrong too. It's alright, it's not like anyone can hear me, I am two floors higher than everyone else. I turn the tap off and grab a paper towel to dry my hands on. Oh, I think excitedly, I should go and ask the DJ if we can have some karaoke.

I'm half-walking, half-dancing as I leave the bathroom and I walk smack bang into a man. He grabs me by my upper arms and stops me from falling, but instead of being grateful that he stopped my fall, I'm more furious at the fright he gave me.

"What the hell do you think you're doing wandering about the building and lingering outside of the ladies' bathroom? Especially the lingering. Are you some sort of pervert or what?" I demand hotly.

The large warm hands leave the tops of my arms and I look up at the man. He has dark hair, dark eyes, and a flash of stubble across his chin and cheeks. He's good looking, um, very good-looking. Not in the boyish handsomeness of Jeremy, but in a mysterious and sensual way. I feel butterflies in my tummy as he raises one corner of his mouth in an amused smile.

"That's a lot of questions," he remarks, his voice low and smooth and kind of hot.

"Start answering them then," I mutter, crossing my hands under my breasts.

"I heard someone absolutely slaughter *The Edge of Glory* and came to see what was going on. No, I'm not a pervert."

Ouch, he heard me. I can feel the searing heat rush up my neck, but I've got a lot of wine inside me, and I don't back down. "And why is that your concern?" I challenge.

His amusement widens into a proper smile and his eyes

sparkle as he looks at me spitting fire at him. "I'm Blake McIntyre. Your CEO."

Oh God! How embarrassing. I know I should apologize instantly. My God. I can't believe what I've done. Not only did I not recognize him, but I've also just accused the CEO of the company of lingering outside the ladies' room and being some sort of pervert. I open my mouth to apologize, but it's not an apology that comes out.

"Well fuck me sideways," my mouth blurts out as if independent from my brain. "I've always expected you to look older in person."

His surprised expression strikes me as funny and I start to laugh. Even though I'm laughing, inside, I am horror struck at what's happening. I am kind of waiting for him to fire me when he suddenly throws his head back and breaks into a deeply sexy rumble of laughter.

"And you are?" he asks when he stops laughing.

"Ella," I say. "Ella Henley. I work in marketing."

A speculative light comes into his mysterious eyes. "Well, well, well, if I had known I had people who were this much fun to be around, I might have come down to the party."

Pre-order your copy here:
Propositioning The Boss

ABOUT THE AUTHOR

Thank you so much for reading!
If you have enjoyed the book and would like to leave a
precious review for me, please kindly do so here:

Surprise Proposal

Please click on the link below to receive info about my latest
releases and giveaways.
NEVER MISS A THING

Or
come say 'hello' here:

ALSO BY IONA ROSE

Made in the USA
Middletown, DE
06 April 2023

28380394R00175